The Sitter

'...a wind blow ... ... fields which seem already to smell of bread.'

The Sitter is a perfect evocation of late Victorian Norfolk, a fine-spun tale of love and learning, in an age of seismic change. This book charts a lost world that once seemed so sure, capturing the pull of the old in a narrative fresh as the day.

With historical scholarship worn light as silk, and an unerring feel for human emotion, Caroline McGhie spins her story's web, drawing us to the innermost world of each character.

An exotic stranger emerges from a cloud of steam, observed by an old railway worker and a curious young lad, and we are pulled back to the heyday of railway, all senses alert. The story unfurls with unflinching attention to intimate detail - brutal working lives, the everyday bravery of fishing families, changing landscape through the East Anglian seasons – all are intricately depicted, with humour never far away, in achingly poetic prose.

If you liked... L.P. Hartley's *The Go Between*, Sarah Perry's *The Essex Serpent*, Jessie Burton's *The Miniaturist* or J. L. Carr's *A Month In The Country*... then you will love The Sitter.

Jess Streeting

THE SITTER

A Novel

CAROLINE McGHIE

WATERLAND BOOKS

First Edition May 2025

Copyright is reserved to the authors and artists, their heirs and executors.

Cover photo: Seated Female Nude – Jean Louis Marie Eugène Durieu (1800 - 1874) (MET, 2005.100.41)

Back Cover: Train by Tom Grayling

Design/typesetting by Nick Stone

Published by Waterland Books, 2025

ISBN 978-1-7396034-1-0

Waterland Books, Norwich, Norfolk

www.waterlandbooks.co.uk

Printed in the UK

For Dick

"So we beat on, boats against the current borne back ceaselessly into the past."

F. Scott Fitzgerald *The Great Gatsby*

CHAPTER ONE:

THE SPECIMEN

Steam tumbled skywards as the train beat onwards to Swanton Stoke, scurrying through black turned fields towards the end of the line. It was late in the afternoon on the last day of October and only one passenger remained on board. When the train pulled out of London it had been crammed with people, seated according to their tickets and their incomes, in first, second and third class. Men and women, old and young, bowlers and bustles, gloves and bags and flouncy hats, jostled for space. People imagined themselves elsewhere to make it bearable. Then one by one they left, taking their dreams and disappointments with them. The only way for the train was forwards. The future could not be undone. The iron horse skirted high cliffs and rounded coiled creeks, turned inland for the last two miles and pushed on to its final halt in a large railway works. White smoke thinned to nothing and revealed the solitary figure of a young woman stepping tentatively onto the platform, carrying a brown leather bag.

Nobby Stokes caught sight of her out of the corner of his eye and jerked his head up for a sharper look. He didn't need anyone to tell him about the wonders of rail, that it could make and lose fortunes, shift goods, shrink time, rule his every waking moment. But today it had delivered a surprise in the form of a living, breathing painting. The woman's hair was like burnt sugar, yards of sweet shining caramel, stippled with gold and copper. It was severely pulled back but unwilling strands escaped and swung round the white oval of her face. Her ashen pallor put him in mind of a spirit. Either she was from another world or she was so short of sleep that her skin had become luminous. One tiny hand fluttered around her waist like a feathered dove, pecking at the gathers of her skirt. The other hand was bandaged. It was the end of Nobby's shift and he was on his way back to Sebastopol Road where he shared a room with his landlord's son. He was bone tired. One thing he knew about burnt sugar was that it was too hot to touch. He banished her from his mind. A couple of hours later as he drifted to sleep he remembered her eyes, those heavy lids and that solemn gaze. They seemed to reveal and conceal at the same time, offer a gift, then take it away. He rolled over. He thought she had probably fallen asleep on the train and found herself carried to the end of the line by mistake.

᪐

I have arrived in a village which is Godforsaken or Godgiven. It is unlike anywhere I have known before, neither the docks nor the East End of London. It is full of men in cloth caps, all busy about their business, but there is no threat or competition in the air. I feel quite safe. I can hide myself away here. No-one would think to visit such a place unless they had a reason.

The day rewinds in my head. The hundreds of miles travelled in a single day. The river valleys and baggy farms I've passed. The places that slipped by which I will probably never see again. I am up to my neck in sadness. It pricks me with a thousand pins. I put my body on the train as if it were a parcel or a sack of vegetables, placed myself in a corner seat and let the machine take me where it willed. I thought to myself that if a steam train can shrink the country to nothing in one journey, then maybe it has the power to change a life in one day. I will go where it goes, to the end of the line, to a place where there is room to be numb. I press my nose to the train window and watch hedgerows stream past. I imagine I am a dandelion head floating off into the sky, except I am more spent than any dandelion. Suddenly I was cold. My blue cotton dress was not enough to protect me from the breezes skipping off the railway track. The train pulled on, uncaring, unthinking.

When we arrived in Highcliff, I thought we had reached the end of the line. Porters sprinted along the platform, dressed in blue serge frock tailcoats and pill box hats with fresh carnations sprouting from their buttonholes. They reminded me of the doorkeepers at The Savoy Hotel in The Strand. They loaded themselves down with bags and boxes so that the well-to-do owners could walk unencumbered and blather about 'taking the air' and 'promenading'. Is the weather still warm enough to take a bathing machine and will the water be as cold as last year? Beside them I was a shell on the seashore, worth nothing, wanted by no-one, looking for an ending at the start of a new century. Like one of *his* shells in his glass case. A specimen. I asked one of the blue tailcoats if this was the last stop but he said no, the train had a short way to go to Swanton Stoke, where it would stay the night and re-fuel. He said there was a hotel of sorts where I could find a room. So I stayed in my corner seat for another ten minutes while the train clacked along and came to a halt in what appeared to be a veritable hive for railway workers, as full of purpose as a swarm of bees. I had the impression that everyone, apart from me, knew why they were there, what they were for, what they would do tomorrow. It was almost as if I had arrived in another country.

My legs shook as I stepped onto the platform. The engine snorted and rolled steam around before it was taken away for the night. I found the way out of the station into the road and a boy dashed across my path. I called out and asked where I might stay for the night. "Excuse me!" I was so wrapped in misery that I was surprised my voice still made any kind of noise.

His eyes turned to soup spoons when he looked at me, as if he had seen something strange. He wasn't afraid.

"The Hartley Arms, Miss. I'll show you." He ran ahead, bony legs dangling from his short trousers, weighted to the ground by heavy boots. He said his name was Jack Stamp.

※

I peer through my hotel room window. As the sun goes down the clouds boil up and wrap it tight, leaving just a slip of amber, glinting through a slitty eye. The universe is saying *look, look, I am still full of wonder, no matter how unhappy you may be*. The gas lamps come on in the street below and I can see inside one or two front parlours before the curtains are drawn. Across the way a sulphurous glow comes from the railway workshop, where men move about in the lamplight casting black shadows. There is a murmur of voices and a scrape of shovel on coal and metal. If I ever see hobgoblins, they might look like this.

※

The night is over scarcely before I have shut my eyes to lie there without hope of sleeping. A hooter blasts before six in the morning, then again five minutes later, then again. After that comes the sound of feet, at first a few men stamping along the early morning pavements but soon an army is on the move. My sense of foreboding turns to curiosity. I peep through the window and watch men streaming towards the railway works, leaning up the hill, heads bent, none of them speaking. Dawn lights their ghostly faces as they press forward, like a shoal of blank-eyed fish. I am stiff from my journey and stretch out my neck and shoulders as I watch them funnel into the entrance of the railway works and hear their boots on the steps, sounding like a thundering waterfall.

※

Jack Stamp left the lost woman at the Hartley Arms and darted off down the main street, past the houses on the right with indoor lavatories, and the houses on the left with outdoor lavatories. He skidded left into Sebastopol Road, his heart pattering in his chest. At last he had something interesting to put in his diary. He'd seen a vision. She was not like the Virgin Mary who had showed herself hereabouts a few centuries ago when the sky turned wobbly. Her appearance had made people come every year on bloodied bare feet, carrying heavy wooden crosses, to the spot where she had hovered. This was better than that. This was something from the outside world that made his spine tingle.

He loved his diary. It was his secret self, the place where he could be who he wanted to be. He loved the touch and feel of it, the glossy brown leather bindings and tissue-thin pages. But often all he had to write in it was *went to chapel* or *helped Father chitting the potatoes*. Each day he opened a fresh page. At the top of each one was a note about an event in history which had happened on the same day of the year in another decade or century. It made him think about human strivings and how time was layered like that French pastry he couldn't remember the name of. Sometimes it described a useful thing that he should know; then it left space for him to write about his own life. The introduction was crammed with facts like the longitudes of the tropics that girdled the world, the countries ruled by the British Empire, the dates of famous battles won by the British, the number of miles between London and Edinburgh. The end pages were full of weights, measures and tables. One day they might come in useful.

༄

October 1 1900
(1661 Yachting becomes an English pastime. King Charles II beats his brother James, Duke of York, racing from Greenwich to Gravesend)

Flies in Amber
Amber is immeasurably old, for it is really the fossilised gum of extinct trees. Very often insects were caught in that gum and you can see them today – three million years at least after their death. Egyptian mummies are merely things of yesterday compared with flies in amber.

A frost came down in the night and touched the rooftops of every house in Sebastopol Road. I share a bedroom with Nobby Stokes. But he is often away on the railways, travelling all over, sleeping in the platelayers' huts or even in the railway coaches when they are stopped. I am lucky because I could be sharing with more. Others do. Everyone in this town has lodgers and Nobby isn't bad. It seems there are at least seven people in every house and only two or three bedrooms in each so the village is bursting. As I have no brothers and sisters, I am odd really. I don't have to sleep with my older sister in my face or my younger brother's elbows in my stomach. Never mind the smells. This isn't a place where big events take place. My parents do the same thing each day. But today is different because I saw a beautiful ghost arrive in Swanton Stoke. The evening train from Highcliff delivered her like she was a gauzy insect that needed a leaf to hide under, so I showed her the closest thing to a leaf which was the Hartley Arms.

I woke this morning longing to be more good than I am. Father is a stickler for goodness and rightness. The back of his head, which is shaped like a square box with grey hair stuck at angles, is all goodness and rightness. He works so hard and talks so much about duty that I have no doubt he will go to heaven. I listen to him go out in the mornings, long before I have to be up, at the same time every morning, six days a week. Sometimes the sound of him on the stairs comforts me back to sleep. Sometimes I think of him as a puppet and his duties are pulling his strings. On Thursdays and Saturdays I help him on the allotment where we grow leeks and carrots and peas and potatoes. Where women are not allowed. Sometimes he is pleased with what I have done but I wish he was pleased with me more.

My bedroom window gives me a grand view of other houses along the road. Today they are covered in frost, as if Father has sifted them with icing sugar. I can almost reach out from the window and touch the homes of Soapy Hardcastle, Boney Craske, Jockey Skillings, Toby Girling, Weary, Spuffler, Magic. In winter when the lamps are lit I can see inside if I want to. Since I was born they have all been there, going out and coming back just like the trains do. The early turn is from quarter past eight in the morning to quarter past seven in the evening and the late turn is from noon to eleven at night. Nobby is a lad porter and does alternate weeks. Each day he pulls on his clothes in the dark, his cord trousers and cloth overcoat and cap. He leaves his rule book under his pillow. His job is to collect the signal lamps and make sure they are cleaned and filled and changed twice a week. Then sometimes he is sent far away, fifty-one gates away to Bressingham Junction box. You see, I can tell you all about working on the railway but I cannot be one of them. Father wants me to be like him, a baker.

But I have different ideas so I linger over the professions listed in my diary. "The Colonial Service. *Indian Civil*. Aged 21-24. Examination of University standard. Colonial Police (Hong Kong, Ceylon, Straits-Settlements, Malay States). Pay rises according to State. East and West African Police Forces. Age 22-35. Medical Exam only. Pay varies. Pharmaceutical Chemists take the exam of the Pharmaceutical Society of Great Britain; training may be obtained at the School of Pharmacy, Bloomsbury Square, and at private establishments. Many qualified men set up privately." What does that setting up privately mean? Where is Bloomsbury Square? It sounds a beautiful place, full of flowers, no soot off the trains. I know it is an hour by train from Highcliff to Norwich, then more hours from Norwich to London. I have so much to learn. But the more I find out the more I discover there is to know. So maybe it is better not to find out at all. I don't think Billy minds much about learning. I don't think Billy minds much about his dad either, not the way I do about mine. He has been my friend for ever.

I push past sheets on the washing line in our garden to reach the hens, feed them and search for eggs. My frozen fingers open their stinking coop and scatter the corn. But it is a kind of den in there, and sometimes I think it would make a good place to hide. I can hear the pig in the yard next door, snuffling about. I smell his stink. I am also in charge of catching the rats but I have Gyp to help me and he is a good terrier. Sure enough he has left a dead rat with a glass eye on the kitchen floor. It is stiff as the stuffed birds in the glass domes at Swan Hall I saw at Christmas. I wrap the corpse in newspaper and resolve to keep a tally of dead rats in my diary.

Mother and Father are away at the bakery until late this morning. I am not needed to help, so I can meet up with Billy. The ice should be good enough down at the bottom meadow to make a slide.

"I'm going to be an engine driver," says Billy.

This is the way all our conversations start. We set off to make an ice slide and find a stretch where the meadow has turned stiff, into crystal swords. We need water which has pooled and frozen in a long strip, and we need space to run up to it. Billy knows what he wants to be. And I don't. Since engine drivers are kings, he manages to be a bit royal just by saying it. And by saying it he is already on the way to do doing it. It makes me feel a bit of a girl. He might end up as a coach trimmer or a shoveller or an office clerk or a boiler-maker-finisher or any number of things which aren't so good. But that is beside the point. And I might do much better than him at school. But that is beside the point too. He is the one with *the big idea*.

"You could run in the Olympics or you could be a gardener?" he says encouragingly. "Or a preacher?"

Yes, I can run. Faster than anyone in the town as a matter of fact. But Bloomsbury Square sounds easier to get to than the Olympics. All I can think of is Father's stern face. I don't tell Billy about the diary because I don't think he would understand the pleasure of opening leather covers and turning thin pages.

Off we go, running like demons, like winter lions. We run all morning along the ice slide, making it glassier and shinier and faster. Billy finds it and Billy leads the way, telling me which end to scrape and polish first. Then we wander back up through the allotments to the Rec to look for dead things. We collect as many dead things as we can find, frozen or starved. But it turns out it is harder than we think because creatures hide away to die and you can't find them under the ice or frost without digging and burning your hands with cold. Then we revisit our secret path, which means turning left after the Chapel, ducking right immediately after, into the back gardens of the bigger houses in Colville Road where the doctor lives, and the station manager and the foreman. Billy's ears are pricked and even the hair on the back of his head listens for noises. I follow in his footsteps, as excited as him. We make it better all the time. At first it was just the doctor's garden. We slipped into it through a gap in the fence, far enough from the house not to be seen, straight into the bushes. We couldn't breathe for a bit and didn't look at each other for a good long time. But there we were, sat behind someone else's redcurrants looking into their rooms, shelled like peas out of a pod into a bowl of other people's secrets. We were crouched on foreign soil but now all-seeing, panting like Gyp when he is tired out. At that moment, it was the most thrilling thing I had ever done.

We sat a whole afternoon, scarcely moving.

*

October 12 1900
(King John attempted to reach Kings Lynn in the East of England by crossing The Wash but the tide came up and he lost all the Crown Jewels in the mud and whirlpools)

Another sore throat means I am not at school again. This means I will miss scripture, book-keeping, more book-keeping, French and English. I am now third in class and I want to keep my place. I keep a record of my test results in my diary too. I must get better before woodwork on Wednesday because there is something I want to make.

The day of the ice put me in trouble. Father said I had wasted my time all day long. Though he didn't know where we had really been. He and I sat up reading the Bible until late, him reading and me listening and Mother darning in the corner. I know the words so well. Isaiah 44 verse six to the end. They are almost like music to me. Then we prayed together. Him praying and me listening and Mother darning in the corner. He said that Grace was restored. And we finished the way we always do.

> *Oh let me see Thy features,*
> *The look that once could make*
> *So many a true disciple*
> *Leave all things for Thy sake:*
>
> *The look that beamed on Peter*
> *When he Thy Name denied;*
> *The look that draws Thy lovers*
> *Close to Thy pierced side.*

I am not so sure about Grace except it is obviously very important. I know that it makes Father feel better. I go to chapel with Father and Mother every Sunday. So, I know that Grace is for the ordinary man. And that we are ordinary. It isn't just for people who live in big houses any more or just for people who belong to the Church of England. Grace is a thing for all of us. And I know that, through hard work, day in day out, I can have dignity. It doesn't mean that I will wear the fine clothes or have the smart hats of the dignitary. Because dignity and dignitary mean different things, though they are very similar words. The only dignitary I know is Lord Hartley at Swan Hall. He has his own station platform for getting on and off the train and he lives in a house with terraces to stroll along and lakes to put bridges over and woods with deer running through. And he grows oats and barley and turnips and grass. And there are near forty servants in his house, butlering and bobbing and curtseying and baking and cleaning out fireplaces and feeding the horses and the dogs. I know, as I have been to shoots and run through the woods and fields to scare the pheasants up into the air for them to shoot at. Those are grand days with hot soup and bread at the end of them. But I must always be careful when I get home not to say too much. For if Father thinks I have been too interested in the world of fine things, then he gets his Bible out and we sit up late again.

~

"You haven't told?" says Billy. We are sitting in the bushes at the end of the doctor's garden.

"No."

"You're sure?"

"Mmm."

We are getting bolder. We move along the back of the garden on our hands and knees. The gooseberry bushes are difficult to get round because of the thorns. So we move very slowly. We reach the fence of the next house along. Billy starts to worry the boards to see if they will budge. They won't but he thinks they might if we brought a jemmy. Our hearts are racing again. The garden beyond is attached to the house owned by Mr Massingham, the foreman of The Works. Mr Massingham! You don't know what this means. Mr Massingham wears a bowler hat all the time and has a mouth so tight that I'm surprised he can fork anything into it which hasn't been mashed for him first. His eyes are blue and made of steel. He cracks the whip in this village. The older boys cut his hedges and do jobs for him, as this way they might get jobs as apprentices. Men who fall behind or turn up late for work get punished by him, so he is like an angry God who has taken human form. By him and with him and through him we are given Grace surely?

He negotiates the price of every job which The Works carries out. He has a direct line to the nobs up in the railway sky. And we are planning to jemmy his fence.

Billy looks at me. He is testing me. He has had the big idea again. I am dancing round him in a pink frock if I don't do something quickly.

"Yes. I'll do it."

So there it was. The task was set. I am to find a jemmy, steal it, and apply it to Mr Massingham's fence.

꧁꧂

Rosie Etherington put on the scuffed boots and the blue summer dress she had worn the day before. She opened her small leather pouch and counted her money. The cloudless sky of yesterday had allowed ice to cover the ground overnight, so she wrapped a shawl around her. She had no plan other than to find out whether she could stay in this place for a while. The army of men had walked the ice off the main road so that she made her way along it easily, past a large building called The Railway Institute which she thought must be a kind of men's club, then on past a house with a notice on the door. It said patients for Doctor Mawson should wait in his front room. Another notice outside the next house said the front parlour turned into a bank on Thursday mornings. There were a few shops but nothing much more to see. She concluded there was nothing wrong with people's stomachs in Swanton Stoke. They ate enough to keep two butchers busy. One was full of hanging geese, the other had a chorus line of pigs' trotters dancing across the window. The smell of warm bread wafted into the cold air and drew her to a baker's shop. She had little money and no appetite, besides which she was put off by the couple behind the counter, a man and wife who looked as if they had forgotten how to smile.

She turned into Colville Road, which was wide enough for a horse and cart, and admired the pretty terrace houses of red brick which must be homes for the better-paid. Round the corner she found the Recreation Ground, where a row of six ducks waddled out, lifted their behinds and pecked at the iced puddles. She slipped along on the other side of the main road and turned into a street where the houses were very much smaller, with front doors arranged in pairs and outhouses in the gardens. They were so tiny that if she stood on tiptoe she thought she could touch the first-floor window sills. A street sign told her this was Sebastopol Road.

Then she turned into a road which ran along the railway track and found a church which was unlike any church she had known before, made of corrugated iron, painted bright red and yellow. As she stepped towards the graves she felt the women who had gone before her call silently, willing her to be comforted. *We understand weakness, we understand strength.* The gravestones themselves stood as monuments of human sadness. She passed Ethel May, Queenie Muriel and Matilda Etty, all lying obediently in the earth beside their husbands. *Reunited,* read the last line on each of their stones.

Far off, through the trees, she caught a glimpse of a big house and some kind of tower or folly. She didn't want to stray far. Winter had shown itself and soon the night would drop like a lead lid. In London she had never been conscious of the earth pivoting away from the sun as winter arrived because city streets shut out the natural world. But here the land stripped itself bare and stretched itself flat against the sky. Here all was ice and mud and parsnips.

As she made her way back to the Hartley Arms, a woman stopped to ask if she needed help. She jumped nervously but gathered herself to own that she was looking for somewhere to lodge. The woman said she was called Mrs Massingham and asked gently who she was and what her circumstances were, where her parents came from and why she was here. The older woman listened to the younger woman with a kind but puzzled expression, her breath turning to steam in the frosty air. Then she smiled and offered the young woman a room in her house. It was one of the better houses in Colville Road. Rosie Etherington felt relief sweep over her. They agreed she would spend one more night at the Hartley Arms, then move next day to her new lodgings. The friendship of a total stranger had lifted her mood. It seemed she was *meant* to stay. She was beginning to realise that, though her heart was a dead thing, she must continue with the endless process of being.

She slept no better through her second night at the Hartley Arms. Scenes from the recent past leapt out of the dark and danced around her.

༄

Was it just three months ago that I entered the department store Draper & Trotter and Edward dazzled me with wonderful things? Was it really so short a time? I saw the famous 'walking skirts' which exposed the ankles. He told me this is what the *new woman* should wear. Some preferred to call it the Anti-Microbe Skirt so that it could be seen as something clean and decent which didn't sweep up all the dirt into its folds. So much time was spent by so many people in London in the long battle against dirt, especially the piles of horse dung, some fresh and steaming, others hard as nuts rolling underfoot. There they were, these skirts, on full-size wax figures with heads and hands.

"We will do as they do in Paris in the *grand magasin,*" he said, boasting and laughing at himself at the same time, in the way he did. "We will walk around wherever we want and look and look. And we don't have to buy." He smiled at me and my heart leaped into his mouth.

"See. All the shop assistants are silent. They don't ask us to buy. They don't expect us to buy. We have come only to look."

We didn't even have to ring a doorbell. We walked in under awnings which fluttered like women's underthings, flashing pink underneath. We plunged into the smells, which were so full of different things you couldn't tell leather gloves and perfumery from cut hams and cheeses. I was swept up. Unbuttoned. Violinists played jauntily somewhere above us. I gawped at gowns that had weeks of work in them, hats waving feathers, furs from the Ukraine, glittering mirrors from Russia. There were huge glass cabinets filled with household goods, rugs and cloths hung over upper galleries, chandeliers scattering light all over the place as if we were in a palace. Objects had come from all over the world, just for us to look at. Everyone was filled with desire and the building hummed with quiet murmurings. A large sign said:

A Convenient Rendezvous! We are pleased to find that many Ladies make our Warehouse a place of meeting in Town. It is very central, and in any case a place of call, and it is big enough to be private! Of course, the spot of meeting should always be named – The 'Blouse' Room! 'The Millinery!' The 'Flower and Perfume' Gallery! The 'Ladies Outfitting' Room! The 'Tea Room' or any other of the magnetic points in our Huge Emporium.

"You would think that we were all permanently in a state of surprise, wouldn't you?" I said as I counted the exclamation marks.

"Ah! Yes, my dear. How observant you are." His eyes twinkled and looked away towards a row of headless, armless busts which had stiff white shirts on, ruffled with frills and pleats, buttoned high to the throat and pulled in tight around the waist. He took my hand and led me onto a moving staircase like a dragon's tail which took us up and up, to where anything could happen. He stood one step above me on the tail and I wanted to reach my head up to his. The escalator brought us very close. I wanted to slip my fingers round his coat buttons and open them up and slide my fingers inside. But I didn't. We came back down again. There were gasps and squeals. A man in uniform stood at the bottom with a tray of smelling salts and tiny glasses of Cognac to revive our spirits.

꧁

December 1 1900
(AD 60 or 61 Boudicea led heroic uprising against the Romans and was defeated)

A Raft Made Of Eggs

Mother gnats, or mosquitoes, are very clever at the art of egg-laying. They do not lay their eggs, single, but in batches of a hundred or more, all glued together into a little circular raft on the surface of a pool or waterbutt. This egg-raft is sometimes moored to a water-weed, but even when it is not it is as safe as a lifeboat. If you plunge it beneath the water it comes up dry as a bone, and if you turn it topsy-turvy it immediately rights itself. The baby gnat emerges through a trap door (at the bottom of the egg) into the water.

Each scrap of information tells me that there is so much more I don't know. I am filled with fear about all that there is to learn.

Yesterday an owl left a pellet for us to find. It was a parcel left for Billy and me to open out and unpack. We sat on our haunches, knees in our chests, and prodded with black fingernails. It fell open and inside was a collection of tiny bones, thin as eyelashes, toenail clippings white against the dark brown of the pellet. We started to push them apart. We tweaked out a bone and decided it was a jaw.

"Do you think that's a shrew's?" said Billy.

"Could be."

"That one's a thigh," he said.

"Could be. Lots of thighs. Femurs. Tiny skulls too. They hold them in their gizzard as they can't digest them, then pack them in a ball and sick them up a day after." I know this because my diary told me so back when the blossom was on the trees.

He looked at me, unimpressed and impressed at the same time. He wishes I wouldn't do that, make out that I know more than he does.

If a jeweller had made it in gold he would be an artist, I thought. It would be a treasure if it wasn't made of bone and squashed mammal fur. It was a keepsake, a thing full of reminders of what had gone before. We sat for an hour or more with our mouths hanging open, working out exactly what the owl had killed and eaten. The pellet was a record of time folded up and pressed small, and nature had done it without any skills at all, just by digesting and regurgitating.

Then Billy kicked it away into the hedge and it was gone for ever.

"You haven't forgotten, have you?" he says.

"Uh. No." He won't stop reminding me about stealing the jemmy until it is done.

And now my throat is sore again. Each time I swallow my spit, it has to pass a bee which sits down there and stings. Carefully I write into the front leaf of my diary that I am living at Longitude 1.2 East and Latitude 52.38 North. I know that sure enough. That is a fact. There is something wrong with Mother. That is another fact.

CHAPTER TWO:

THE JEMMY

Heavens, I can't complain. I might feel buried alive but I still breathe and eat. My life feels as if it is over and yet, like a hen which has had its neck wrung, I still walk and talk. I didn't expect this afterlife to be peopled with humans who are gentle and kind. The Massinghams have taken me in, or to be truthful Mrs Massingham has. I have a room with a white lace bed cover, a jug and ewer decorated with tiny pink roses, and beyond the window is an apple tree dropping its leaves. And Mrs Massingham has arranged for me to visit Mrs Eden, who would like someone to talk to. A companion.

"There is scarcely a body here with whom she can discuss the new department stores, fashions and latest designs," says Mrs Massingham, who is as round-faced and friendly as Mr Massingham is not.

Her hips are so broad that she must stand with her feet wide apart to bear the weight. Her ankles are strong enough to moor a boat in a storm, her skirts severely starched and her grey hair combed up into firm loops around her ears. She has bound my sore hand again and it is healing well. While she was tying the bandage she asked if there was anything else I might want to tell her, and said I was not to hide things from her. I could not think of anything that would be right to tell. But I wanted to lay my head on her bosom. At that moment it seemed like the safest place in England.

I think she must wake with an apron already tied around her waist. Today I find her in the kitchen organising a chopping board, apple corer, peeler and filling a bowl with water. She adds a dash of vinegar then picks apples from a basket, pares the skins, shucks the cores and slices the sweet white flesh with the confidence of someone who has spent half a century of autumns making stewed apple.

"How anyone can abide London I don't know. Not that I have ever been, of course. But I have heard enough to know that I wouldn't like all that noise and everyone with something to sell," she says. "I wouldn't like the horse manure all over the roads. Nor the smell of it. Lord knows how many tons a year, I hear. And the trams on top of it all. No wonder people are moving out faster than you can catch a cold."

She steers herself back to the real reason of our talk as another fan of sliced apple flutters into the water. No less than the wife of the overlord of the railway has asked to see me.

"Mrs Eden is too refined for the likes of us. The Edens hobnob with the lords and ladies who have made a tidy sum out of allowing the railway to cross their land."

She drops her voice and the tone is kindly. "But the Edens don't *really* belong with them. So Mrs Eden is a little...well...lonely I think. At any rate, she made enquiries when she heard you had arrived and had some knowledge of things outside."

❧

Before the week is out, I am in the Edens' house which is altogether bigger and finer than the Massinghams'.

"My husband has done the best he can to save the men from their previous lives, from themselves really," says Mrs Eden, back straight, face pale, lips thin. A maid has laid tea before us on a low table and bobbed out of the room backwards.

"When we first came to this place, it had such a bad reputation. The wildest of men, those who had failed in previous lives, were sent here because it was so outlandish and so... well," her grey eyes survey the lace and pomegranate patterns on the curtains, "...isolated."

She pours tea and offers sugar.

"My husband, Jonathan that is, decided that if he was to do any good and make the company work properly, then he must come and live among the men, immerse himself in their lives and ways in order to understand them. And he *must* bring the Bible to them."

She sighs. The bulk of her crinoline on the chair behind her bottom forces her upright like a perching bird.

I'm not what she believes me to be, but she is not one to puzzle over others because she is so thoroughly wrapped up in her own dilemmas. I don't admire her pieces of fine mahogany or the painting of a glistening horse on the wall, which I suspect is a copy of a Stubbs and was probably her husband's choice. Yet I'm surprised at the sense of sadness coming from her. This tells me I'm not as numb as I feared. The maid polishes and brushes in another room, scraping chairs back and forth. With each tick of the grandfather clock in the hall I measure Mrs Eden's loneliness surer than I can weigh the grains of sugar in that silver bowl before me.

But perhaps I am only seeing my loneliness reflected in hers. Who is to say? Who is to care?

"Jonathan tells people that his wife left her beautiful London home for an outpost manned by uneducated labourers and brigands, whom he is determined to mould into better men." She takes a sip of tea. "He is pleased with me, you see."

I am taken aback at the intimacy that buds between us, even before my cup has touched my lips. It must be because I am not of one of them. I belong to no-one. I have no tribe. She thinks she can collect me like another ornament, a porcelain Bo-Peep for her mantelpiece. And I must confess she is right about that. She can.

"It must have been very exciting in the early days?" I want to keep her talking.

"Oh yes. It was." The memories come thick and fast. They excite horror in her, a kind of thrill that can be had from experiencing danger second-hand. Her mouth quivers and smiles.

"My husband would come back covered in mud from his trips along the wilds of the East Coast, exhausted but unable to sleep because he was so exhilarated. He would take my hand as he described new stations being built which were no more than a shed with a single platform. Not even a proper signal box. I would dress specially to please him and we would take dinner by candlelight. He'd tell me of places that the railways hadn't yet reached, where he could travel for miles in a dogcart searching for the construction parties."

She raises her eyebrows. "Not everything was done by the book. Jonathan told me some of rum things they did like running locomotives along the *streets*."

She thinks she is being daring. "Once, the geese got in the way and no-one thought to move them. The men were laying tracks across a wide common, miles from anywhere. When they finished they went home and each one took several dead birds to pluck for the pot."

She laughs and fiddles with a ring on her slender white finger. "Jonathan has never minded this kind of behaviour but he is tough on them when they get into fights, or drink liquor, or don't arrive for work on time. But the geese? He didn't mind that at all."

She tells me the men were only too willing to leave their farms for the railways because the agricultural depression had brought them to their knees. On the land they were lucky to get twelve shillings a week *if* the work was there, but on the railway they got eighteen shillings and the work *was* there.

I listen hard. There are no children in this house. Something about Mrs Eden's poise, tight waist and perfect fingernails, tell me she is a stranger to posset and runny noses. The whole experience of sitting in this drawing room, hearing about the warp and weft of someone else's life, looking at the precious things which set her apart from everyone else, is a novelty. I've travelled a long way in a short time and I've woken in another story. It is not what I thought might happen when I cast myself out. She smiles at me as if I am a poor kitten that she has rescued from the cold.

"Jonathan had been hoping to go to America soon after we married, to join a railway company there. But once he was involved here, he didn't feel the need to go abroad any more."

She is proud of him. "He took to the challenge of working for a small company struggling against powerful competitors, fighting over different routes for the lines, pushing on inch by inch. He used to talk in his sleep, muttering about rails and sleepers, bricks and ballast. It provided him with adventure in the same way the Gold Rush did to all those greedy souls in America."

She looks at me as if she has suddenly remembered I'm here, sitting quietly in my chair looking at her beautiful rug.

"Now tell me, my dear, are you aware of the Paris International Exhibition, and have you seen anything of it?"

Surprising though it may seem, I am able to offer my thoughts.

"And what do you think of the Arts and Crafts movement?"

I have already spotted her love of lilies and knitted greens. It is easy for me to chatter on about William Morris and John Everett Millais. I tell her that taste is changing now that the Frenchman Claude Monet has taken his easel out of the studio and on to the bank of the Thames, there to paint London in swirls of blues and yellows.

"Oh," she says. Not sure.

"He is making room for feelings and dreams, so getting a likeness in his pictures is not so important." The words tumble out of me. "At the same time, artists are picking up new ideas from the camera. They want to capture a moment, take everyone unawares, catch them in their ordinariness. There is so much happening. It is changing composition altogether."

A mewing sound escapes from her. I have disrupted the ordered way in which she approaches life. I've tried to bend light itself, which she long ago decided travelled in straight lines. I haven't gone so far as to talk about Millais' *The Knight Errant*, not dared to mention his lusty horseman in shining armour pulling his sword to cut free a naked woman who is tied to a silver birch. I don't imagine she warms to nudity in art. I tap my bandaged hand and change the subject. We move on to talk about the books she likes, and she despairs of the governess novels which are now so popular but are beneath her.

"It is always the same. These governesses have ideas above their station. Families take them in, the men of the house get lonely, they take advantage of them, and the women are either undone or move up through society like sewer rats."

Her opinion is like a slap to my face. I feel suddenly dizzy but manage to look away quickly and focus on a magazine lying open on the table beside her. The headline reads *Why Women Lose Their Looks When They Marry*.

She starts to chatter about her favourite places in London which she treasures like old and dear friends. She leans forward.

"And darling Liberty's. How is it? Have you been to tea there recently?"

It so happens that I have.

Though she urges me to stay longer, I am overwhelmed by the need to rest so I make my way out, treading gingerly across the mosaic floor in the hallway with all the colours of the world stamped into it. It is so like another I have known. I could draw it in my sleep.

"Come and spend time with me. Three days a week. Would you like to? I need a paid companion. Come and take lunch with us on Sunday so that Jonathan can meet you. There may be something else you can do for us too."

❦

Rosie returned on the following Sunday. She had slept well and realised that, if she must continue to live after all, then she must find ways to be useful. Mr Eden was as kind to her as his wife had been. The only difference was that he *bestowed* his kindness as a monarch might endow his subjects. As soon as lunch was finished, he excused himself, announcing that it was time for him to go into the garden.

A few minutes later, Rosie heard an unusual clacking and puffing sound, then a shrill whistle. Through the window she saw her host ride past, sitting bolt upright on the engine of a miniature train. He nodded and waved. Toot! Toot! Mrs Eden said it was very important to let her husband relax in this way. It meant a great deal to him. The track ran to the bottom of the garden, circled a copse and vanished for a few minutes, then made its way back towards a miniature engine shed. The engine, the track and the shed were perfect replicas of the ones at The Works, except that they were a third of the size.

Mrs Eden turned from the window and offered Rosie a monthly sum that was almost enough for her to live on. As she gratefully accepted, Rosie suddenly felt she might faint. Mrs Eden asked if she was feeling dizzy, but Rosie assured her she was fine. She couldn't possibly explain that the transaction they had just made together had brought home to her the fact that Edward had never paid her for anything. No money had ever passed between them. Only friendship, then affection. She subsided into the chair for a moment and put her head in her hands. Behind this thought, floating in like a light behind a curtain, was the notion that this was perhaps why she had become so confused about how they were, one to the other, he and her.

*

Night after night she was woken by noise from The Works and the comings and goings of the trains. The village lived by the trains. There was no need for clocks or timepieces. As the darkness of winter deepened, the gas lamps glowed longer and she became accustomed to the sound of men scraping and clanging, the blowing of whistles, the hissing of steam, the roar of the engines. Often she lay in bed waiting for the approaching dawn, and it was at these moments that the memories of the past chose to come back to haunt her.

In the evenings she sat down with the Massinghams and forced herself to swallow large helpings of rabbit stew and apple pie. She couldn't throw off the feeling that she was living behind a wall of glass. She was not the person people thought she was. She was an imposter. She hadn't lied to them but she hadn't told them either. Mrs Massingham was warm and watchful, as if she saw in her someone she would like to have been if she'd had the chance. She liked the company of a younger woman with a waist small enough to hold in two hands, and hair which reached her bottom when she let it down. Much of her own day was spent helping other people, delivering to the needy, visiting the sick. This was in contrast to Mr Massingham, who felt himself a martyr surrounded by lesser men. When he came home each evening, he didn't ask his wife how she was or what she had been doing. Instead he delivered, in a long low monotone, a list of all the problems he had faced during the day. Mostly they consisted of other people's misdemeanours and the challenge he faced in deciding how to punish them. Docking their pay? Blocking their advancement? The men who were late, the boys who misbehaved, the jobs left undone, the mess not tidied up, the shoddy workmanship, the train which left three minutes late. This was his catalogue of woes.

Rosie began to walk out in all weathers. She was irresistibly drawn towards the sea and to Staithe, a village with a windmill and a tiny harbour where boats took shelter. She walked whenever she could. One evening as she stood admiring the colours at the edge of the creek, the sky turned monumental. Dark purple squalls rushed off the sea, and the mill turned silver as the curtain of rain lifted for an instant and light sliced through the sails. She turned back, heading inland, walking briskly to keep ahead of the storm. Another day she walked down to the sea and found a huge tide had poured in overnight, spilling over the banks of the creek and flowing along the little roads through Staithe. The water had lifted the boats up out of the creek and tossed them wherever it wanted. All was strangely still now, mirroring the sky, doubling the landscape. She felt quite disorientated, seeing boats where they shouldn't be and roads turned to rivers. There was mud in the gutters, mud churning in the lanes, mud silting up the narrow channels that ran down to the creek. She walked and walked in the hope it would exhaust her and keep her memories at bay, but they forced themselves upon her all the same.

⁂

Last time a mosaic hall floor took my breath away I was carrying my drawings, tied between boards and tucked beneath my arm. My, what a house that was! It was my first visit, the first time I met Edward. And he was all boyish and delighted, and ushered me into a dining room where a whole bay window was filled with ferns. Edward Stafford Clark, society artist and cartoonist to *Burlesque*. I brimmed with my own foolishness and spoke his name with a faint heart. His hands waved and fluttered like a musical maestro conducting the orchestra of photographs on the walls. There were woodland scenes, nymphs scantily adorned in wisps of muslin, Egyptian scenes of camels kicking up desert sand, laughing soldiers, theatrical tableaux with models dressed to look like nymphs or monsters. More than a hundred photographs hung from the rail around the dining table alone. Above them was a display of the prettiest blue china plates. He was bursting with expectation, desperate for appreciation.

I was able to comply without any effort at all.

"The House Beautiful," he said. "This is my intention. William Morris's golden rule. Do not use anything which you do not know to be a pleasure to yourself, and which you do not believe gave pleasure to the man who made it."

He bounced from foot to foot, his body straining at the buttons of his shirt as if it refused to be contained. He stroked his small beard like a much-loved pet. This, together with his careless flamboyance and the ongoing command and control of his shirt-tails, created the impression of a dervish who was never still.

⁂

"Yes, yes," he said. "*What* fun! This is something you must see. It's just the very thing." He showed me a gas light which had been adapted for electricity and was raised and lowered by a pulley.

"Now even when the smog is so yellow and grey that we have to have candles *in July*, I can switch on the light." He fussed round, switched and pulled and laughed. How he laughed!

"Yes. Yes. I can see you are *impressed*. I can see you *understand*. Ah yes. I see you have the *sensibility*. Now watch this." He pointed to a fan, hidden in the ceiling, which carried unwanted smells away through a pipe and out into the street just above the pavement.

"*Ha*. Yes. Yes. Oysters, fish, pigeon, beef and mutton, mutton, mutton. Always, mutton. The fumes are whisked away. And what of *this!*" He reached up to a contraption in a hole in the wall which looked like the tip of a pipe.

He bellowed into it. "Freda! Freda!"

I heard feet on the stairs. Then more. Then more again. And again. And again. Like descending scales on a piano. His eyebrows danced with joy. "Yes. You see it! The top floor is up so many flights of stairs, so this contraption saves us much exhausting mountaineering. I can call our maid from here and bother is saved. There is so much delightful newness in the world."

Freda landed panting in the doorway. But the way she spoke to him was more like an elder sister than a servant.

"Oh Sir, be quiet, won't you," she said. "The mistress is asleep. She is feeling out of sorts, as you know."

"Just showing off, Freda. Just showing off to my visitor. You know. Of course, we mustn't disturb The Duchess."

Freda tripped away and he turned his eyes, bright as lamplights in the fading day, back on to me.

"Come, come, come, come," he said. We stepped through a door into a small Morning Room where stained-glass windows caught the sun. It reminded me a little bit of church, though the images were not of Christ on his Cross but of minstrels, stars, shields and swords, gleaming in ruby and sapphire, emerald and gold.

"Oh!" I was almost speechless.

"It is marvellous, isn't it?" He sucked in his breath and puffed out his chest as if he had just received the Order of the Garter from the Queen.

"This is Marguerite's Morning Room. The Duchess. Of course, of course. But this is where we will look at your drawings."

He laid my boards on what I presumed was his wife's desk. I was quite dumb then, not thinking, yet able to move and do what he told me.

He bent his head over my work and stayed silent as he shuffled it back and forth in his hands. The clock ticked. I stared about and saw I was surrounded by proper paintings. I recognised a sketch by Kate Greenaway and then some oil paintings which looked as if they might be, could they really be, Van Dyck?

"You have a real gift, my dear. These are good likenesses. I should like to see you again. And your work, too. Return next Thursday and we can talk some more."

His gaze was intense. It raked my face and my body. His world was full of shape and colour. His voice so full of promise.

"No. They are not Van Dyck," he said. I was turning away but swung back as he had penetrated my thoughts. "I couldn't afford them. Of course, of course. But The Duchess *will* insist on having proper paintings. And these are very like. As you noticed."

He didn't call Freda again but saw me out himself, though not before he had taken my hand, turned it over and examined it as if it were a special object he would like to paint.

I couldn't hide my calluses from him.

So I rode on a cloud to the underground station. No, I was carried along on a shaft of sunlight. All I know is that I didn't walk. I don't know how time manages to stop and start like that, or how things go gliding by without you seeing them. Often since then I have pondered how meeting one person, in one moment, in one house, can turn a life right inside out, as quickly as a little rennet turns milk to junket. It is not something you would ever read about in a history book, unless of course the meeting was between Cleopatra and Mark Antony. History books care more about the dates when people died.

༺ཨ༻

November 27 1900
(8BC Horace, Latin poet, died)

The morning is so dark it could be midnight. As well as book-keeping and algebra at school today there will be woodwork. I love the smell of the shavings, the planing and the fixing. The feeling that I can do what I like with it.

My plan is to make a railway signal like the ones on the tracks, with a base, an upright and a lever to flip the flag up and down. But I get nowhere with the planning because every time I consider how to do it, my thinking is pushed out by the bad thing. I cannot do the bad thing without the risk of getting myself into big trouble. I could be seen, I could be stopped, I could be sent to hell for ever. But if I do not do the bad thing, I will never be able to look Billy in the eye again. So I will be in hell then too. Either way I will be in hell for ever. Word will go round. I will have no friends. If Father finds out he will send me to damnation. I will have undone all the good I have tried to do, the prayers I have said, the tests I have passed at school, the good deeds for Mother. All my strivings. But somewhere here, under my covers where it is warm, I feel little wriggles of excitement. Now how could that be? That badness could be thrilling? Why aren't the dark clouds of Satan circling my bed and making me look dark and sly? I sense that one way or another it will show on my face soon enough.

It reminds me of the day when Billy's younger brother Terry was at Chapel one Sunday, all scrubbed up and fastened into his best short trousers, holding on to his mother's hand. Then a boy came up to say that his Uncle Bob had died falling backwards off a cart. Terry's face lit up and he started to laugh. His mother gave him such a look and squeezed his hand until his face twisted up with pain and then she marched him home. That is when I saw that there were different ways of looking at things. The way we were supposed to look at them, and the other way which involves dancing on the moon or, if you wanted to, seeing things upside down.

The oil lamp shines in the kitchen. Soon Mother will want me to fetch water from the pump. She'll stand at the bottom of the stairs with a chipped tin jug, telling me to get a move on. On this side of the village we have to make do with oil lamps and water from the pump at the end of the road. We are called The Privates because the houses weren't built by the Railway Company but by the landlords who rent them to us. Billy lives on the other side of the main road in a house built by the Railway Company, with water and gas laid on, so he doesn't have to fetch water. The Railway Company takes their rent off the men's wages.

*

"It will have to come from the engine workshop," says Billy. "Maybe at night when they are busy and it's dark. I'll do it for you if you like."

"No. I can manage." Maybe he is beginning to think there is a bit of glory attached to it. Perhaps he's realised that a baker's son doing something more daring than a boilermaker's son might put him in the shade. But he is busy picking a scab on his knee, so he might not be thinking anything at all.

"It's Mr Massingham you have to watch for," he says. Billy is back being the expert again.

"Yes, I know."

I know also that the business of getting hold of the jemmy is now more important than whatever it was we wanted it for in the first place.

"Night would be good," he says again. "You could pick your time according to the shifts. The engine shed is the place. The cleaners work from seven in the evening until six in the morning, but they stop at midnight to eat their pies. You might have to watch out for the knockers when they go to call up the four and five o'clock shifts."

"Yep."

"People sleep deep after midnight," he says. "So maybe early morning is the time." This village can give the impression of being awake all night. It is almost more awake at night than it is by day.

"Yep."

"No-one'll notice. It'll be easy once you do it."

"Yep."

He chucks a stone across the ground, then tries to hit it with smaller ones.

"Shall I come too? Be your lookout?"

I think about this. But not for long.

"I could accept that."

We are in the school playground, at the front behind the iron railings. I can see Father's shop from here.

We talk and plan, and we are better friends than ever. Billy is really excited and I am too.

On the way home with our friends, we come across Rough Jimmy. He moves from village to village like a pile of old clothes that can walk by itself, a felt hat pulled down over his ears, brown hands buried in the rags. Occasionally he pulls them out and we secretly admire how black his fingernails are. The hat is a battered thing which he turns up at the brim so his grey hairs stick out on either side. Then his beard takes over like a huge badger's bottom, grey and white whiskers all tangled together. He has been a woodcutter all his life, but now his eyesight is going so he splits branches for kindling and helps with the harvest. We like him. He tells us stories.

"What do yer all want to do when yer grow up then, eh?" he says.

"An apprentice fitter," says Skinny.

"I want to work in the trim shop," says Barney. He is keen on drawing, and on not getting his hands dirty.

"I don't know. Maybe a clerk," says Dudley. He wants to do better than his father, a labourer who once worked on the railways in India and now makes concrete signal posts. My wooden post will look like one of these. Every five years Dudley's father turns decorator and paints the Railway Company houses. All in the same colours, so we know where we all belong.

"Engine driver," says Billy. As if that tops them all. Which it does, really.

Rough Jimmy's misty eyes turn towards me.

"I think my father will want me in the bakery," I say. "I'm not sure."

He twinkles and his face creases up like a piece of old leather.

"So you all want to be at The Works do you, except young Jack who maybe wants to be there too?" He chuckles and spits in the dirt. "Well, let me tell you." He leans close and we can smell cellars and mushrooms on his breath. "When you get as old as me, boys, there won't *be* any Works."

We think he is a bit of a magician, Rough Jimmy. When we hurt ourselves, he rubs our sores with special leaves. When we make camps in the hedges, he brings pieces of wood for us to use. He appreciates our work. He sees the craftsmanship. He admires the roofing and the tunnelling. He scratches his nose, which is covered with dark pulsating blood vessels, and pulls at the badger on his chin. I fear that crows might suddenly swoop down and snatch tufts from it for their nests. And he takes an age to tell us about this or that. He isn't rushing anywhere. Nor does he owe anybody anything like everyone else in this village seems to do. So when he says there might come a day when there is no Works, we wonder if he has seen the future. Seen it like he says he sees the harvest moon rising up over the fields, big as the sun, a rose yolk on the dark blue sky. A weightless bubble of promises and losses, he says it is. But the end of The Works! He might as well be talking about the end of the world. Our world, at any rate. In my head I can hear Father's preaching voice. *The Lord giveth. And the Lord taketh away.* And looking at Rough Jimmy with new eyes I think he looks very like one of the prophets from the Bible, mostly like John the Baptist, who fed on wild locusts and honey. Rough Jimmy probably feeds on wild rabbits and honey. Father tells me to stay away from him and I don't need to ask why. But it strikes me that Rough Jimmy could be a sort of John the Baptist in disguise. And then I have the awful thought that Father might turn away from John the Baptist if he happened to meet him, just because he was a hairy old man who wore dirty clothes. Father says cleanliness is next to godliness, but he is more likely to put cleanliness *before* godliness.

"You're dreaming again, tiddler," says Rough Jimmy. He laughs and shuffles away.

⁌

The sky is darkening when I poke my head round the corner at The Works. Billy is somewhere behind me, near the road, being the lookout. The gas lamps light up the polished bodies of the carriages, and the workmen's silhouettes cast huge shadows against the sheds. The place is peopled by so many giants, it is difficult for me to sort human from shadow. There are maybe twelve engines lined up for maintenance. A filthy, stinking job. The cleaning lads are busy with wads of cotton waste. They guard them fiercely and hide them from each other as there aren't enough to go round. Waste to them is like gold dust. A funny sort of gold dust is all I can say.

Up on the coal stage I can make out the bent backs of the shovellers and hear the scraping of their spades. The stage is level with the footplates, sandwiched between coal wagons on one side and the track on the other. The shovellers work to a rhythm, shifting coal from the wagons into huge iron tubs. With a screech of iron on iron, the tubs are then raised by a crane that swings them round and tips the coal into the engine. A great roar goes up. They curse each other if there is no water in the glass when they fire the engines. It means they have to fiddle about pulling the washing pipe out, fixing it to the hindsight, removing the plug from the boiler face, re-filling it and then starting all over again. This slows them right down, and it means they go home with faces as black as men from Africa. I know these things without even knowing how I know them. I have known them for as long as I can remember, most likely from listening to Father's customers.

The men bellow to each other above the noise. "It's no mystery how you get on here," I hear one of them shout. "You keep a date, keep a promise, keep time. And when the signal is down you stay there until it changes. Those are the rules."

"That's not what our Lord and Master says," comes the reply. By which he doesn't mean God but Mr Jonathan Eden. "For he believes what the Duke of Wellington used to say, which is that education without religion makes men clever devils. You can keep your time all you want, and your promises, but it ain't no good without chapel. Keep off the liquor, do the chapel, and you'll be all right."

Mr Eden came down from on high to dwell among us here in Swanton Stoke and live in the biggest house with his pretty wife. Everyone here owes him for everything. The list of owings gets longer all the time. They owe him for apprenticeships, they owe him for their houses, they owe him for the school, they owe him for the chapel, they owe him for their days off, their wages, their lighting and their heating. And sometimes people owe the company more than they should. We all know when that happens because they take in even more lodgers and the waiting to use the outhouse in the morning takes an age.

The shovellers, the crane, the screeching and scraping go on all night as hundredweights of coal are shifted and turned into miles of travel yet to happen. The shovels they use are huge, with scoops as big as a man's chest, too heavy for me to lift at all. Engines roll in one after another. I can sit and watch them for ever. It is what the making of the world could have looked like. Gigantic dark ghosts, strange lights, groaning monsters. And God said, *Let there be light.*

"Come on. What are you doing?"

It is Billy panting behind me in the darkness.

"I've been waiting for ages. Get on with it."

"If anyone asks what I'm doing, I'll say I'm bringing a message."

Billy looks at me as if I am a bit daft but truthfully I have shocked myself at how easy it is to pile one wrong on to another. Now I will have to make up a message and make up a reason for bringing it. With all this extra complication my brain starts to seize up like an old engine.

"Just get on with it," Billy says. His eyes are popping and his breath in the cold air steams like a kettle.

A dribble of smoke appears from an engine. A dull glow comes from between the wheels as the steam is raised. A pale finger draws the faintest line across the sky, the first hint of dawn which we and they must now work against. Though there is time enough before it signals the moment for the knockers to go running through the streets and throw handfuls of dirt at the windows.

In the end it isn't so hard. I slip inside the back of the shed. The heat hits me and my eyes smart in the smell and the noise. I stand out of the light, quite still. Everyone is hard at work, banging and scraping. Being invisible, I can take time to look around. A pile of tools lies just beyond the third engine on the left-hand side of the shed, and I think I can see something that looks like a jemmy. I move very slowly. No-one even looks up. I lift the jemmy and creep back, slow like a sleepy snake, smooth as water flowing down the plughole, nothing jerky. I am sure to be found out and yet I am not. I have my prize. Billy is waiting outside panting, his eyes shining.

"Got it?" he says. He doesn't want to make out any more that it's a big thing. "Come on then. Job done."

We crouch at the corner of the shed, then run across the yard, hugging the gloom. Above, the half-light of dawn fills with will-o'-the-wisps and turns ghoulish as a graveyard. My ears throb and my throat is so dry that my tongue won't work. My blood fizzes like the bicarbonate of soda that Mother spoons into me when I am sick or queasy. Sip slowly and sit still, she orders. Billy turns off down his road to the right. He gives me a silent salute and walks away. He almost swaggers, like it is the middle of the afternoon and he is just strolling along and might even start whistling. I slip left into Sebastopol Road and reach for the half biscuit which I have saved in my pocket to feed Gyp so he won't bark when I go in. I tip-toe up the stairs, carefully avoiding the creaky boards, and I am under the covers before I hear the knockers go down the street.

I can't stop shivering. I think two things. I did it. I did it. I did it. *Also.* She saw me. She saw me. She saw me. Just before I turned off down Sebastopol Road, I thought there was a movement in the air around one of the gas lamps. It was her skirt. She stepped out, slow as you like, all wobbly and see-through like a ghost. But I was speeding so fast I didn't think. I just saw her and she saw me. The lady I took to the Hartley Arms. Her face lit up with surprise when she saw me. And I was filled with wonder when I saw her. Then I turned the corner and was gone.

And she was left standing there, all beautiful and covered in silver in the lamplight.

❦

November 28 1900

(1721 Cartouche, highwayman, executed)

Earth-Shine

When the new moon is very young, you may often see a faint image of the whole round globe as well as the slender and brilliant crescent. This is a sight which is sometimes described as 'the old moon in the young moon's arms', and astronomers say that it is caused by earth-shine. This means that, while the crescent itself shines by direct reflection from the sun, the rest of the moon's surface is really reflecting only the small amount of light which it receives from the earth.

What did he, Cartouche the highwayman, steal I wonder? Jewels and gold and handkerchiefs. And women, perhaps? The jemmy is only borrowed. I clean the hens out before school, working hard to do something good which may earn me a kind look from Mother. The hens screech and flap and stretch out their necks. The bottom of the hen house is a carpet of dung which Father will dig into the earth at the allotment and turn into leeks and potatoes. I am giddy because I am tired, but also weak at the knees now that I have learned how many hours a night is made of, how time moves while I sleep, how dark turns to dawn and the earth carries on turning. I have not thought of time like this before, as big as the universe or as small as a hen's egg, depending on what you do with it. Mother's face is drawn tight. She has bruises round her eyes, which look inwards instead of outwards. I try not to breathe in the bitter fumes from the sour yellow, grainy, straw-filled cake at the bottom of the chicken shed and stick my head out now and then to suck in clean iced air. No, she is not angry with me but she is not happy either. The chickens are better for having their shed cleaned but Mother is not. I feel as if I have committed a sin and have not been found out but am being punished all the same. The lady in the lamplight keeps floating back to me like the moon slotting in and out of dark clouds.

I must try to remember these things which my diary tells me, the old and the young moon, now you see it, now you don't. I check the page at the back where I record the results of my tests at school. At the beginning of term I was fifth in class for everything, and first in Mathematics. Then I slipped to eighth and tenth and then back to second and first. There is also space for marks in Classics, but we don't have a lesson called Classics. There are tables of Latin and Greek verbs which aren't really helpful as I can't read the letters in foreign. I realise more and more how much there is which I may never understand. Over the page is the list of how many rats we have caught. It is a competition between me and Gyp.

CHAPTER THREE:

THE READING ROOM

I have found another way to make myself useful, part of my beginning or my ending. I am helping out in the Swanton Stoke library. All is quiet but for the gas lamps hissing in the street outside, casting hazy circles of light down the hill. In fact it is unusually silent. As if nature is crouched out there in the dark, like a wild animal waiting to pounce. The wind has dropped, the birds are mute, the leaves in the trees have stilled. I am alone apart from the strange wide-eyed boy, the one called Jack who crossed my path when I first arrived. From half past seven until nine o'clock we work together to check books in and out of the library.

I can't help noticing that my young companion is strangely nervous.

This is like no other library I have known, not that I have known many. The books are not on open display but are shut away in the back room, where they're not arranged in the usual way, by author in alphabetical order, but are filed numerically. Each one has a number, from one to three thousand. Every single one of them has been read by the Methodist preachers to check their suitability. Some have pages torn out where the content was deemed unworthy.

"Well, Jack, what is your favourite book?"

"The one I know best is the Bible, Miss," he says.

Little clouds of anxiety skip over his face and I suspect his unease is due to the fact that I saw him slipping down the street in the dark the other night. No good is what he must have been up to.

People who come in wanting to borrow a book must give the title and author to me, which I check against a numbered list. I fetch the book and Jack scrambles up a stepladder to a big indicator board which holds thousands of keys.

Each key is painted green at one end to show the book is available, red at the other to show it is taken. Jack's job is to find the key bearing the number of the chosen book, and turn it accordingly.

"I'll find you something exciting," I say. I think he needs cheering up.

My choice for him is Robert Louis Stevenson's *Treasure Island*. He needs a good adventure story to take his mind off his worries. It will also give him a boy's eye view of rights and wrongs, and therefore should not upset his parents too much. I have identified them as the grim-faced couple I saw behind the counter in the bakery. I'm also confident that if the book has survived the scrutiny of the Methodist readers, it is unlikely to cause a revolution.

Jack looks afraid and thrilled all at once. He fingers the deep crimson cover, embossed lettering and spine so stiff that it clearly hasn't been opened much. He climbs the ladder, turns the key, settles on a stool and starts slowly and gently to turn the pages.

Suddenly the wind gets up. It lets out a roar and circles the library, whipping the trees into a rage. The gale turns our little building into a tiny ship on a stormy sea, miles from human habitation. We carry a cargo of thousands of words, and the only deckhand I have to help me through the tempest is this under-sized boy with his nose in a book. Rain follows, battering our vessel of knowledge, and the sheer passionate force of it makes me feel shamefully aroused. I realise no-one else will come through the door tonight. I glance up at the indicator board and am staggered by how poorly it represents the store of imagination and thinking in this room. It has more in common with the arrivals and departures board at the railway station.

✺

Again I find myself seated at the smartest dining table in the village, feeling very much out of place. But here we are, with the ticking clock and the fine cutlery and Mrs Eden's face delicate as a bone china teacup. I have time to study Mr Eden's weathered face, his clipped white beard and moustache, the massive dome of his forehead. This house of ornaments and manners is a far cry from his 'travelling office', the railway carriage adapted for his personal use, in which he hurtles about to inspect his men, signals, junctions, bridges, embankments and the tracks themselves.

"Drink, my dear, is the demon which stalks the land," he says. "But not the railways, I would hope. A man who drinks cannot call himself a true railwayman."

"When a man weakens and turns to drink, it may be because he lacks spiritual fulfilment, or is without answers to the great questions in life. My belief is that the gap is easily filled with something as small in its obviousness as it is huge in its scope. The Bible itself! The frailty of man creates the very conditions which allow us to fight for his soul."

I ponder these statements and decide to speak.

"I wonder whether turning to drink *is* actually an indication of a spiritual need." My voice is small against his mighty torrent of certainty. "Or could it arise more from an emotional or a creative need?"

It doesn't matter if I say something untoward because I'm from outside. And, because my heart is shrivelled, nothing truly matters to me any more. Who knows? I might decide not to stay here but move on, climb aboard Mr Eden's great railway to another place, another community. But for now it seems that people want me here. His eyes look up sharply and his forehead darkens. His gaze flickers between me and his wife. He digs his long white fingers into his mouth, extracts a fishbone and lays it carefully on the edge of his plate.

"Quite so," he says. "Quite so. Men are men but they have beating hearts. We neglect their softer side at our peril. It is our duty to educate, to show them how to live, to teach them discipline and skills. And we are fortunate to have noble women, evangelists among us to bring the Gospel into their lives and change their hearts."

I am not one of these noble women.

He warms to the sound of his own deep voice. He relaxes and does what he likes best, which is to recall the early years. He remembers when he fell asleep on an engine while he was standing bolt upright and crashed through the station gates and thank the Lord no-one was hurt. Or the days when he herded gangs into the fields and the first spades went into the ground to build the line to Highcliff. He is still proud that he managed the work himself and didn't employ contractors to do it for him. He kept the price down to no more than ten thousand pounds per mile.

Those early days have left his face wind-scoured like the men's.

"Highcliff opened three years ago, but I have not rested since and nor shall I," he says. It was at Highcliff that I saw the jaunty porters, the suitcases, the well-dressed visitors and heard them talking about bathing machines on my journey here.

"The next thing is that we must build links to the Midlands. And we must continue our efforts to attract more passengers and goods."

He pushes his plate away. "At Highcliff we bring thousands of people straight to the beach, to the sea and the sand, the cliffs and the new hotel. Great work is being done and some are growing rich. But we are still only at the beginning. There are many more miles of railway waiting for approval in Parliament."

I can't help wondering how the two great giants of our time – Christianity and Industry, or rather God and Commerce – have become such good friends. The whole of the last century was devoted to expanding them both, hand in hand. Though, according to my humble reading, the Bible never asked to be twinned with the making of fortunes. It was Edward in his London house, with his endless poking fun at things, who set me questioning these ideas. Edward opened my eyes, then left me staring into the nothingness of a future without him like the eyes of a dead woman. But I can see that for Mr Eden the two great beliefs work marvellously together and have created an Empire to bestride the world. His railway brings order to chaos. His God makes people obey his rules. His work makes money and creates wealth for others. Yet it strikes me that his plan to bring visitors, with all their desires and pleasures, bathing machines and swimming dresses, could lead to new kinds of sinning and new types of shock. For the moment, at any rate, he is disposed not to see this. He cleans his nails and waits for the plum crumble to be brought to the table.

The past plays out in my mind when I am alone. How did it all happen? On the Thursday, as Edward requested, I returned to his house. Goodness, yes, I was back with more of my sketches at the home of Edward Stafford Clark! I dressed in my prettiest things, put on my best boots, washed and pinned my hair. I hoped that through him I would get the opportunity to improve myself and leave my sewing. I wanted to escape the tailor's dummy, the stitches and the swatches, the encasing of bosoms and imprisoning of waists. I longed to take up my pencils and step into a world of observation, colour, light and shadow. How I longed for it! I had nothing else, no status to preserve or fear losing. But I remember I was a little wary of the enthusiasm he had shown for my work. I thought, but only for a second, that I would almost prefer to live with incessant yearning and the prick of hope, than with success and the burden of expectation. Dreaming of becoming an artist might be easier than becoming one. But nothing quenched the sense of adventure that coursed through me as I approached the house.

Yet even before I reached the door it became clear there was turmoil within. Which bell-pull to use? The one for visitors or the one for servants? The sound of chaos told me it didn't matter which one I pulled, so long as I made myself heard. There were bangs, squawks and the sound of furniture being pushed around. Was he moving house? I was confused. Had he forgotten his invitation to me? Had it been made in a moment of rashness. Hundreds of people must have sought his advice and patronage, but I supposed that not many *women* eager to earn their living as artists would have plucked up the courage. Women were the subjects of works made by men. They gazed out of the pictures. They did not create them. Or they saw painting merely as a hobby and made nothing more than pretty landscapes.

I needn't have worried. Suddenly he was there at the top of the steps, opening the door himself, ignoring the straitjacket of social hierarchy, bouncing on his hamstrings and rushing me into the hallway.

"Take care!" he cried. "The Duchess will never forgive me if they are damaged!" Freda and the groom, whose name was Arnold, were taking down the curtains in the Morning Room, folding them in piles and carrying them to the back of the house. They grunted under the weight and sighed with exasperation as they snagged them on the antlers of a moose's head that hung in the hallway. There was much teasing and laughing. They didn't question what they were doing but hurried on, racing against time, as children do when they fear being caught. A sense of joy and naughtiness filled the air.

"The table! The table!" Edward shouted. This, too, was cleared of ornaments and carried out. It was a small Moroccan table, made of ebony inlaid with ivory. "Freda! The feather duster. For the tail. Arnold! A saddle and a whip!"

I was so bewildered, I thought they must be preparing for an evening of theatricals. I remember how the sunlight fell through the windows into shimmering pools of green and gold. I remember the house being so crammed with pictures and objects that it felt like a shop.

"Ah, my dear. Just the very thing. Yes! How very wonderful to see you! Just the right time," he said as I pressed myself against the wall, allowing him to pass without brushing my body.

If this was a show, then he was the magician.

Things were fetched and carried while he directed operations with shouts and exclamations. He, Freda and Arnold worked together, bound by an invisible sense of purpose, buoyed up by good humour.

Freda's forehead was beginning to shine as her hair escaped from her cap. "The mistress has gone shopping, so we have time to do what the master wants. She doesn't like him involving us in his games, Miss, not that they are games. They are real work," she giggled. "And we don't mind a bit."

Steps at the back of the house led to a courtyard where a large shed stood. Edward pressed his hand into the small of my back and pushed me through the door into its dark interior. The brightness of the day was shut out by the curtains, and it seemed that a space had been cleared at one end for a performance. The saddle brought out by Arnold was thrown on a table, and he solemnly mounted it as if it were a champion racehorse. He had changed into a fine pair of riding boots and flourished a whip. Freda lay on the floor beneath, her brow puckered in concentration as she raised the feather duster and swished it like a tail. They were as happy as children preparing an amusement for their parents.

All at once the atmosphere changed. The shed walls closed in. Edward stood quite still and held up his hands to command attention. He stood before a camera mounted on a tripod, the shining eye of the lens cloaked in a black cloth. For a few moments there was complete silence and nobody moved. Then he lifted a large glass plate, inserted it, lifted the black cloth over his head and the work began.

Even then I did not fully understand what was happening.

"The indispensable fifth wheel, the third eye, the invaluable adjunct," he announced.

The playful mood had gone and his tone suggested he was sharing something precious.

"It is a marvellous thing." He flicked his hand as if removing a cobweb from the air. "This is how it is done. There is no other way for me, with so little time in hand, working week in and week out against the clock for *Burlesque*. Deadlines. Deadlines." He sucked air through his teeth, pulled his beard and stroked his lips.

"Drawn by Friday morning and delivered just in time for publication. Men who draw against time must use what means they can. And this is a marvellous means! Don't you think, my dear?"

I hesitated.

"What exactly am I looking at? This scene here today?" I asked.

"Ah, yes. This is to catch the creasing of the britches around the knees, the fall of the light on the boots. And the composition! The angle of the tail. The shape of the saddle on the horse. Hours of time saved in an instant. You don't look quite sure, my dear?"

His eyes bulged fiercely, half-amused, half-challenging. I saw a man at the centre of his own stage, a man driven by what he could see, a man exploding with pictures inside his head.

As soon as Edward had finished with his camera and plates, Arnold and Freda carried everything back into the house and put it back where it belonged. A wooden box was returned to its position on the Moroccan table. I stepped over to look and found a small blue butterfly pinned inside. The blue was so intense, I wondered if it might be made of cloth. But I had only to touch it to know it was real.

He came up behind me and I whirled around.

"Art out of tables and feather dusters?" I whispered, confused by his proximity.

"Yes! Yes! It doesn't matter what the material is. What matters is what you do with it. What happens to it in your hands! And your hands, if I may say so, are exquisite." I put my right hand behind my back because I didn't want him to dwell on the hard pads on my thumb and fourth finger.

"The eye and the hand, I agree," I said. "But the mechanical eye I am not so sure about."

His face came very close to mine and he lowered his voice.

"*Nothing* is what it seems. Everything is a trick of the light. We only ever see fragments of things, pieces of each other. We sift and we keep. We store and we turn it into something. That something may be a record, it may be entertainment, it may be art. It may be kept in a scrapbook or framed for posterity. Or it may be lost for ever because no-one has understood what it means. But there is, in my opinion, no reason why the gathering process may not be done with the invaluable adjunct."

He tucked his shirt in again and tried to straighten his wayward clothes. "We live in the age of the machine."

I stayed silent. I was absorbing a sheaf of new ideas, an intoxicating mix which I would never truly get to know if I remained among the hems and seams of my normal daily life. He hung on my silence. His eyes roamed.

Then he wagged his head back and forth as if I had said something interesting, and raised his hands.

"You are quite right," he said. "There is debate about it. It is perceived by some as treading a dangerous line between art and documentation."

He threw me a sideways glance. Perhaps he imagined I was thinking more than I was.

"I was only listening to you," I said. But he was too caught up in his train of thought to take notice.

"Ha! The powers in the land might object, mightn't they? The taste-makers? Well, take it from me. Sometimes the Royal Academy is frankly more than a little pompous. In their pompous way the powers-that-be call these *études photographiques*." He put on a lah-di-dah voice and jutted his chin.

"They say that, in the interests of integrity, the idea must precede the stimulus. But what I say is that the idea and the stimulus can work hand in hand. *Do* work hand in hand! Could Wordsworth have written his verses without walking the hills and valleys?"

CHAPTER FOUR:

THE RAILWAY SIGNAL

December 7 1900

(In 1783 William Pitt became British Prime Minister and Chancellor of the Exchequer at the tender age of twenty-four)

Billy and I crawl into our secret passageway through the back gardens of Colville Road. The jemmy tucked inside my jacket burns with triumph and guilt. I am amazed people cannot see it through my clothes. We move gingerly round the gooseberry bushes and crawl up to Mr Massingham's garden fence. We are afraid of the great punisher, even though he is married to a woman we would be glad to have as our own mother. Her apple pies are the best in the village. The truth is that our interest in the Massingham house has doubled now that the mysterious lady has taken up lodging there.

The jemmy does the job. This afternoon I am Billy's equal. Three boards in the fence swing away and we slide through the gap. We are in! Buried in the shrubs at the bottom of Mr Massingham's garden, we have an uninterrupted view of the back of the house, kitchen, morning room and back bedrooms. In silence we swivel our heads, surveying the new territory we have invaded. This must be the lawn where they take tea in the summer. The bed of flowers, ragged now the summer is gone, is where Mrs Massingham must cut blooms for her vases. Over there is a birdbath where she has put out bacon rinds and bread crusts. Oh Lordy! We can see *her*! She is in the window of the kitchen, head bent, elbows working like pistons.

We dare not even whisper. We are turned to stone like the birdbath. We scarcely breathe.

Mrs Massingham is scrubbing clothes on her washboard, rubbing and pummelling, arms white as the fat on a cold lamb stew, shaking with the effort. She turns away to a steaming copper and drops in the laundry to boil. Her broad shoulders heave as she turns the dolly.

And then Miss Etherington appears.

"That's the lady," I whisper to Billy. I have not told him I saw her on the night she arrived, or on the night I stole the jemmy, but he knows I helped her at the library on the night of the big wind.

His eyes pop, he breathes in quickly and leans forward for a better look. I guess he is not going to say anything just yet. But then he does.

"My Ma says she is no better than we."

This takes me time to consider. Billy's mother has gaps where some of her teeth are gone, her hands are rough and raw and the best thing about her is her pastry.

"She says she don't know why these Massinghams and Edens have taken up with her. She's just a stranger who came on the train with all the rest of the cargo, like the sacks of grain, the cattle and bags of soot and bones." He crosses them off with his fingers.

"Mangolds, swedes, coal and coke," I chime, getting into the game. I think of more. "Hides and skins, hay and straw, potatoes, machinery, manure and fertiliser, fish and crabs." Our whole world is made of things coming and going.

Our attention has strayed. We have, for a moment, forgotten the purpose of our great expedition, which is to watch grown-ups and see what they do when we are out of sight. Miss Etherington comes up behind Mrs Massingham and they talk in a low murmur. I can see the detail of her pale grey-blue gown, the tip of her nose. Her shawl is the colour of cornflowers. All of a sudden, I am struck by a bolt of lightning and in the flash I know she is the most beautiful thing I have ever seen. Or ever will. She is delicate as a butterfly, a miracle of nature. I have a strange sense that she might change my life.

Mrs Massingham drops a blue-bag into the last rinse to make it *white-as-white-can-be*, which is what my mother says when she does the same. Then the door bursts open and Mrs Massingham comes out, hauling baskets of wet washing to the wringer. She turns the iron handle, feeding sheets through the rollers before hoisting them to finish drying on the line. By this time her grey hair has fallen round her face, her cheeks are flushed, and dark patches of sweat have appeared beneath her arms.

Even if we wanted to move, we couldn't. We can't do anything that might make her look up. We are trapped like rats in Gyp's teeth. Miss Etherington comes out to help her and we hear them talking.

"Sometimes, when they prime the engines and put too much water in the boiler, it gets in with the steam, goes into the cylinder and *whoof*! It shoots out the top and comes down in a black mist," says Mrs Massingham. "That's when you hear all the women in the village shouting 'shut the box down' because they don't want their washing covered in soot."

Miss Etherington makes a sympathetic noise. Mrs Massingham keeps turning the handle and starts to pant. She pauses and gives Miss Etherington a funny look.

"Art classes at the Institute? Whatever will Mr Eden think of next?"

"I have a little experience. I think I am able to do it."

"Do you, dear?"

Mrs Massingham looks at her as if she had just flown out of the sky and perched on her mangle. Miss Etherington smiles back and laughs lightly, her throat opening like a bird in full song.

"I do. And the money would be handy. Mr Eden says the men must be educated and that it would be foolish to neglect their artistic as well as their spiritual needs. He is keen to keep them here, so he wants to improve their conditions in every way he can think of."

They carry on turning and lifting in silence. Eventually Mrs Massingham speaks.

"He is eager, more like, that they come to your art classes rather than ride the engines to Wellmouth, fill themselves with ale and ride home again pickled as the eggs in my waterglass."

She puts her hands on her back to ease the strain, spreading her feet like the hands of a clock at ten to two.

"Well, well, well. It may end up causing more trouble than it's worth," she says. "You take care, my dear."

December 11 1900

(In 1282 Llewellyn, the last native Welsh prince, was killed which made way for Edward I of England to rule Wales. Llewellyn's severed head was taken to London and displayed on a spike outside the Tower of London)

Why Bread 'Rises'

There are little egg-shaped cells which look like spectacle lenses when you magnify them and they are really microscopic plants. Actually they measure about one two-thousandth part of an inch in diameter; yet, though they are so very tiny, they have been given the ponderous-looking name of Saccharomyces cerevisae. It is due to the hard work of these busy little plants, which the baker simply calls yeast, that a loaf of bread 'rises' and 'becomes light'.

It is Sunday and the rule is that we don't work on a Sunday. I blackened my boots last night, as I can't be dubbing them on a day of rest and couldn't help noticing the iron heel plates were wearing thin. Normally on a Saturday Mother takes two dozen eggs out to sell but yesterday she didn't. Usually she walks to market with her basket, stopping to talk to everyone along the way, picking up bits of news. Instead she sat by the fire and her breath smelled like rotting brussels sprouts. In the afternoon she cut our old clothes into strips. *Spread, smooth, snip, pile. Spread, smooth, snip, pile.* Then she rested her head on the back of the chair and stared at the ceiling, all the stains that need painting over. Then she carried on. She took some old flour sacks, unpicked and washed already, then knotted the cloth strips into them to make rag rugs for upstairs. When I go to bed, my toes brush over shreds of Father's old shirts and Mother's undergarments and skirts. It is like walking on the past.

There is no baking today either, as the Lord said Thou Shalt Not Bake on a Sunday. Except that he can't actually have said that because I can't find those words anywhere in the Bible. We will eat slices of tasty cold pie instead. Mother usually buys pie at the market. It is shaped like a loaf with a hard pastry crust, filled with pink and purple meat topped with dark brown jelly. We eat it with pickled onions. Before that I must go with Father to prepare the chapel and light the candles. The day is dedicated to reading the Good Book.

"Each stone in this building was laid down by a great man. An ordinary man but a great man, just the same," Father says to me.

He says the same every Sunday, and I know he means I am to feel blessed even though I am only a boy and I am the son of a baker. Put an *n* in that and I could be the son of a banker. This is what I think but I do not say.

There are people in the village who can point to the walls in the chapel and say where their families laid their stones. The walls are covered in plaster now, so they can't be too precise, but they know it as well as they know the backs of their hands.

"There was no organ in the early days," Father says. "The preacher read out the hymns two lines at a time and Billy's father would start the tune."

He tells me this every week too, proud of their singing, men taking up the low notes and women taking the high. These days an organist walks four miles to play here each Sunday so we count ourselves lucky. We've been provided for. We can move mountains with our singing. We almost turn into angels. Everyone stands up in their stiff collars and best clothes smelling of rosemary and lavender, which is meant to keep them fresh between outings. I can't help noticing they manage to smell of lack of washing too.

Travelling preachers also walk from far away to stand in our pulpit, and Father looks forward to a special one called Peter Codlin whose name is known all over Norfolk.

"There is none better than him," he says.

Peter Codlin draws crowds. Everyone turns out to hear him. He is a fisherman from Highcliff with hair that froths like waves on a stormy sea, a jutting beard and a Guernsey that looks to have been knitted with rope. He has piercing blue eyes but he is blind, so he is led to the pulpit by his daughter. When he speaks we are swept away on claps of thunder, hosts of harpists and a longing for Grace, which you can have even if it is undeserved and that, at least, is a good thing. We pray strongly that we will be spared the wrath, the burning sulphur and the plagues of locusts. Once, when he told us the story of Jonah and the whale, I truly felt that he was Jonah and that the whale must have been very brave to swallow him whole and keep him down for three days and nights.

"And Jonah prayed unto the Lord his God out of the fish's belly, and said, I cried by reason of mine affliction unto the Lord, and he heard me; out of the belly of hell cried I, and thou heardest my voice."

In that instant we saw Jonah, wrapped head to toe in seaweed in the pit of his misery until he was vomited onto dry land. It made my body shiver all over.

Some of the travelling preachers make us laugh. One pretended the pulpit was an ark and he herded imaginary animals in two by two, then slammed the door shut so firmly behind Noah that he couldn't open it again. He pulled with all his weight and the door flew open so suddenly that he was thrown onto his backside and lost all his dignity.

But today the chapel is full of echoes. It is only a small square block of a building, plain compared to the other church in the village, the tin one painted bright colours. Inside our chapel everything is wood or white-painted plaster.

The central pulpit overlooks the pool, covered in boards, where the immersions are done. Two staircases lead up to the gallery which runs round three sides so that people up there can look down on the heads below and see the bits of hair they have forgotten to brush. There's nothing in the chapel which is not useful. It takes Father's mind away from just thinking about his work, the reason he was put on this earth, which is to put bread on other people's tables. Sunday is the day when he lifts his head up and reaps his rewards. Instead of the baker who sells loaves, he is the superintendent of the chapel who greets the preacher, reads the lessons and tells his customers about the bread of heaven, the bread of life, the bread which turns into flesh. Sometimes I think the stories adults tell each other are harder to believe than the stories children tell.

My father never stops thinking about service to others.

"Business without the ideal of service is like a wide but shallow stream," he says. "It makes a fair show but is not deep enough to be useful."

Every day he rises at three in the morning, no matter the weather. Even if it is tunnelling off the North Sea across the fields, or if ice has crawled up inside our windows, he is always up. He heads into the street like a ghost, making his way to the bakery. Mother is often with him. Though she is small for a mother, she is strong. She hoists the sacks of flour and carries them in for him on her back. Soon enough, clouds of flour pour in and out of his mixing bowl, gathering in his hair and eyebrows, in the creases round his eyes and in his ears. He sets the yeast aside to ferment with warm water and sugar, wrapped in his long apron which reaches his ankles. I have seen him stand at the big wooden trough, the length and width of an altar, and mix the dough so tenderly, he seems to be willing it to live. But when he knocks it back he takes full charge of it, cutting and thumping. Then he kneads, pummels, stretches and pulls, the dough and his body working together as if he is in communion with his Maker. After that it is left to prove in the trough, a breathing white body. Only when the firemen start stoking the engines does Father feed his oven with logs and chippings from The Works. He never pauses for a moment of rest.

"I test the heat with a piece of bread to see how fast it browns." This is what the mothers in the village say to each other. But my father knows his ovens better than that, so he has no need of pieces of bread to tell him what's what.

The kitchen heats up even as the icicles grow outside. The flour settles over the floor and works its way into his lungs. The dough rises out of the trough and tips over the edge. It is slapped and sliced and put into tins like little black coffins lined up for a funeral. The oven doors are levered open and his face burns red in the furnace. Sweat streams down his cheeks. By the time dawn breaks he has been up for hours and his job is still not half done.

"At least we do not live in London, Jack," he says to me one morning when I am helping. "There are times during The Season when the work never stops. So many folk are there to attend the balls and the parties that bakers must work round the clock."

A slip of newborn sunlight cuts through the haze of flour as he turns his hands. When there is no school he likes me to be there and I try my best.

"We are blessed to be here, Jack. The bakers in London don't live much into their fourth decade. With so much work and so little sleep, they don't last as long as those who eat their fare."

As the first trains leave the station, warm loaves are laid out on the shelves. The rest are piled into baskets, loaded on to the handcart, taken from door to door along the streets and up to The Works. He won't be finished until midday.

December 14 1900
(1861 Prince Albert died at the age of forty-two)

Pouring water. It is not the rain itself but the eternity of it that worries us. I wake at night and hear it stroking the rooftops. When Father goes out to deliver the bread, the wheels of the handcart turn up ribbons of mud, no-one wants to be a delivery boy today.

At school we take mud in on our wet boots and are kept in all afternoon to do woodwork or sewing.

The railway signal I am making has a simple upright, fourteen inches long, that fits into the base. I plan to attach a long wooden flag with a pin so I can lever it up and down. But how to make it happen? Minty Morgan is the Swanton Stoke expert on signals and he is proud as can be that he was one of the first in the country to make one with poured concrete. As it happens he uses it to make window frames too, and he's been all the way to India to use it for building telegraph poles for the Indians. But my signal is nothing like his. Mine is more like a ship's mast. It has two extra uprights at the top to bear the signals, and five levers down below, with a small dolly signal at the side connected to the top by a ladder, high as any cabin boy would have had to climb on a ship. Minty Morgan is a clever man, even though he is a labourer and not an engineer.

I decide I will take a piece of wire and loop it round a pin at the base, then bend it into a lever. I'll run it up to the top so that the lever will pull the signal. I think this will work.

As evening settles and gas mantles light up the windows, it seems the rain will never stop and, if it does, all the world will have to be wrung out and hung on the line. Water pours off the fields, making pools in the lanes for us to leap over on our way home. At night the rain gets heavier, drumming its fingernails, never letting up, turning the gutters into fast brown streams, silencing the cockerels and deepening the stain on my bedroom ceiling. Morning comes and it is one of those days that will stay half-dark as if the end of the world is nigh. The men head into The Works through the wall of wet, rain stabbing brown holes in the ground all around them. Word gets out that the regular coal stage hand hasn't been able to get in and Soapy Hardcastle has a hard job of it, stepping in to fill the tubs and crank them up by hand. The night shift ends and the men move to the canteen to eat their bread and cheese with cold tea. They must be wondering what the day will bring. Then night falls again, with thick ladders of water hanging from the sky. It occurs to me that Father might even build an ark of his own if the rain doesn't ease. The hens would come in useful.

"The passenger train will have to stand in the station for the night," Father says as he comes in, wet and tense, stamping his feet in the hall. "The bank has washed away at Pig's Grave. The rails are hanging in the air."

He reaches for a clean apron. His face is set, his task is clear. One look and I know what he expects. He doesn't need to say. We head into the night, hair streamed wet, to the bakery. Inside, our clothes steam. We work urgently, reaching for the knives, bringing in firewood, pulling in sacks of vegetables, setting the largest pot on the stove.

"The bridge is washed away at Blackwater too," says Father.

His book of recipes is open. The headings are firmly underscored and the instructions written in his perfect handwriting. It is a Bible of sorts. There is no room for questions tonight. Cabbage and bacon soup for a hundred people is to be made.

25 quarts of stock
4lbs of onions
10lbs of cabbage
8 oz of butter or fat
4 lbs of bacon bones or trimmings
36 white pepper corns
4gs salt
1 faggot

I chop cabbages until my arms ache, but there is no let-up. I weigh salt and pray that he won't ask me to chop the bacon bits. I remember the pig being killed along the street, the sound of squealing as the knife was stuck into its belly. Its legs quivering for a long time afterwards.

Father is baking for the world. He is on the Sea of Galilee feeding the five thousand. He has been sent a good deed to perform and he will not fail.

We take the steaming soup in the handcart to the station. Tiredness is of no importance. This is another night which I may see all the way through, same as I did on the night I took the jemmy. We feed some of the passengers from the platform, handing bowls of soup through the windows of the train. Others we feed in the mess room. Their faces are grey, their hands shake, they are the same as all other human beings who are cold and have nowhere to sleep. It doesn't matter how smart our clothes may be, we are all alike when we need to lay our heads down and fill our stomachs. All are truly grateful, blessing Father for his goodness. And Miss Etherington is there, helping to feed people, so I know she must have good in her too.

CHAPTER FIVE:

THE FIRST HAND

Rain can do awful things. It ended the first part of my life. I can't say that things since then have been hard, though. Unlike so many, I've never gone without food, clothes or shelter. I've always found a way to survive. I was born in the room above my parents' grocery shop in Windsor. They served customers tea and sugar in twists of brown paper, and dry goods from jars behind the counter. But, as I grew older, the joy I had given my parents turned to anxiety. My father would turn my chin up to him and stroke my hair and say he feared what would become of me. I don't keep many pictures of those days in my head, but the rain of recent days has brought back to me the great flood of 1894, when the Thames flowed across the meadows, ran through the streets and crept up to Windsor Castle.

I remember looking out across the new-made waterland, trees spearing the surface, thinking it looked other-worldly. I remember, too, the men who came in flat-bottomed boats, propelling them forwards with tall poles. One of them moored against our shop and my parents handed me over. I put one foot in the boat, stumbled a little, then pulled my second foot in. I sat down and gripped the side as we glided away across the mirror of water. No-one said goodbye. Somewhere inside I understood that my parents had not come with me because they needed to stay and protect the shop from thieves. The boatmen took me to a church hall where women were handing out soup. Other large and small children were there too, so I played with them. I was unthinking, excited to be in a new place with new friends. It seemed as if I was there for a very long time, but perhaps it was only a matter of days. I almost forgot about my parents because I was quite content. The rain came back the following night, and the one after, but in our safe dry place we rolled ourselves up in blankets and whispered and laughed until we fell asleep. I didn't know yet that my parents had sat on the roof growing weak and cold, or that they had drowned when the water rose. When the waters drained away, they were found curled together, stiff as boards. All I knew was that after a week, or three or four, I was placed with a milliner and dressmaker in a good house in Clapham. The sale of my parents' effects paid for a room, and for the privilege of working with other girls, learning a trade as a seamstress. I found new friends in Elsie and Nelly, who were grateful for the chance to work with a needle and avoid going into service like their sisters.

"We have been spared raking out fires and emptying pisspots!" they boasted as we sewed.

Mrs Garbutt, whose house we shared, was a good woman, unlike many we heard of. We slept together in the room under the roof, swapping stories, often weeping with laughter as we clutched each other in bed. Our few possessions were kept in boxes under the beds. We worked so diligently at our stitching that we soon had hard patches on our fingers. Some days we fantasised about the people who might wear the clothes we were making. Didn't Mrs Pettigrew have a waist as big as a whale? To which grand ball would her beautiful daughter wear the rosebud dress? What handsome young man would be first to lay his hand on this tight bodice, finger the stitches we had just put in? Some days we worked in silence on dresses that had to be finished in no time at all. We had bread and milk at breakfast, pudding at midday, and hot drinks to keep us going on days when we had to work late.

Mrs Garbutt's was not like other establishments. She wasn't impatient with us. As we picked up our cloth and needles each morning, she didn't say *any girl can sew*. Because she was kind, her Third Hand, Second Hand and First Hand took their example from her and taught us well. I learned to work with expensive silks and gauzes. I loved the feel of them on my lap, the light that glinted off them. I became quick and nimble with buttonholes, frills, lace, tucks, gathers, darts and inserts. While the other girls moaned and put down their work when they got tired, my fingers went on flying. My stitches, even and tidy, settled like flocks of little birds in exactly the right place. But, as the months passed, the work took its toll. Elsie's wrists began to ache so badly that the pain never left her, not even on her days off. In the afternoons she began to get bad headaches. Very soon I was made Third Hand and was given more difficult work. Then I was Second Hand, helping with new girls. Finally I became First Hand, deciding which pieces of work would be done by the others while taking on the trickiest pieces myself. Oh, how I loved the delicacy of it! I inserted the tiniest stitches, small as the whiskers of a mouse, into the most delicate stuff, created gathers which twisted and flowed like a mountain stream. If you believed you could do it – you could do it! Elsie and Nelly said it was because of the way I looked that I had been made First Hand.

"She wants to put her finest in the window," they said, and laughed as they put their hands in mine.

We were just girls then. We made friends with another girl called Verity, who worked for a dressmaker across the Common. All the houses in these parts were newly built, ready fitted with aspidistras in the windows. It felt as if all London was expanding, houses marching across fields and orchards on the edge of the city. On rare afternoons when there wasn't any work to do, we would link arms and walk past the aspidistras, to call upon Verity. She worked for sharp-faced Mrs Blunt, who was known sometimes to keep her girls up all night. Ladies could come as late as midday to choose their fabrics, then leave while the cutting was done in the afternoon. They returned for a fitting at six in the evening and expected the dresses to be ready first thing the next morning. Mrs Blunt kept the work room cold, and I was sure this was why Verity's nose was red and she was always coughing. She got very thin, and dark rings appeared round her eyes.

"We work under the gas light until the air gets too thick," she said. "When we open the window, a freezing wind blows in and my lungs turn to muslin. The lady customers don't notice we're dizzy with exhaustion. If they knew how tired we were they would ……oh, I don't know…. Sometimes I think they see and it adds to their pleasure. They all swish away in their carriages glowing healthy and happy."

Her cough became slow and deep.

Verity stopped talking because it took too much energy, and she stopped coming out with us. She was sent home to Gloucestershire to rest, and returned with stars in her eyes. She was going to be married, she said. But quickly she fell ill again and then one night she just died in her bed. No-one knew why. Then we spied an anonymous letter in Mrs Garbutt's Times newspaper about a poor seamstress who died in her bed and the inquest had looked into what could have caused such a tragedy. We thought Verity might even be the subject of this letter. The inquest found she had died from 'apoplexy', a medical word which I have never truly understood. All we ever knew was that she had a sudden fierce headache and went to lie down. We looked at it every which way and could speak of nothing else. Then we learned, little by little, that poor Verity had a broken heart, because she had discovered that the man she was engaged to was already married. She had lost the will to live.

༄

December 22 1900

(In 1880 the writer George Eliot died. Her real name was Mary Ann Evans but she published all her novels under a man's name)

I wonder why a woman would pretend to be a man. I will ask Miss Etherington next time we are at the library.

Father doesn't need to watch me. He has eyes in the back of his head, so he can sense when I am not working my hardest. Sometimes I hear him speak in my sleep and I think he is in the room and his voice is coming from the corner. He and I were up before dawn this morning, when the frost twinkled all the way up the street. The trees threw black arms against the sky, and the hedges around the fields were all tipped with the gold of first light. Father doesn't notice these things because he is too busy planning each moment of the day. There was no sound from Mother this morning, but she now takes a hot brick wrapped in a flannel up to bed with her so I know she is suffering. We hear the knockers going to wake up the men for the four-o'clock shift, and again for the five o'clock. Soon the hooter will go.

Christmas is nearly here and there is mincemeat to be made. Father is already shredding beef and shovelling ingredients into the bowl. They look like piles of jewels – gold, rubies and diamonds all heaped on top of one another. It is the Christmas harvest.

15lbs of beef
36lbs of sugar
12lbs of apples
15lbs of suet
42lbs of currants
10lbs sultanas
6lbs of peel
8 lemons
½ oz of nutmeg
1 oz of cinnamon
1 oz of mace
1 oz of cloves

Mother has had to come to work because she is the one who ices the cakes. The task is bigger than anyone knows, for each one takes more time than my railway signal has taken me. Each night when she came home she was in bed again with a hot brick before Gyp could say hello.

"I've done my last. I'm never going to do another cake. I got the one for Swan Hall done this afternoon and it was worse than herding cats," she said.

"The icing sugar burst out of its bag and flew round the bakery. Then, when I mixed it with the egg white and lemon juice, I worried about the consistency. Would it set or would it run off? There are so many hazards when you ice a good Christmas cake. Two layers of white marzipan, two coats of white icing. Some of it got on my face and in my hair. Even making the icing bags was difficult, folding the greaseproof to the right size, snipping the ends, inserting the nozzles."

She paused to look at me, and I was afraid she was lining me up to do the next one instead of her.

"What sort of decoration did you do?" I asked.

"Little S-shapes in three layers all the way round the top. A wavy line all round the middle, scrolls round the bottom and stars over the top."

I fetched her a fresh hot brick and she clasped it to her neck.

December 23 1900

A winter moth

The peculiarity of this little moth is that she has no wings – or rather that such mere wing-tufts as she has are no use for flying. She is very common in gardens and orchards at this season, and climbs the trunks of the trees to lay her eggs on the twigs. When you see what are called 'grease-bands' tied round tree-trunks, all smeared with a sticky concoction and covered with struggling insects, you can be sure that they are put there to trap these wandering wingless moths.

Billy and I are back in Mr Massingham's garden. We feel quite at home there now, seeing the world back-to-front.

We hear shuffling down the side passage and hold our breath, thinking we have seen a pile of compost come to life. It is Rough Jimmy, wheezing and coughing. He doesn't know we're here because he blows his blackened nose on his fingers and examines the result. He wouldn't do that if he knew we were watching. Then he wipes it down the side of his trousers. Pieces of cloth wrapped round his ankles are beginning to unravel and trail in the mud. He knocks on the back door.

Miss Etherington opens it and speaks to him kindly, as if she knows him.

"How did you fare in the rain?" she says.

"I were up the line near Pig's Grave. A platelayer's hut."

She vanishes inside and comes back with something wrapped in a cloth.

"Here, take these. They're freshly made."

"Thank you," he says, stuffing them under some sacking tied around his waist.

But he isn't going anywhere just yet. He leans against the wall.

She folds her arms and she isn't going anywhere either. They talk like old friends.

"It were a horrible sight. You wouldn't want to have been there. The bank at Pig's Grave got up on its hind legs and moved across the track, and water poured off the fields. The rails lifted up like broken twigs. Then an engine came out of the darkness and ran over one of the platelayers from out west. They had to take his leg off the track, careful as they could, put it in a box and send it to the hospital. They say he didn't make it."

Billy and I turn to each other, raise our eyebrows and feel important. I am secretly relieved that Billy did not know this before me. I am also glad that this terrible thing did not happen to my room-mate Nobby Stokes. But this might explain why Nobby has been sleeping badly. The last two nights he has cried out in his sleep and I have coughed hard and turned noisily in my bed to bring him out of the dark dreams that upset him so.

January 2 1901
A new diary for the New Year. It is very like the first. The leather is etched with tennis rackets, boxing gloves, golf clubs, a football and a bicycle, with a pleat to fit a pencil down the spine. The inscription "Charles Letts School-Boy's Diary" on the front looks as fine as words on a tombstone. I turn the first page and find a tea-coloured print of the Duke of Wellington at the Battle of Waterloo. He sits on a very big horse carrying a telescope and leather gloves while corpses lie all about and between the hooves. I turn to the lists of important facts.

> *The date of Empire Day – May 24.*
>
> *The distance between Lacrosse goals –*
> *not less than 100 yards and no more than 130 yards.*
>
> *Ramadan begins – February 22.*
>
> *The Battle of Waterloo – June 18 1815.*
>
> *The Zulu War – 1879.*

I look once again at the entry requirements for good careers for boys. Marconi wireless telegraph, barrister, medical practitioner, dental profession, veterinary surgeon. Then come tables of Latin, French and German verbs, trigonometry, logarithms, conductivities, comparative temperatures, chemical names of common substances, winners of the England Lawn Tennis Championships, cricket championships, rugby football.

I close up the old diary but, before I put it away, I take a last glance at my tally of rats.

> *1 trapped*
> *1 Gyp got*
> *1 trapped*
> *I think Gyp got one*
> *1 Gyp got*
> *1 trapped*
> *1 trapped*
> *1 Gyp got*
> *1 trapped*
> *1 Gyp got*
> *1 trapped*

January 7 1901

I have seen Miss Etherington out walking. She walks and walks and walks. As if she is haunting the marshes. She wears the leather off her boots, willing the sky to lift her up in that sad way she has. She is drawn to the water, always. To Staithe, to the creek and the mud and the stiff white sails of the windmill. When I cross her path she calls me by my name and asks me where I am going. I say to the wide-open smile of sand to the west. She asks if I will show her and so we walk together. She and I. The spirit and the dull boy.

A little smile crosses her face when she asks me if I know about Mr Eden's train in his garden.

"Oh, yes," I say. "As if the village doesn't have enough tracks already. And there is another that people forget to count. It runs from the water tower and carries things around The Works."

I look at her, a bit sly. "Sometimes Billy and I go there and jump on the hand-trolley and pump it round the track. If we get caught we get a bang on the ear or a boot up the backside."

She opens her throat and laughs.

I take her to where the sand makes a desert, with the sea on one side and pinewoods on the other. We fall silent as the dusk creeps across the sky. Our feet sink into the dunes and I breathe easier, even though I am so close to her. The sea is soft blue-grey velvet, folding and unfolding. It looks like the edge of the world. We walk along a line of crushed razor shells, gazing across the emptiness to the scribble of trees against the sky.

"We are tiny beings painted on a huge canvas, single brush strokes on yellow and grey," she says.

"Are we, Miss?" I squint and try to see what she is seeing but I'm not sure I do.

"It isn't what you see, Jack, so much as what you feel. How you interpret things. The trees could be the edge of a forest. They could be filled with menace or filled with hope. They could be painted in green, or blue. Or purple, even."

I put my head on one side to show I am listening. But really I am just loving the sound of her voice, the way she talks to me as if I am a friend. Not the kind of friend who makes ice slides, but one to think with, as if I am more than my short trousers and tally of dead rats.

"There is more to see. In a few minutes," I say. I am mad with courage for a moment and take her hand. She willingly gives it and we half-run towards a fresh-water pond which shines like pewter in the winter light. Then they come. I knew they would. This is their time of day. This is their time of year. First comes the sound, and I watch her puzzled face because she can't work out where it's coming from. Then we see them. Thousands of geese are flying out to sea where they go to sleep at night after feeding on the fields all day. At first just a few threads appear, hundreds of feet above us. They make flights of arrows in the sky, one flight touching the next, followed by another, floating on top and beneath each other, all the time moving out over the water. Soon there are thousands of them. The occasional straggler loses altitude and comes close by, squawking like a rusty hinge. We stand and watch until our necks ache.

CHAPTER SIX:

THE DEVIL'S THROAT

January 15 1901

(In 1759 British Museum opened)

How Winds Come

In every lamp that burns you may see an illustration of how Nature makes her mighty winds and gales. Air is always rushing out at the top of a lamp-chimney, and always rushing in below – that is why there is always an open grating there. Similarly when any part of the earth is heated by the rays of the sun, the air over that region rushes upwards; and as Nature cannot bear a vacuum, other air rushes in at once to fill its place. Then we say that a wind has risen.

We set off on an expedition to visit Mother's sister at Highcliff, and this is not normal. Usually we go in summer when it is all crabs and parasols and I can run with my cousins in hot sun on the beach. Sometimes it is covered with pebbles, sometimes with sand. We never know which it will be. Tom is now fourteen and working at the boatbuilders, so he doesn't come so often now to jump the waves and dodge the horses pulling the bathing machines. But there is Filch, Reg, Ron and Skinny. Anne is only small and a girl, so she is not much use. There is little Squawler too, who can turn grown women into nodding dafties, or she can go bright red and bellow louder than the hooter at The Works. If we can, we boys get out to the cliffs or the beach. But now it is deep winter in the nothing-to-be-said-for-them weeks after Christmas. Mother and Father have been murmuring and keeping something secret from me for a week or more.

Father tells me that in the old days, before the railway came, members of the family couldn't see each other unless they hired a horse and cart and the journey would take the best part of a morning. Now we get there in a cough and a sniff.

Our tin heels rap along the narrow alleys, cobbled houses leaning towards us against the weight of cold. The sea is a grey slab humping and growling in the distance. Clouds are building into black mountains and the wind is doing its best to tug our clothes right off.

Mother's sister Mary is the kindest woman alive, always dressed in black, buttoned to the neck, clean white apron over the top. There are so many widows in this town. Each one has sat by the kitchen table for hour upon hour, waiting for her man to come back, walked the cliff path to scan the sea for specks on the water. All the women wear black. Even those that don't have husbands wear black, and those that do have husbands wear black, as if they are preparing themselves for what might happen in the future. Aunt Mary has eyes like oysters, large whites couched in round shells, and her white hair is tied in a knot at the back. Her husband – he is not my uncle by blood but I call him uncle just the same – is Henry Squinty Clink. They all have nicknames round here, just like they do at Swanton Stoke. Squinty's eyebrows foam like waves capped with surf. One eye looks straight at you, and one peeks through the tiny window in the living room or up the stairs in the corner. I never know which one to look at.

"Come on," say the cousins. And we are off, running down the alleys, wind clawing at our faces, flying past the mess of fishermen's cottages, the yards, the sheds, the boats, the crab pots and coiled ropes, out on to the sea wall. It is like being on the ramparts of a mighty castle. Smart hotels are being built so that Highcliff soon will be as refined as the French Riviera, or so they say. We press our noses to the window panes of one hotel front, all of us in a line, laughing at the neat white tablecloths laid out for nobody in the winter. In summer they play music and couples lock arms like crabs stuck together, dancing and remembering when they were young.

We lean on the wind and think we might fall if it dropped. The sky turns odd browns and yellows and shakes its fist at us.

"Let's go pick stones," says Reg. And we are running along the ramparts, down the steep slope to the beach where our feet turn on the pebbles. The moon could be like this. Blues, browns, greys, pinks, blacks, whites and all the colours in between.

"It's the blues we're after," says Reg. He should know. He's been stone-picking all winter. His fingers are tougher than a boot heel, his skin is split, his nails have gone. It is the coldest job on earth but it earns extra money for the family. When he finds a blue flint he puts it in the pile by one of the big hotels. When the hoard has grown to about the size of a house, it is carted onto a train and sent to the potteries at Stoke-on-Trent.

"I like the ones with the holes in," I say.

"The hag buns. Keep the witches away," says Reg.

All the colours make us dizzy. We have to lift our heads and look out to sea to get our balance back.

Then we dodge home like skiffs on the high water, racing up the alleyways, sniffing pots on the boil through the back doors. On the way we bump into Flinty Daredevil.

"Here comes a weird one," says Reg as he spots him on the gangway.

"Hello lads," Flinty says. He is unlike all men I can think of as his face is completely without whiskers, smooth as an egg. When he speaks, he sounds more like a son of Lord Hartley's than like Uncle Squinty, and there is something about his mouth that is like a girl's. He cuts his slop shorter than most and doesn't wrap up against the wind in oiled skins and cloths but stands tall and thin in the bite of the wind with the expression of Paul before he was stoned by the people of Antioch.

"Weird. In many ways?" I ask.

"He's not one of us," Skinny says, his words snatched away by the brewing storm.

"Go on."

"He went to that posh school where the lords and ladies send their children to meet other children who are the same and will run the country." Skinny's nose is running fast now so he wipes it with the back of his hand.

Though the blast from the sea half-shuts my eyes, I look back at Flinty Daredevil and notice his very long legs. His thigh boots must have been specially made to fit and to show them off. The cloth tied round his head would do for a Sunday service.

But we are off again, boots clattering on the cobbles. Tom first, then Filch, Reg, then me, then Ron, then Skinny, strung out in a line. We turn right, back down to the sea wall, to shelter between the houses. Lamps are being lit and the windows begin to glow. We stop by Small Spratt and spy him sitting at his table lighting his pipe, smoke circling his beard and the great mole on his huge nose, which gave him his nickname. His house is called 'The I dunno' and the shed at the bottom of his garden is called 'Nor do I'.

We pause to catch our breath.

"That Flinty Daredevil is having a big boat made," says Tom. Uncle says Tom has done well for himself at the yard, building boats for the fishermen.

"His is special," Tom says. "It has a mast thirty feet tall and a huge fish hole. The cabin is fourteen-foot long with a coal stove. And get this. It has wooden beds built into the side."

We are impressed by Tom being so knowing, and puzzle over what the beds are for.

Then we run down to the sea wall again and watch the waves washing around the new pier. This is only half built and looks like bits of railway stuck together. The sea is churning round the footings, pulling at the girders, sending clouds of spray into our faces.

"Do you remember when the old jetty went?" I say.

"Storm of ninety-seven, weren't it?" says Tom. "The poor old thing were made of wood, not iron like this big one. It were all the ladies' fault. Their thin heels got stuck in the gaps between the boards but gaps were what let the waves spill through, so the jetty could stay put against the force of it. But the ladies went on wanting to wear their heels. So extra planks went over the gaps and the next time a good storm blew up, the floor was ripped to pieces. That were the end of it."

We all nod at the madness of women. But I am interested in this new structure because I know, from making my railway signal, that it must have needed many drawings before a thing could be done. It is much more complicated than a railway signal.

Out there in the rolling water is a lost village, worn away by the tides until it sank into the deep. We boys look at the weight of water on it now and fall solemn. We've heard fishermen say they hear the bells of a church at low tide and we've heard them remind each other not to hit the sunken spire when the tide is low. I can't help thinking that the spire would have crumbled long ago and made homes for the fishes and the crabs. But it is not for me to say.

"Get on back home. This is lifeboat weather."

The voice is Piglet Long's. His hat is pulled low over his head but his beady eyes fix on us and his white whiskers bob like a bird's tail. His brother drowned one day when he went crabbing in a calm sea and the weather changed. Piglet turns his weathered hands this way and that to make a living. In the summer he moves out of his house and lets it to visitors. He takes them fishing in his boat. He puts tents up on the beach to shield them from the hot sun or the cold wind. Visitors love him, and treat him as if he is their oldest friend or part of their family, even though they see him for only two weeks in the year. Piglet loves them back, but for his own reasons. When they're here he's up with the sun and down with the moon, joyful as if angels and archangels were singing around his hat.

"You know why I loves them?" he says. We wait for the answer, which we know already.

"I loves them because it's like keeping piglets in a pigsty. I keep them well, I charge them well." His eyes gleam like washed pebbles and he chuckles.

"I don't fatten them for killing, mind." He waits for a minute, looks up at the raging sky and down again. "I farm them for profit, then I let them go again. That way I get them back again the next year and we start all over again."

It is the poor luck of the visitors that they do not know they are being farmed and fattened, and that their good old local friend is dancing a little jig around their purses. We laugh at them too. Just like he does.

❦

We are squeezed in tight around the fire while the wind whistles through the cracks in the door and windows. Father has gone back to his loaves and the early-morning handcart. He says Swanton Stoke will starve without him. Mother keeps saying sorry and looking down as if she has sinned and he is her Maker. His jaw is set but he speaks gently to her before he goes.

Aunt Mary's oyster eyes are calm as you like as she clicks away by the fire. She has five steel needles with points at both ends so that she can knit round and round the body of a man to make a Guernsey in hard dark blue wool.

"What you making this time, Aunt Mary?" I ask.

"Lightning. For Big John Tandy. His wife died a year ago."

I see it now, the pattern of lightning down the front of the Guernsey, picked out in the light from the window. Her hands work wondrously fast, a special thing which I know I could never do.

"March will put everything right," Aunt Mary says to my mother. I have never seen Mother so pale and small. For several days she has scarcely spoken. It is as if her mind is in another place. She is a shadow that falls across my path, but it is a shadow I do not want to look at in case of what I see.

"When the crabs crawl, the bills will be paid," Aunt Mary says. "Nothing is paid for here 'til the fishing season. Until then six pennies of bones with onions and carrots goes a long way. This is what I've put by, my dear. We'll have you right in no time."

She reaches into the basket where she keeps her balls of wool and pulls out a tin box. She takes money from it and tucks it carefully into her apron. Then she lays Squawler in a basket. The child's red cheeks flake and her nose bubbles but at least she is quiet. Aunt Mary covers her with a blanket and puts her knitting away. The two sisters wrap their shawls round them and step through the door into the moan of the wind.

❦

Uncle pulls his leather boots over stockings of coarse greasy wool. He throws his slop on over his Guernsey. That always seems clever to me, making a thing specially to keep the wind out. Mother says it is nothing more than calico made strong with boiling in the tanning copper. The oilskins hanging up by the door are the same, but they'll have an extra rub of linseed oil to keep the tide out. On goes the sou'wester too, an upturned boat which he'll wear all evening in weather like this. No-one thinks it strange. A man sitting at home wearing a hat bigger than a lady's bonnet. We all know the reason. The sea has roared.

"It is the Devil's Throat," he grunts. All I can see of his face is the nose poking out under the brim.

"There's hundreds of miles of sea rolling in here from the North Pole," he says. "When the wind moves round to a north-easterly it piles the ocean up like nobody's business. I'll never forget sixty-six, when near a thousand vessels were lost around this corner in six months. The sea chased ships into the graveyard. It was terrible. Terrible! They were sucked in by the currents around Hosiery Sands and broke their backs. Like floating coffins."

He sits back down in his chair.

"The sea will have her way."

It might be hard for me to sleep at all tonight.

"We must listen for the hooter," he says. He may be talking to me but on the other hand he may be talking to Reg, and because of his squint I don't know which. The hooter isn't the one for The Works at Swanton Stoke but is the one for the lifeboat, which might be called out if the sea gets too rough. Grown-ups, it seems to me, like to have hooters everywhere. I wonder if London is full of them. But then Miss Etherington told me it was full of the sound of bells on a Sunday morning.

"Well, then?" he says. I have missed something he has said.

"Are you going? Or are you not? This is lifeboat weather."

For one moment I am a rabbit under a stick. But then I realise he's looking at Tom, who must go to the top of the cliff and look out into the black boiling sea to search for the lights of ships in danger. Tom is up to it. He will go without a word.

When the call comes, Uncle has been sitting in his sou'wester half the night, listening and waiting. Reg and Filch are in the same bed as me, with Reg's cauliflower toes in my face. When Uncle growls and says he's off, we're all three woken and scuttle downstairs to the kitchen, but he is already out of the door. We pull on our clothes, all the layers we can find, take up a lantern and head down to where the boats are pulled up on the beach. The clothes are almost not worth putting on. Any warmth in them leaks out before I am there. The shivers that shake my body will soon be nothing, I know, when my backbone turns to ice. But we are high on excitement, trembling with fear. Others press through the flashing dark, bodies bent, heads down. I hear men shouting, feet pounding over the cobbles. We are all pulled in the same direction, drawn by what must happen next, down towards the beach, towards the waves, towards the boats, towards the heaving waters. *And the mountains shall be molten under him, and the valleys shall be cleft, as wax before the fire, and as the waters that are poured down a steep place.*

Down the steps we come to where lights cluster and shouts fly on the wind. Words are lost before they are said. Small Spratt's wife, thin as a boy under her shawl, hurries along with his life jacket, a bodice made of corks to keep him bobbing in the water as few of the men can swim. Small Spratt left home too quick to take it with him. Others have gathered, all boots and sou'westers, lunging out of the darkness, lamps lighting their faces so they look like walking corpses fresh dug from the churchyard.

They are all there. Uncle Squinty, Flinty Daredevil, Piglet Long, their friends and their neighbours, cousins and brothers, circling the *Heather May* drawn up on the beach. The sea is throwing itself on to the shingle like a monster, belching water and foam, sucking pebbles off the shore with a horrible grinding noise, then throwing itself down again with the weight of a falling cliff. The men shout that they have seen a light out on the Sands, though I cannot see it however hard I try. I see only white mountains of water heading towards me. The men start to heave the *Heather May* forward. They push, pull backwards, heave forwards again, urging each other on. Others work to pull it forwards, leaning on each shout, hauling so hard on the rope that their heads hang only a foot from the stones. In all there may be forty men, pushing their stomachs inside out, dragging the boat towards the danger.

"The light is two miles off," says Filch, teeth rattling.

Two miles off, and all they have is their muscle to get them there. I can't believe they'll have an ounce of strength left by the time the boat reaches the water. The water is a good way off yet and the boat seems heavier than the sea itself.

I cannot imagine I will ever become a man like this

"They say it is a Dutch vessel, over a thousand tons, with a cargo of wood. It has ploughed into The Sands, which means it could be breaking up in this sea, or it could be listing," Filch says.

The men keep shouting. The sea keeps boiling over like milk from a pan. And somewhere out there, men are holding on to their lives with nothing more than a prayer. *For thou hadst cast me into the deep, in the midst of the seas; and the floods compassed me about: all thy billows and thy waves passed over me.* That's Jonah for you.

The boat is close enough now to be hoisted onto the iron wheels that will roll it into the water.

"What now?" I ask Filch. My shout turns to the mew of a kitten in the tempest. "How can they get it into those waves?"

His eyes are full of not believing too. He doesn't answer.

The wheels sink in the sand and the men push harder into the water. They push into the impossible. They push for the lives of the men at sea as well as themselves in the *Heather May*. Flinty Daredevil, smooth jaw, is at the front. He is into the water up to his knees, then up to his waist, urging them forward. A huge wave comes from nowhere and they are all thrown back with the boat, like fish, twisting and flipping on the shore. At once they are up again, Flinty Daredevil at the front once more, straining and heaving on the bows against the surf that spews them out again and again. Flinty Daredevil shows no fear. He turns his smooth face back to the spitting waves, and the look on his face is like that of a saint who has seen Paradise.

"She's a good boat, that one. Forty feet," shouts Tom, pursing his lips, showing that he knows a thing or two.

It looks no bigger than a kipper on the seashore, with no better chance than a kipper of saving anyone.

"She's got these two tanks that fill with water to stabilise her. And the centre-board is a large fin made of iron. When they put that down she'll never turn over. She's worth the struggle, see."

Our faces are whipped with spray and wind, our mouths frozen to our cheekbones.

"It's happening," says Tom.

Suddenly the *Heather May* is deep enough into the water. She shoots off into the angry spume, scattering men in the water. Our eyes flick from one to the other. Figures roll wildly in the water, each one hanging on to a rope. They haul themselves into the boat, flinging their legs over the sides. They lift the oars and begin to move together against the snow caps of sea. We cousins look at each other, understanding that they have cast themselves out beyond help. The sea looks not like one sea but like many seas, all heaped up until there is no end to them. The boat is suddenly high on a wave, then vanishes in a canyon beyond.

"Pull, my boys!" We hear through the tumult, coming from the boat on a shawl of foam. The world has turned murderous. The sea and the air are so powerful, they could kill us with one spit. *The waters compassed me about, even to the soul: the depth closed me round about, the weeds were wrapped about my head.*

If this is God's instrument, I think to myself, then I'm not so sure that God is all that my father says he is. On board the men start to move as one, swivelling their oars like tiny spoons in a simmering broth, two to each oar, and the boat rears up over another fold in the sea and drops into another chasm. We will not see or hear of them again for many hours, not until dawn arrives and the night is over.

We sleep and we don't sleep under the blankets among the fleas. The sea rolls through our ears and wind flies round the bedroom like screeching cats tied nose to tail. I pass a good hour believing Mother has been carried away in a ship and lost at sea. By the time we are fully awake, Aunt Mary has the kettle boiling and wet clothes steaming around the fire. And there is Mother, resurrected in a chair beside the fire. I go to hold her skirt, as I haven't done for many years. She smells of oil of cloves. She looks at me and her face has collapsed. She has become an old lady in one night, in one storm. It is a shock to find a mother with no teeth, let me tell you, but it is also like having a prayer answered. I can now be certain of two things. She is not going to die and she is not going to be able to chew her meat.

The day is blustery, as if the wind is trying to dry all the wet from the night before. I am out again with the boys on the clifftop, looking across the sea, which is tamer and kinder now, for any sign of the lifeboat. We sit with our knees under our chins.

"Did you know she was having them out?" Skinny says.

"No."

"'Er mouth looks like a cat's behind."

"Yours isn't much better."

I'm quick to reply but I'm not offended. I like being with my cousins, one of a crew, not having to listen out for Father's anger or Mother's silences. She has never been one for long speeches but her words may now come even less often. I like it that my cousins speak their minds and don't mean anything more than what they say. But I know I will never be like them. They assume I'll follow Father into the furnace of breadmaking. It is an odd thing that, although all our mothers can bake bread when needed, the world still needs a baker. Father's view is that his work is not women's work but a calling. Other men such as platelayers, stokers, firemen, carriage-makers, engine-drivers and fishermen spend their days joking, eating and talking while they work. They get through life together. But Father, he works alone and fills his loaves with the goodness that everyone needs, alone with his troughs of dough. And that is what he wants me to do too.

January 17 1901
(In 1756 Mozart was born)

Why ice floats
Although ice is nothing but water in a solid state, it is always less heavy, bulk for bulk,

than the water from which it is made. This is explained by the peculiar fact that water invariably expands just before it freezes, so that a pint of water always makes rather more than a pint of ice; and this ice, being greater in bulk than the water itself, is therefore less dense, and so it floats at the surface instead of sinking down below.

There is so much to learn if I am somehow to make a life away from here. I've seen enough cold water expanding before it freezes to last me for a lifetime. What I would like the diary to tell me is why the sea *doesn't* freeze? The *Heather May* came back but not until Aunt Mary had sat in the kitchen, hour after hour, waiting for news of Uncle Squinty Clink. All the women were doing the same. They hung on time until the waiting wore their nerves and tightened their skin and shrank their stomachs. But she never cried. She held Mother's hand and stroked her hair and stoked the fire. And when Uncle eventually came through the door, moving like a sleepwalker, weighed down with water, red hands swollen and trembling, she didn't waste her breath. She went to the pot where she had prepared bacon and onion dumplings and filled a bowl to the brim. She watched him remove his slop, his Guernsey, his boot stockings, every stitch of which she had made herself. The *Heather May* came home safely with all the men on board and six Dutchmen they had pulled off The Sands.

CHAPTER SEVEN:

THE STRIPED HORSE

Without needing to open the curtains I can tell the snow is lying thick on the ground. There is something about the silence and the light. The hooter sounds just before six and I wonder when and if the trains will start. They do, of course. The screech of metal on metal, the huff of steam, the connecting of place to place has to go on.

The sky is the colour of metal, striped with shards of purple and pink. Trees, fences and rooftops stand out black-on-white, every branch and twig iced with snow, shadows falling long at sharp angles. More snow flurries arrive like ghostly ballerinas dancing over the rooftops. When they stop they leave flakes swirling upwards and sideways. The sky darkens, shuts us in, cutting us all off from each other.

I burrow into my bed and I am back again spending one extraordinary day with Edward Stafford Clark. This day starts early with a bright spring morning and we are out together before the London gentry are awake. We step briskly past cream stucco terraces with shiny black doors. The number of each house is painted boldly in black on a pillar with a scroll top creating an aura of grandness. We are almost skipping as we pass a street sweeper, skirt lavender beds trimmed with box, admire flowers held aloft by stone lions and water splashing in the fountains. The birds are singing their throats out.

What was he wearing that day? I remember. He wore some sort of heavy coat and he actually pranced, his calves tight and his heels reluctant to touch the ground. I am there again, in our dewy wonderland where everything seems newly made. Heaven knows, this is an unusual arrangement. He has asked me to work with him, not just to observe but to make sketches of my own. I take a precious day away from my stitching. And this is an even stranger thing. His plan is not for us to work with grooms and tables and brushes for these precious hours, but with animals.

"Getting the likeness is just the same as with humans." He crackles with excitement, his hands running through his hair and pinching his moustache. "I have a very important commission to design an invitation for a grand dinner. I intend to depict the great and the good seated round a large oval table, each one represented by a member of the Animal Kingdom. Ha! We are all, are we not my dear, creatures of the Animal Kingdom?"

He thrills to the great concoction of naughtiness he has in mind. I'm more than nervous about what is required of me. I'm not at all sure that cheekbone and neckline are quite the same as fang and fur. In fact, I'm liquid with anticipation and fear. Am I here for my skills? Is it something to do with my small hands which he keeps admiring? Or is it my companionship he wants, for it seems partly to be so. Dare I think that? Am I about to be plucked from my world into his, much like he might pick a winkle from its shell?

At this intoxicating hour of the morning, the Zoological Gardens are closed to visitors. Nonetheless we're given special permission to enter what he calls the Animal Kingdom. We are immediately hit by the stench as keepers scurry past with carts of dung, which they tip into the canal. There is rush and bother everywhere, cages being unlocked, brushes at work, greetings exchanged.

Edward is welcomed by the head keeper Augustus P. Reynolds who, it turns out, is a man like no other. Taller than most, he dresses in a top hat, black coat and tails. He speaks with the sweetest, gentlest voice, but all the while half his mind is listening to the animals. It strikes me he is a reluctant member of the human race.

Their conversation reveals that this is not the first time Edward has come here for inspiration.

"Two giraffes in this morning, sir. Arrived from the London Docks. Walked it themselves, all eight miles, bringing their Arab handlers and enough members of the Metropolitan Police to make you believe there was Royalty about," says Augustus P. Reynolds. "Fine creatures, they are. Magnificent. Good markings. Long eyelashes. Bad nerves. We're keeping them quiet now. After their travels they need rest."

He turns and is off at a trot, leaning towards the day, a man who has much to do and many creatures to care about.

"Ah. A charming man, perfectly charming," Edward says, as his eyes dart here and there. "He lives here, you know, among the beasts. Last one to bed, first one up. Knows when snake eats snake. Bothers when an elephant has an abscess and lances it himself. I've seen him do it, standing under the tusks, in the stench of its breath with a steel rod and hook, pulling on the gum until the beast shrieks and the pus pours out. They trust him, these creatures. Elephant even comes back for more."

He throws me a little sideways look.

As we move towards a screech of monkeys, I stop by what seems to be the most unusual tunnel. Edward has already read my thoughts.

"Yes, you are right to admire it." He flaps his hands. "Decimus Burton, the man who laid out this marvellous menagerie, designed a tunnel to match those houses we've just passed. A classical portal, Doric columns. No less than these beasts deserve." He leaps ahead.

"For, you see," he beckons me on. "This was meant to be a place of great romance, a place where you could visit the arid wastes of the desert, climb the Himalayan heights, gaze in horror into the dark corners of the jungle, watch in amazement at a slow death happening inside the expanding stomach of a python, marvel at the bottoms of the baboons."

It is a test. I am sure of it. He has come out with a word which gentlemen do not use and I've not flinched or blushed, fainted or blanched. He uttered the word *bottom*, willy-nilly, as if it were any other ordinary word. I turn away to calm my mind, which is reeling with all these associations of nether regions and curling snakes.

"Other members of the fair sex with their petticoats and parasols will be here later in the day, clutching their handkerchiefs to their noses," he says. "But I'm glad to see you are not like them. In my view there is nothing so provocative as pretended embarrassment to plant suggestions in a man's mind."

He takes my arm. "Well, what shall it be? The world's first Insect House, the small cats, anteaters and sloths, the Bear Pit? The Reptile House, which they built with the money from the sale of dear Jumbo?"

Everyone remembers Jumbo. The newspapers were almost hysterical when he was sent to America even though Queen Victoria had asked for him to stay. Mr Barnum said he had fifty million people over there waiting to see him in his Greatest Show on Earth. In spite of the fuss, Jumbo was sold and the money was used to build the Reptile House, where snakes are kept warm with blankets and stoves.

There is calm among the animals. The tiger slinks around its cage, letting out deep moans, stomach swinging just above the ground, with paws the size of frying pans and a tail as long as its body. The llamas seem to be made of spare parts from other animals, woolly like sheep but with soft muzzles like ponies and pricked ears of donkeys. Instead of hooves they trot along on fully separated toes. Some of them wear woolly stockings covered in chocolate or cream, and they have perfected the art of smiling.

The wit of the Elephant House takes my breath away. It could be a row of oversized cottages with quaint chimneys and tile-hung roofs, except there are busts of rhinoceros and elephant over the doorways.

"You are quite enchanting, my dear," says Edward as the sun's rays start to warm our backs. "This is a mirror image of the world we live in. I believe it shows that this great city of ours has reached a very high state of civilisation. We care for creatures which, in another age or another place, would be hunted for the sheer joy of killing or eating."

"It feels to me," I say, "that the animals might even believe *we* are the captives. They see us prowling the same paths every day, having no apparent purpose in life but to point and squint at them. They may also believe humans to be inferior to them, there to clean and feed them. While the animals remain naked, they see the lower orders cover themselves for shame."

I can't believe I'm speaking so confidently, but something seems to have happened since we entered the Zoo. I don't feel bound by the rules that exist outside.

We take up our positions with our sketchbooks and work alongside each other among the caws and grunts. We become utterly absorbed. I am with the ostriches, working in pencil, picking out details that might suggest human characteristics. He doesn't need my interpretations. He needs only a likeness but I believe it helps if I can work on aspects that will interest him. I try to grasp the swoop and stiffness of an elastic neck, the bulk of the body feathers (which would serve well as a woman's bustle), the train of extra feathers down the back. Suddenly the ostrich lifts its behind, releases a stream of yellow muck, then shakes herself as a lady might shake her petticoat. Its little black eye seems to say that it is possible to be rude and dignified at the same time.

I move to the vultures and capture their black cloaks, orange gizzards, white rimmed eyes and shoulders padded with white feathers. Ah, then the flamingos! Absurd pink powder-puffs on slender stems, with curling necks. Several of them standing in a row like notes on a stave. Who is he going to make fun of with these? How will he use my sketches?

We come together, he and I, by the monkey poles. A chimpanzee lies on a bed of straw with huge forearms, tiny legs and a bright pink groin exposed for all to see. His cross-hatched black leathery face is sandwiched between ears like teacups. While the mouth stretches from one side to the other, the nose is no more than two little indents and the eyes brim with sadness.

"Which one of us shall do this one, my dear?" he says.

I have no appetite for drawing the chimpanzee with all his bits on display.

"The ladies love the danger of those manly fingers," Edward says, laughing. "They might lose a purse, or a handkerchief, a hat or a bag. Oh, the thrill! But not you, my dear."

Normal visitors have started to arrive. An older woman in deep red full skirt with black trim has raised her parasol against the winter sun. A young woman in pink silk sweeps towards the Monkey House. Men in top hats and black coats take their companions' arms to keep them safe. Small children run hither and thither, pointing at the monkeys when they use their tails like extra legs. My head is now brimming with naked bottoms.

"You are thoughtful," he says.

"Oh. I'm a little tired, that is all."

He steps back, pulsing with pleasure. He is an unstoppable fountain of joy and I am out with him alone. He has taken my arm and walked with me, yet he is a married man. I've not set eyes on his wife but I have leaned across her desk and heard him call her The Duchess.

"It is a wonder! In any other age we would have persecuted these creatures. But in this time of new and great ideas, in this new century, we have decided to keep them for pleasure and for study. What do you think?"

"We keep them because we believe ourselves to be better than them," I reply. "Just as a Duke believes himself better than a chimney sweep. It's the same, isn't it?"

"So serious, my dear?"

"She is right." Augustus P. Reynolds has come up silently behind us.

"The great Charles Darwin, who supplied us with specimens from his travels, God rest his soul, made a habit of sending me questions. There is one that I often ask myself when I'm here alone. It is this. If God did not create the world, or man, then man should surely not set *himself* up as God of the Animal Kingdom?"

He adjusts his top hat, as men do.

"He wanted to know, too, if I had ever crossed a donkey with a zebra. A curious question, you might think, but not when you consider it was from the Great Man Himself. I had to say I hadn't tried such a thing."

His smile is warm and kind.

 "And I've recently had a similar enquiry from the African explorer Sir Harry Johnston, who has heard rumours of a dark-coloured horse with stripes on its legs. The two questions may lead to the same answer. Turmoil of the times we live in!"

He hasn't finished with Darwin. "The Great Man held his big idea back for twenty years because he knew it would turn society upside down and make a mockery of hierarchy. He sent me a copy of his book. And it was just as Miss Etherington hinted. Idea too big. Too big an animal for the cobra to swallow. He suggested, didn't he, that it was like committing murder?"

I breathe deep. I am in a new universe, far from thread and stitch, night coughs and sore backs. I am teeming with exciting thoughts and new ideas.

"The murder of God?" I ask.

"Pleased to be of service, miss," says Augustus P. Reynolds. He bows, clicks his heels and doffs his top hat. "Servant to the Great Man Himself."

❧

Rosie never could have imagined when she left Mrs Garbutt that she was on her way to a morning of such significance, that she would find herself drawing caged animals and discussing the Almighty with men of knowledge. But she knew then that she must leave Clapham to step up in the world. She found an establishment in Marylebone High Street which was a first-rate house. She showed samples of her work to Madame Juliette, as she was known (though all the girls knew she was called Mrs Bullen), and she was taken on almost immediately. London seemed to be swilling with money. It seemed as if the whole capital was in love with fame and wealth. Old districts on the river were being revived and made fashionable.

The facade of Madame Juliette's house consisted of a series of magnificent plate-glass windows, each one bisected by a brass bar. Displayed in the centre was an exquisitely embroidered handkerchief, a sampler of all samplers, a promise of what could be done within. Rosie was taken to the 'premier magazine'. Everything was half French and half English, and therefore was superior. She couldn't help being impressed as she glided across the room on a cushioned carpet of purple, the colour of dark summer irises. Big as a ballroom, it was lined with wood panelling, every alternate panel inset with a huge floor-to-ceiling looking-glass in a gilded frame. When she looked into them, myriad images were reflected back. Customers were flattered and dazzled at seeing themselves multiplied. The counters were of polished ebony and everything that could be gilded, was gilded.

Madame Juliette watched her closely and gave her encouragement. Unlike her fellow workers, Rosie earned enough to take a room nearby and live out. She was never late, and put in extra hours whenever she was asked. Every day she wore the black glacé silk dress she been required to buy from Madame Juliette. She was more than willing to take on extra pieces at times of general mourning, when half the city needed new black clothes by the day before yesterday. She met extra demand during the Seasons, between April and July, and October to December. She worked from dawn until dusk, and sometimes back to dawn again to make dresses of the like she would never see again. She covered the sloping shoulders of the aristocracy. She accentuated the necks of the great and the good. She came close, physically if not actually, to respectability and to money. Some of her work was worn by minor royalty. On days of rest, she began to read novels and to carry a sketchbook. She started to use her eye and hand, the same eye and hand that served her for pin tucks, in a different way. Early in the year, before the spring rush for new dresses turned to a fever, she took a course in drawing 'for working women' she had seen advertised. She journeyed out to Whitechapel to a large red brick building with airy rooms and high ceilings. There she was invited to draw a different person each week – one week a flower seller, another a coachman.

Above the door in the studio was a white board with beautiful black lettering:

It is the mission of art to gladden human life, to attract men to goodness, to lift man's ideal, to suggest hallowed emotions, to witness faith, to lend wings to the soul, to bring heaven nearer, and help faltering men to the throne of God, where all his servants shall see him and see his face." J.D. Sedding 1886, Liverpool Arts Congress.

One day she lingered and looked into another room where an artist in a billowing smock splattered with paint was working at an easel. She eyed the piles of canvases, some rolled, some lying on racks. Big old chairs in the process of losing their stuffing stood among pots, brooms, a hammer, a pair of bellows, two large wicker baskets, piles of chalks and pencils. Nearby was a table covered in drawings of noses, eyebrows, lips, nostrils and frames of hair, but nothing you could call a whole face. In the middle of the room the artist's model sat very still, her face and neck stiff as a china doll. The painter's palette was daubed with colour, duck-dirts of turquoise, mauve, aquamarine, cream, yellow, black. Rosie was surprised to find the artist was a woman. She had never seen a woman paint before. There were no women artists she could think of. Every woman of leisure drew under willow trees in the summer, just as every woman of leisure played the piano, but she could not think of one who worked at it. The woman sketched in the eye sockets, laid a foundation of blush for the sitter's cheeks, darkened the outline for the nose and corners of the eyes. She dabbed the paint with her fingers to make the nostrils. The hair was many shades from lemon to burnt biscuit. But it was the flesh that surprised Rosie most. She had no idea that skin was made of so many colours, from purple to green, white to bitter charcoal.

Another day she was drawn by the noise of hundreds of women talking outside. What was happening? A banner bearing the words Votes For Women had been hoisted over a doorway, and smartly dressed women in full skirts and flowery hats were handing out leaflets. The crowd pushed past her into a hall to take their seats. She slipped in at the back to watch and listen.

The hall fell silent as a woman mounted the stage to speak. She urged the audience to show their intelligence, to remain polite, to obey the law. "We must be peaceful and avoid confrontation," she said. "We must win our case by honourable means. We already have the support of many in the House of Commons. It may take ten years. It may take twenty years. It may take thirty. But in the end, we will win. Our time will come. I believe it will be sooner rather than later."

The audience murmured its appreciation.

"Let me quote from Fanny Burney's *The Wanderer*, written almost a century ago."

Why, for so many centuries, has man, alone, been supposed to possess, not only force and power for action and defence, but even all the rights of taste; all the fine sensibilities which impel our happiest sympathies, in the choice of our life's partners? Why must even woman's heart be circumscribed by boundaries as narrow as her sphere of action in life? Must she be taught to subdue all its native emotions? To hide them as sin, and to deny them as shame? Must her affections be bestowed but as the recompense of flattery received; not of merit discriminated? Must everything that she does be prescribed by rule?

"No!" came shouts from the audience. "Bravo!"

"But women must earn their place. They must become economically independent, they must know their minds, they must not represent themselves as slight of learning or physically weak. They must not play the part that men for so long have written for them."

As Rosie slipped out of the hall she wondered who made their fine clothes and the flowers on their hats. On her walk back to Madame Juliette's she became acutely aware of the women she passed. She thought a good few weren't as lucky as she was. She thought of women who were forced to make extra money by selling their bodies, and of others who took in shirts to sew for slops. She kept her distance from them, from anyone poorer than herself. She smelt their desperation, saw the sores on their faces. She was afraid of the abyss. She yearned for a life without worry.

Months later in the studio at Whitechapel she felt possessed by something much bigger than herself. Smelling the paint, handling the charcoal, feeling the paper, studying the sitters, made her feel she had found exactly where she wanted to be and what she wanted to do. For the first time for as long as she could remember since her parents died, she felt cherished. Not by a person but by the act of sketching. Her drawings attracted praise, as her needlework had done at Madame Juliette's. She thought then that if she could be successful with one skill, then why not in another? She needed a patron, a tutor. It was this that led her to the door of Edward Stafford Clark.

January 22 1901

The Pound In Our Pockets

The pound was probably first thought of in Continental Europe centuries ago and the idea was that it was something worth the price of a pound of silver. The symbol we use for the monetary pound is also thought to be a speedy flowery version of the letters lb which we use to represent a pound in weight. Silver coins have been around for a long time, as long ago as King Offa and the Anglo Saxons, but the first pound coin did not appear until 1489 under Henry VII and was called a sovereign. Henry VIII reduced the amount of silver in each coin drastically in what became known as the Great Debasement but Elizabeth I increased it again. Since then the silver content has gradually diminished.

Well, according to my diary no-one important has ever died on this day. Until today. In my best writing, I make up for that. *Queen Victoria died.* A copy of The London Gazette with the word *EXTRAORDINARY* across the front page has arrived on the late train. Beneath it is a line which explains it all. *Her Majesty the Queen breathed her last at 6.30pm, surrounded by Her Children and Grandchildren.*

Father brings it home and I try to feel sad but I cannot.

"Sixty-three years she has held us together. Eighty-one years old. Now we start the new century without her," he says. "The shops will be hung with black and purple banners. The fences will be painted black. The funeral will be a sight to see."

All I can remember about her is that she had an upside-down face. Her eyes, her mouth and her cheeks pointed downwards. She's always looked like a black beetle to me, her clothes like closed wings, her hats like feelers. But I don't say this to Father.

Last time I saw a picture of Queen Victoria she was sitting in a carriage in Ireland, wearing a pair of dark spectacles and holding a black umbrella with flowers on it. My memory is probably wrong as it is more likely a footman was holding the umbrella. That was a year ago. She went to Ireland to thank the Irish for dying in South Africa while they were defending the Empire against the Boers. And in return the Irish thanked her for thanking them for dying.

～

My room-mate Nobby has returned from travelling up the line with fourteen other men. He took his lodging basket filled with cooked meat, cakes and pastries, all baked by Father. But since he came back, he hasn't slept. I have a bad cough and shooting pains which pulse in time with the trains as they come and go. Nights and days are difficult to tell apart because I sleep in both and I am awake in both. He and I both lie awake at night. I know he's awake because you can't scratch yourself if you're asleep and there is always a flea somewhere. The snow has been on the ground for five days and I feel like a carriage which has been shunted into The Works for overhauling while the rest of the world carries on. This always happens when I'm ill.

"Was it a hard trip, Nobby?"

He grunts and blows off. This is usually a good sign. He may talk.

"How far did you get?"

"Out towards The Wash," he says. "You could just see Lincolnshire across the water. The lights of Skegness, maybe. But not for long as the snow came down again. We rode the engine out there."

"Was it cold?"

"Was it cold, lad? Was it cold? You don't know what cold is. My fingers went, my toes went, my nose went. So many lumps they were, hanging off my body. But we lit a fire at night to warm ourselves."

"What happened there, Nobby?"

"What happened, lad? What happened? You don't know what happened? No, that you don't!"

"You going to tell me, then?"

"Am I going to tell you? Oh Lord, forgive us!"

There is a long silence but I have time and can wait all night if need be.

"It was the snow what did it. White upon white. White like the wastes of Russia as far as the eye could see, with black trees here and there poking out. Froze our food, froze our drink, turned everything to iron."

I wait to see what he decides to say next, if he decides to say anything at all.

"We didn't really see it at first. It was like we'd imagined it in all the black and white out there, track and snow, track and snow. But we saw it all right, lad. We heard the whisper on the tracks before the train appeared. We heard the engine coming, then the sight of it in the distance and the line of the train, dirty against the snow, moving towards us, the steam puffing. It was that strange. It was like, I don't know, like looking at our own future before it had arrived. We all looked up. And then we saw it all right. Bright red all over the front of the engine, sticky mess, mashed all over it. Some on the wheels too."

"That'll be a nice piece of venison on the plate for someone's supper tonight,' says Lumpy to me. And we laugh and our breath turns to steam in the cold. It was the last train out that night. The temperature went down like a stone when darkness settled."

We are sealed in together in my bedroom. He carries on speaking and his voice floats up towards the ceiling.

"We are up before first light next morning and soon enough the first train comes through, curling round the fields like a trail of ink dribbling over a white sheet. And we squint through the grey at the engine – funny that we all do that. In spite of the laughs about the deer the night before, see? We are all worried. We are none of us certain. So we look at the front of the engine to be sure, not saying a word to each other. And there it is again, more of the same mess all sticky across the wheels. Not red any more but blackish."

I let the meaning of what he says sink in.

"So what do you do, Nobby?"

"What do we do? We have no choice lad, do we? We lay down our tools and start walking. We follow the track back up through the snow. Sometimes it comes up to our ankles, sometimes our knees. We walk a good forty minutes, snow round our legs and in our boots. We might be on a wild goose chase, but there again we might not."

I stay quiet. It takes my mind off the pains shooting through my body.

"Oh, we find it all right. The body laid by the track, stiff as can be. It has been hit twice by a train, see. Parts of it are like an exploded blackberry pie. Bits of flesh are stuck to the track, bits have flown into the snow. And there he is, somebody who is no longer anybody. Though who he was we do not know. Somehow, lad, it isn't like the big thing it should be, with drums rolling. It just seems dirty. Messy and sad." He turns in his bed and thumps onto his side. "I can't help thinking he may have survived the first train and lain on the frozen track all night, waiting to be hit again in the morning. Who knows?"

There is nothing to say. Nobby's breathing gets heavier. He can fall asleep now he has told his story. My head is full of dead bodies, eyes dangling on white crystals, fingers lying in the snow, clothes soaked with blood. Which is real and which is not I can no longer tell. What he said and what I dreamt afterwards have made another sort of pie with all the ingredients mixed up. I'm on the track with the pains running up and down but the pains are from the wheels of a train instead of from the fever. I drift on them, waiting for the morning and what it might bring.

CHAPTER EIGHT:

THE MOROCCAN TABLE

I have been keeping Mrs Eden company all morning as expected. Today her dress is expensively tailored to look plain, tight over her tiny breasts, synched at the waist, a touch of lace. She moves like a bird, long white fingers working quickly, beaky chin stabbing the air, grey eyes watchful. She's keen to talk about herself so doesn't expect confidences in return. In truth, I think she wouldn't welcome them, so she learns nothing of me. Today she's picked grasses from her garden in order to paint them.

"At least if I can do this, then I can feel I have done something at the end of the day," she says. The clock ticks. She is an orchid in a land of common daisies.

"When Jonathan comes back from his travelling office he kisses me on both cheeks and for a moment he can forget those outlandish men who are so dear to his heart," she says quietly. "I like to tell him what I have done in the day. He constantly worries that I have renounced the better things in life to be with him. I would not wish it otherwise and yet he continues to be concerned about the effect on my nerves. Though he is consumed with his railways, the men and their deliverance from evil, he is nothing but tender to me."

She continues, almost as if she is talking to herself. "I never cease to wonder at how generous Jonathan is to those men. Ragged though they are, he sees good in their souls. He finds time for them. He listens to their troubles as a father would listen to his children."

There is an awkward silence which I don't fill.

Then she surprises me with a laugh, a high silver tinkle. "Last night at supper he told me about one of his workers, a lamplighter or a coal shoveller or who-knows-what because I forget. He was late into work and Jonathan called him to his office. The man was the worse for wear, green around the eyes and swaying, so Jonathan asked him to explain himself. The man said he'd been to a funeral the day before and had been overcome with distress. Please Guv'nor, he said, it won't happen again."

She carried on and her eyes began to twinkle. "He shifted from leg to leg while Jonathan looked at him with all the disapproval he could muster, and asked whose funeral it was. The man said the funeral had been that of his poor wife's husband."

I laugh too, and the room is startled by the unexpected noise.

The maid Molly arrives to check the menu for supper. Smoothing her apron with swollen fingers and wiping sweat from her forehead as she pushes her hair back into her cap.

"We have George Childs to dine with us tonight. He is the owner of the windmill at Staithe. We hope you will like him," Mrs Eden says, her grey eyes holding steady on me for slightly longer than they should. She waves Molly away.

"The mill stands out on the marsh, on a channel which boats find difficult to navigate as it has been silting up over the years. It is a pretty sight in the summer when the white sails stand out against the blue of the sea and the rustling reed-beds."

"I know it."

"There, then," she says and steps back to admire her handiwork.

"George Childs," she adds, "is a man of reasonable means."

❦

The supper table gleams with silver. I am touched by the Edens' kindness, the way they have generously included me in their arrangements. But I am beginning to think that kindness always comes tied with ribbon. My task is to understand the message bound up in that ribbon.

"The railways are the future." says Mr Eden, who smells faintly of carbolic soap. He coughs, which is a warning that a lecture is about to follow. "When lines are laid, whole trade routes open up, industries flourish, towns are built, people are civilised."

I nod and smile, using all my good manners. Vegetables hang for an age on the end of his fork while he delivers his discourse. The rest of us try not to eat too quickly or our plates will be empty long before his.

"As we speak, thousands of workers are building the Trans-Siberian Railway between Moscow and Vladivostok. It may have taken many years already, indeed it has, but one day it will be finished. Tsar Nicholas II wants to extend it right across Manchuria, through the Chinese territories, and transform the map of the great frozen wastes."

He says the word *Chinese* as if he were pronouncing a horror.

"In America the railways created a giant steel industry," he continues. "In Pittsburgh last week Andrew Carnegie hosted a dinner of royal splendour for 'his boys', those who have invested in his magnificent transportation network. And, I might add, have made themselves fortunes in the process. The dinner table was made from a T-rail end section, big as a railway junction, covered in white cloths, grapes, pineapples, artichokes, silver and plate, all surrounded by palm trees."

George Childs brims with admiration. He has a handsome face with periwinkle blue eyes, a scattering of freckles and a wide-open smile all framed by reddish blond hair.

"So what about it then, my man?" Mr Eden says. "Staithe to become another Wellmouth?"

I interrupt without thinking. "Wellmouth?"

Mr Childs swivels his blue eyes onto me.

"We've been considering a new railway venture. The loss of business in Staithe, due to the silting up of the channel, has been a problem for years." He clears his throat and marshals his facts. "The proposition is that if we built a new railway to connect the smaller ports along the North Sea, either to the coastal business down the eastern flank, or to the west and the business of the Midlands, then Staithe could flourish and expand as Wellmouth has done. And we would flourish too."

"I see fleets of fishing vessels, ships lined up in the harbour, employment for all the men," says Mr Eden.

"It is an attractive idea, very attractive indeed. Look at what has happened to Highcliff," says Mr Childs.

"Your sister Mrs Birdwood has benefited greatly from the smart visitors who come to Highcliff each summer, hasn't she?" says Mr Eden. "The effects of the railway are marvellous to behold. The people of Highcliff give up their rooms in the hottest months for the well-to-do and they make good money from it, while the Londoners get fresh air and sea bathing, which is good for their health. We are all winners. The difference with Staithe is that we could bring in heavy goods from afar, run a large fishing fleet and give those ports in the West Country a run for their money."

He is getting carried away with his vision and beams round the table.

"You know what they say? That people were afraid the line to the West Country would let The Devil in! It was a stroke of luck that he never bought a ticket for fear of being put in a pasty."

He chuckles.

"I am a mere woman and I know nothing of such things, but forgive me for asking whether marshy ground might present a problem?" Mrs Eden speaks very precisely, which makes us all listen. "In a surge tide the sea breaks its banks. I sometimes see your windmill in the winter, George, and think it is afloat. It is treacherous ground, that place between land and sea which cannot make its mind up. Surely a railway would sink into the mud?"

"Oh my dear, my dear." Mr Eden smiles fondly at her. "Such feminine anxieties!" He pats his white moustache with the conviction of one who knows he is always right.

"People have been imagining this new railway for a quarter of a century. Should it cross the river here, or there? Should it run out close to the sea – along the marsh as you put it – or should it stay on the land and follow the coastal path? Should it run out into the deep water they call The Pit? A quay could be built out there and a branch line laid on an embankment above the flood. It would give boats a deeper mooring *and* connect them to the national railway network."

He takes a sheet of paper and begins to draw the existing railway lines in and out of Swanton Stoke. Above it he sketches the bulge of the coastline pierced by inlets and creeks, shading in banks of sand and mud. Pressing very hard on the pencil, as if to brook no argument, he marks each fishing village with a cross. Then he inserts lines of dots and dashes to show the railway lines of the future, flirting here and there with the sea. We are silenced by the scale of his ambition.

"And here," he says, stabbing his pencil into the paper, "is George's windmill."

It stands on the very edge of the shaded area, a twilight zone which at low tide is half-land, half-sea.

"Land is already being bought and George is already investing in the project."

Mrs Eden's eyebrows have risen halfway up her forehead, all thoughts of sinking railways being forced from her mind. Mr Eden wills her to believe in him as he wills us all.

"Let us offer thanks for this remarkable village, a beacon in the wilderness, a place where men learn how to be men."

"Who raised the money to build Swanton Stoke?" I ask.

"A big question. Though you are displaying a curiosity beyond your station, I will answer it. It is a reasonably well-known fact that Lord Hartley, who owns many of the fields around here, thought the value of his land would be greatly enhanced if it could be used to create a junction between the railways east and west."

Mr Childs breaks in.

"He realised that value could be created out of nothing. The land was almost worthless. There wasn't much more here than a ruined church and a scrubby hilltop. But he pressed his case and argued that a railway would be good for the community. The hilltop was a drawback, of course, because it meant the trains had to go uphill. God knows how much coal and sweat has been wasted on that climb, but it is best not thought of now."

After cold soup, cutlets are brought in and Mr Childs continues.

"Making Swanton Stoke a major railway works, which does everything from building to repairing, has made it absolutely indispensable."

An extra benefit for Lord Hartley, he says, was that the plans gave him a private station with a waiting room and an underground passage which allows him to board a train without having to pass ordinary people.

"So did *he* build the houses?" I ask.

"The railway houses were built *by* the railway *for* the railway. Isn't that right, Mr Eden? And each tenant has to take lodgers nominated by the railway. So, out of nothing, a community was created," says Mr Child. "A new community for a new century. There are more than nine hundred people here now, is that right? It is a new Eden, so to speak." Mr Childs is pleased with his pun.

"So, Lord Hartley is a good man?" I ask.

Mr Childs slices the fat from his cutlet, chews and swallows before looking up to answer.

"He is, it would be correct to say, an astute man. You see, once he had persuaded everyone that this was the best place for Swanton Stoke, and the Bill had been passed in Parliament, he was not quite so keen to sell his land. Some would say he sat on it so that the value rose even more." He looks upon me kindly before continuing.

"Who knows what is true and what is not, but he was certainly an energetic force at the beginning and then reluctant later on. People gossiped. Suffice it to say that he is now inviting developers to bid for pieces of his land and build more houses on the other side of the village. And more money will be made."

"And you might do the same, make value out of the marsh, if the line to Staithe is laid?" I suggest.

Mr Childs pushes his hair from his face. "It is possible, though on a smaller scale because I am not a big landowner. But what I really believe is that it would create value for many."

Value for many, money for nothing. I am confused by such phrases and need to take them back to think about in my room at the Massinghams'.

❧

January 26 1901
(1885 General Gordon killed at Khartoum)

The Candle's Gas Factory
A candle-flame is really a miniature gas factory, for the wax itself will not burn. The heat of the flame turns the wax into gas and it is the burning of this wax-gas which gives us light. The dark patch in the centre of the bright flame is the gas when first made; and if you blow out the candle, and hold a lighted match one inch above the wick, this gas will at once catch fire, and so relight the candle without the wick being touched at all.

Mother has brought me out between the two huge gasholders, each wide as three houses and tall as two. They have enough gas in them to light all the railway houses and the lamps in the streets. Close by is the hand trolley which carries goods round the yard.

"People should have a right to use this to make themselves better," says Mother. "The people in the railway houses pay for it out of their rent. It is deducted from their wages along with the cost of the water and the use of the Institute." She sucks her cheeks and feels her newly healed gums.

I am wrapped up in all the layers of clothing Mother could find, so am forced to move slowly on account of the padding. My chest feels like it has turned to flannel. A little is squeezed out each time I cough but then it only fills up again. Mother wants me to breathe in the sulphur fumes from the tank at the back of the holders, which she says are rich with chemicals given off by the gas-making.

"It makes a good bonfire," I say.

"What bonfire?"

"I mean it makes the tar that we throw on the fire for Guy Fawkes' night."

"Be quick," she says. "They don't like children round here."

No. They don't. But children like to be here for that very reason. We often come to sniff the gasholders and see how much we can take. If she did but know.

The Works are silhouetted against the fading light. Men are busy in the orange heat, no-one thinking about Mother and me out here in the cold. We watch a train pass through and count thirty-two wagons rocking gently from side to side, all with cattle straw sticking out under the doors, dripping slurry as they go.

I put my head close to the discharge pipe and breathe in deeply. Then splutter. Then breathe it in again. And I wonder. If this unpleasant stuff is good enough to stop you catching whooping cough, as Mother believes, then why doesn't Lord Hartley take some of it for himself?

I hope no-one puts a lighted match to my mouth.

◈

February 2 1901
The Colour Blue

The first blue came from lapis lazuli dug from the mountains of Afghanistan. It was ground down by Renaissance artists to make ultramarine, the most expensive pigment. Because it was so valuable it was often used only for the robes of the Virgin Mary. In ancient Egypt they believed the god Amun could make his skin blue and fly across the sky unseen. Some people believe it can protect you against evil so in Mediterranean countries people often wear blue amulets round their necks to represent the protective eye of God.

My cough has gone and on the same day the dead Queen is being buried I'm summoned to Swan Hall. They need me because I am still small enough to crawl through the attics, find mouse droppings and set traps. There are more than a hundred traps for me to check for dead bodies. Those mice are crafty creatures. They slink all the way up the outside along the Virginia creeper and slip in at the top. I don't approach the hall by the front entrance, where I would have passed all the herds of deer and lakes with fountains, but go straight to the back as I know my place.

I climb the back stairs. Attics are places where secrets are kept. Or forgotten about. The roof space is the size of a paddock. Dust hangs in the sunlight which shines through tiny windows set along the floor. The attics are divided into rooms, each one mounded with trunks, boxes, hats, tennis rackets, riding boots, anything the Hartley family has ever owned. When a new generation takes over, leftovers from the one before are stored away and so another room is filled.

The mouse traps are long wooden boxes containing a kind of seesaw which makes the mice slip down inside as prisoners. They are called Perpetual Mouse Traps, made by Colin Pullinger & Sons. My nose starts to twitch and I rise from my knees, sit up and take a photograph from one of the storage boxes. This is Lord Hartley's eldest son, who we all know as Young Joseph, hand-on-hip in front of an archery target on the lawn, together with two women in hooped skirts. They remind me of the sugar figures that Mother sometimes puts on her marzipan. One carries a straw boater, the other a small dark parasol. More photographs slip between my hands – pictures of parties, of the entire household standing on the hall steps, servants in their aprons, and outdoor staff with wind-dried faces holding their spades and hoes. Here's one of the drawing room, crammed with side tables, palm trees, statues and lamps.

I peer out through one of the floor-windows and see Young Joseph himself, walking into the woods. But he is not alone. He has linked arms with a young woman. Her hair is drawn back under a hat of dark felt without any kind of adornment. A blue shawl is wrapped tightly around her. I know her white oval face, her heavy-lidded eyes, that perfect chin. And even from this high up I can see that the eldest son of the big house looks as if he would lay down his life for her.

The attic floors creak. Two pigeons fuss in the eaves before flapping off into the sky. I glance quickly around but no-one is there. I have twenty mice but am not yet half way round. Queen Victoria being lowered on top of her husband must be as stiff as they are. What, I wonder, is Miss Etherington doing with Young Joseph?

༄

Rosie dreamed she was in the great courtyard of a palace in a foreign land where birds trilled all day in palm trees. The dark pink walls of the courtyard were covered in bougainvillea. She was swimming in a pool of water, sun burning on the back of her neck. Ahead of her lay a pavilion furnished with cedar chairs and hung with burnt orange muslin curtains that fluttered in the breeze. They were reflected in the water and broke into a thousand fragments as she swam. Around the pool people lay on white mattresses wearing almost nothing. Rosie herself was entirely naked. She climbed out of the pool, passing the lanterns hanging in the lemon and orange trees, and parted the flaming muslin to find Edward Stafford Clark's little table, inlaid with ivory. The surface was as ornate as a necklace, or a stained-glass window. It was a thing of complication and pleasure.

Someone whispered in her ear and told her that orange came from the high mountains outside the city, where the snow melted in springtime and tumbled through blood red rocks. The table came from the dark alleys surrounding the palace walls, where stallholders hawked sheep's heads, intestines, nuts and prunes, where women turned sweet pancakes on blackened stoves and old beggars shuffled. It came from the din of workshops where metal was hammered, leather cut and glued, lanterns cut from tissue paper. Men and boys sat on the ground, working as if their lives depended on it, which they did. Rosie passed through the workshops and saw a cross-legged man working on a table, marking out the pattern, cutting and chiselling the ivory pieces. She knew that table. She had felt it between her thighs.

She woke and heard the trains and knew she was in Swanton Stoke. Edward told her the table had come from Morocco. He had it shipped from a market to his house and now it kept surfacing in dreams.

CHAPTER NINE:

RHINOCEROS PIE

February 8 1901

(In 1587 Mary Queen of Scots was beheaded on the orders of her cousin Elizabeth 1)

The country is still thinking of nothing but Queen Victoria. It is as if no-one has ever died before. Billy and I decide to get away from the long faces and run up the railway line. Billy dares me to lie under a train.

I lie between the rails while Billy hovers somewhere behind me. I hear him treading on twigs and crouching down. He must have tucked himself in behind the bank, close enough to watch but a safe distance away. I'm as flat as I can make myself with my arms rigid by my sides, the wooden sleepers pressing into my back, rails on either side, legs straight as can be. Up above me the sky is blue like Miss Etherington's dress, and so deep that it could whirl me away into another place. I have never felt more alive. There is a murmur on the lines, the faintest tremble in the track, and I know it is coming long before Billy does.

"Here it is," he hisses a few seconds later. He sounds more excited than I have ever heard him. I am too, but that is because I am the meat in the sandwich.

I stare straight up at the rooks circling above and listen to the engine chattering to itself. It gets closer and I hear steam hissing and snorting from the funnel. In my mind's eye I see the fireman raising his shovel and hurling coal into the fire hole. And I feel the rails vibrate as the engine comes closer. White smoke appears in the blue above me. I lie just beyond a road bridge, so that I am hidden from the driver. And time goes very fast and very slow all at once, to the beat of the engine. I wonder if Mary Queen of Scots felt like this while she waited for the axe. Billy says they needed two goes to get the head off.

And it is huge, big as all the houses in Sebastopol Road, rolling towards me, shining black and silver, dirty, belching, making so much noise that no-one can hear me scream. I open my mouth and the sound vanishes in the screech of metal. I try to keep my eyes open, catch a glimpse of tangled black and then they slam shut. And it comes over and I go under and my body goes into spasms. I am one of Father's loaves going into the burning oven. The wheels carrying their huge weight make walls of iron each side of me. I slit open one eye and see the train's intestines twisting over me. A slip of daylight appears between one wheel and another, and a beat is missed between one carriage and the next. It goes on for a year, wheel after wheel, carriage after carriage, piston after piston. The air is foul and I press my arms hard against my body. I could turn into offal on the butcher's board.

Then it is over. The train has gone. The screeching leaves a fly buzzing in my ear. Then there is silence. Billy stamps up the bank and a blackbird sings nearby.

"You did it," he says.

He sounds calm but impressed.

I get to my knees, and to be truthful I am waving around like a sheet in the wind.

"Yes. Did it." I can't seem to straighten my knees so I am a bit like a newborn calf. I don't want to fall down again the moment I get up, so I play for time.

"Next time it's your turn."

"If there is a next time," he says.

I swallow hard and look up to see what he means but he has already turned and is walking back towards the village.

"C'mon, then," he shouts over his shoulder.

&

I'm awake in the night again trying to understand how things happened with Edward Stafford Clark. I decide to get dressed and walk out into the night. A deep fog has settled, thick and white between the houses. I slip from lamp to lamp down the road, each light burning yellow against the white. I feel as if I'm moving between life and death and have just stopped off somewhere to pause before the end. It is so still I can hear a hedgehog snuffling under a bush. Water drips from the trees and, for once, the trains are still. The wind has stopped its tugging and teasing and crept into a hole to sleep. Unlike me. I find it hard to sleep when pictures jump into my head as soon as I lie down, so here I am walking along the streets where everyone knows their place. Except, perhaps, for me. How have I come to this?

A sudden realisation trickles like water down the back of my neck. I am glad it has come while I am out with the night creatures, not when I am sitting with

Mrs Eden. It is this. I have attended drawing classes. I have viewed the work of great artists, I have spoken with Edward about line and colour and composition, but in all this time I have never seen a naked woman painted truthfully. I have not seen women shown as they really are, with lumps and bumps, hair in their creases and hollows. I admired Millais' *The Knight Errant* without recognising it was a lie, without noticing that the damsel's pubic hair was nowhere to be seen. My heart thumps. What does this mean? Am I right in thinking that artists avoid the sweat and blood and fur of being a woman? They present female parts smooth as marble, pure and innocent as if they're children. Heavens! Some men, who know no better, must get a terrible shock after they marry and find their loved-ones sprout hairy tufts in unexpected places. I am astonished. Then I think of the horde of artists, buyers and the high-ups who accept this lie as a truth. They don't even speak of it. *The Knight Errant* made people angry, even though the damsel had a body as smooth as a rabbit's ear, because she showed too much interest in the knight in gleaming armour. Desire, submission, conquest. The meat was too strong. So Millais painted the damsel again with her face turned away from the knight's hot breath, but still without her pubic hair.

The fog lifts a little and my thinking widens. It seems to me that people spend their lives making rules for each other. Use this door, not that. Eat this way, not that. Be poor, not rich. Paint women this way, not that. If Augustus P. Reynolds studied humans in the way he studies animals, he might find us a cruel species which likes to suppress others, dominate its own kind, fight wars, kill animals, lust after women and expect them to be pure. Anyone who is different does not belong. We are all compelled by these rules which we make for ourselves. No-one else makes them for us. Augustus P. Reynolds told me that Darwin looked for differences in creatures. What did he call the differences? *Anomalies*. That was it. It was in the anomalies that Darwin found his story. I am an anomaly. So is Rough Jimmy. So is Jack Stamp.

༄

February 12 1901

Today Mother isn't taking eggs to market because she has decided to have a Bed Linen Day. The tell-tale signs are there to see. I feel happy because it tells me she is feeling much better but it also means I mustn't get in her way. Not even one small bit.

Calico, which last summer she draped over the bushes to turn crisp and white in the sun, lies piled up on the kitchen table. Sacks full of plucked feathers wait to be baked in the oven to make sure any insects are completely dead. While that is happening, she'll sit at the table rubbing the calico with grease, not caring how mucky her fingers get or how caved-in her mouth is. By the afternoon she'll be stuffing the feathers into the calico, which she has made into bags.

"Pernicious feathers!" she says. "They find ways of sticking out even when there aren't any holes for them to come through." She works hard making sure their quills don't poke out and prick us in our sleep.

I don't know what pernicious means. She knows no better than me but she must think it sounds good.

"You just can't beat a feather bed for comfort and warmth on a cold winter's night," she says. "It's a blessing in the end."

And she makes our blessings. Mother does that.

"If only they were duck feathers. I could sell them for powder-puffs like my sister does. Yet I don't know as I think it right to bring all those little balls of fluff into this world only to snuff them out before they've grown up. To turn their backsides into powder-puffs for fine ladies in London."

I can't tell if she really wants a box full of fluffy yellow cheepers, or if she doesn't. Either way she hasn't got them. I have heard Mother and Father murmuring in their bedroom at night, and think they are worrying about money and need more of it. Father's voice rumbles quietly while Mother sounds angry, which is an unusual way round for them.

I plan to be out of the way today. Baking old chicken feathers will make the house stink.

Soon I'm up and away, over at Lord Hartley's helping with a pheasant shoot, walking out across the brown stubble, encouraging the birds into the air which is known as beating. A pheasant goes up, making a sound like marbles in a jam-jar, wings windmilling. It is a clumsy thing. By the hedge the well-to-do stand still and upright, guns pointing to the sky, all dressed in heavy green coats and caps like it is a uniform and they are birds of a feather too. Another pheasant goes up. Clicks and whirrs. Shots are fired in a blink. Cartridges spin down to the ground.

"Missed!" A voice yaps like Gyp. We carry on.

Cocker spaniels pant and wag their tails, circling the men, bringing in the carcasses.

At lunch we beaters sit on hay bales and listen to them talking about Queen Victoria and how many deer they have, while we eat pasties and onions.

"They're good dogs," Lord Hartley says. I can't help but notice that he speaks more fondly of his dogs than he does of his wife. Chins up, backbones stiff, these people are not like my neighbours in Sebastopol Road.

Dead pheasants are carried off in twos and threes, heads knocking together, as the sun loses its shine behind thin winter clouds.

Then, out of the corner of my eye, in the distance I see Miss Etherington, walking on the arm of young Joseph Hartley. There she goes again.

"He was born with a silver teaspoon in his mouth," is what Mother says.

The pair of them head up the track towards the old Belle Vue folly. And I'm left puzzling over her once more. I remember the bad things I've heard people say about her. Billy's mother said she leads men on with her eyes and there is a danger they will forget themselves.

When I return home Father makes me pray. His jaw is set, eyes buried in sagging skin. He is worried I am getting ideas above my station.

※

Edward asks me to walk with him to the zoo again. As before, we arrive early before the visitors. The morning has come after a long night sitting up to the small hours finishing my sewing. The work Edward is doing, the invitation to the Grand Dinner with the great and the good depicted as animals, is developing steadily. His sense of mischief sharpens as we move from creature to creature. I remember these moments with intense pleasure.

"This will stir them up!" he chortles.

"They'll laugh. But they'll also see what I can do," he says. Then he gives me a darker, more serious look.

"I sometimes feel I do nothing of consequence. But this! This is fun, this is wicked, this will get the tongues wagging," he says.

He strokes his beard and picks up his sketchbook but then is distracted by a photographer who has set up a camera and tripod and is sorting his glass plates in a bag bearing the name Gambler Bolton. He is right by the lion's cage and pokes the lens through the bars. Three men rush up with long poles. One jousts with the lion to keep it occupied, another nudges it closer to the camera, then the third climbs on top of the cage and dangles a piece of meat.

"Ah. The Invaluable Adjunct! Yes, yes. It is the future," says Edward.

"But he is just making a record, isn't he?" I say. "And we are doing something quite else?"

He turns towards me. "But just consider. Think about it. Artists, writers, photograph-makers? We all want to save the moment, store time in a jar for others to see. Who wouldn't want to record this lovely morning with this very beautiful woman?"

"I... I know what you mean of course. I suppose so... yes."

In spite of the flattery, I am not sure he is right.

"Augustus P. Reynolds has done well with those lions, don't you think?" says Edward.

"Has he? How?"

"He's changed the way they live and what they eat. He's brought their cages outside and now feeds them intestines, skin and all the other bits and pieces as well as bone and flesh and sinew. The result is that they are living longer and reproducing better than anywhere else in Europe!"

"Lord! Where does he get all the meat from?"

"Horses. What do you do with an old horse? Might as well have it killed kindly and fed to the lions as anything else. This new diet makes a useful ending for half the horses in London."

My mouth falls open in amazement but at that moment we are distracted by the sight of Augustus P. Reynolds in his top hat, black coat and tails, striding through the zoo with half a loaf of bread in each hand. He is followed by the heavy hooves and armour-plated body of a rhinoceros. It jogs briskly, snout first, ears pricked, skin folding around its neck, small eye fixed upon the bread. Behind it come twenty keepers, each one holding a lead attached to its collar. Augustus P. increases his speed as he approaches the animal's cage and his top hat bobs along with him. The rhinoceros breaks into a trot and then into a gallop, which is a bit restricted by the shortness of its legs. Augustus P.'s long legs, on the other hand, scissor quickly towards the cage, where he vaults the barrier and lets the animal in. Keepers tumble to the ground in heaps but Augustus P. doesn't care one jot what happens to the hopeless humans. His mind is on keeping his contract with the rhinoceros. He leans over, delivers the two half loaves and beams as the creature snuffles with gratitude. As a father would upon his child.

A minute later he is by my side, raising his hat.

"Winter quarters to summer quarters. Time of year. Has to be done."

"What a spectacle!" says Edward.

"A Great Indian one-horned. Lost its mother not so long ago. The naturalist Frank Buckland, good man, good friend, wanted to know what the mother tasted like. You know. The way he wants to eat everything he can lay his hands on in the spirit of discovery." He stops for a moment to listen to a monkey screeching in the distance. Then he carries on.

"He went off to Brighton to give one of his lectures and took the dead animal with him. Minus armour, of course. Stewed it with onions and carrots, topped it with a light shortcrust and fed it to the audience. The general opinion was that it tasted much like tough beef."

"Capital! Capital! I wish I'd been there," says Edward. "And, on another tack, might I ask, how are the elephant droppings?"

"Nothing yet. Give it time," he says.

"Is the elephant not well, sir?" I say.

"Madam," he tips his hat. "The elephant is quite well, thank you. It is merely that a woman dropped her purse while mounting the howdah to take a ride on it, and the elephant lifted up the purse with its trunk and posted it into its mouth. She was *mighty* agitated. Fans and smelling salts, squawked like a parrot. Gave her the money for her journey home. Promised to check the droppings every day to see if the purse comes out the other end. Nothing yet. Give it time."

I almost wish I hadn't asked.

"And how are you, Madam? You work hard. When I see you busying away solemnly with the sketchbook in your hand, you remind me of a heron hunting for fish."

"Oh, I'm quite well, thank you. It is wonderful to learn, a privilege to be here at all."

"Ha, my dear," says Edward. "Such a way with words. And any news, my man, from your correspondents in the Dark Continent? Any more epistles about dark-coloured horses with stripes to the front and stripes to the back, lurking among the natives of the Congo?"

"Well, yes, since you ask." Augustus P. clicks his heels, flicks his tails and looks pleased. "Sir Harry Johnston sent paintings, as good a likeness as those sketches of yours, Madam. Those who thought they knew better have denounced him as a fraudster. As people do. But then the skin and skulls arrived by sea. I opened the package. A treat it was. The Zoological Society will meet soon and pronounce."

"Does that count as another example of evolution at work, according to the word of Charles Darwin?" Edward asks.

"Yes. The Great Man Himself would have been pleased. The world is changing. Turmoil of the times. And time is changing too."

"What do you mean by that?" I interrupt. So excited am I by this world of new creatures, new names, new thoughts.

"The animal world makes sense of everything," he says. "What is time? What is time for? What is the passing of time? Making the world in seven days was a conjuring trick. This slow process of change is what time is really about, isn't it?"

"I thought Railway Time had taken over from God's Time," says Edward, laughing. "To eliminate twelve minutes of difference between London and Liverpool, and thirty minutes between Yarmouth and Penzance, we've all synchronised our timepieces to the London railway timetable."

Augustus P Reynolds bends forward, his face grave.

"No. No. It is evolution, it is change, which makes sense of time. Without change, time is meaningless."

"Now that is a strange concept! I will have to think on that, my man!" says Edward.

"The horn made a good funnel in the top."

"In the top of what?" says Edward.

"In the pie, of course. In the rhinoceros pie."

CHAPTER TEN:

THE LETTERS

February 16 1901

(In 1659 a cheque was used for the first time in Britain when Mr Nicholas Vanacker settled a debt. It was made out for the grand sum of £400 which was a great deal of money in those days)

We are all on the railway bank, lying on the grass after school. We're planning our futures. As usual Billy is king of the railway.

"I'm going to be an engine driver," he says, in case we have forgotten.

Skinny wants to be an apprentice fitter, which means he'll have to work the lathes and make sparks fly. There'll also be duties in the mess room and he'll be the one to go round The Works hooking the tea cans up on a long pole to take in for warming before dinner.

Barney has his eyes on the trim shop. He's never liked getting those long white fingers dirty and he's good at making things. He'll be cleaning and combing horsehair, stuffing and sewing locomotive seats, machining covers and mending window blinds. He'll have to keep the leatherwork on the horse boxes in good repair too.

"The First-Class compartments are better than a naked woman," he says.

We laugh like we're men who are well used to naked women.

"Oh, the First-Class compartment is so soft to touch, so sweet to smell!" he says, outlining the shape of a woman's hips. "Blue Swanton cloth, leather door panels, silk facings on the seats, carpet velvety enough to lie on." Then he lifts his nose as if to sniff the exotic woods from the darkest corners of the Empire and notes of pear-drop in the varnish.

Mother says some of the painting in these carriages is so fancy that it reminds her of a fairground.

"Yer'll start with combing out the horsehair, you daft highness," says Billy. "Twelve hours a day, it'll be. Your fingers won't be soft as cat's paws after that."

Dudley wants to be a clerk. His father and his mother, his four uncles and his three aunts all work for Mr Massingham, and his father is a clerk already, so he is more than likely to follow in his footsteps.

"He seen letters, my Dad, ones which have arrived for the lady. Your lady, Jack Stamp, you dreamer," he says.

"What letters are those, then?" I ask.

They're trying to catch me out but I'm not daft. What they don't know is that I have been watching her from the Massinghams' garden. I discovered that if I wait until dark and crawl past the gooseberry bush, move the loose board in the fence, settle among the shrubs at the bottom of the garden, I can see Miss Etherington carrying the lamp into her bedroom, letting her hair down and gazing into her looking glass. They cannot know this.

"The letters for Miss Etherington. On fine paper. One had a drawing on the back of the envelope." Dudley wipes his nose. "It were a drawing of a giraffe."

Silence follows as we think about this for a moment. No-one has anything useful to say about the head of a giraffe on the back of an envelope sent to the most beautiful lady in these parts.

"It's true," he says.

"Is there a postmark?" I say.

"London."

He is triumphant.

"My Ma says she is no better than we," says Billy.

I have heard this before.

"My Dad says she is maybe no good at all," says Dudley.

"He says she is likely to be a lady *with a past*," he says, full of mystery.

We all sit and think about the meaning of this, but we are no clearer than we are about the giraffe's head.

"Maybe she's a witch," Billy says, giving me the eye.

I roll over on the grass. Five warts have appeared on my leg, in a straight line below my right knee. Billy hasn't noticed but it occurs to me that warts and witches go together and it sets my teeth on edge.

Skinny is not as interested in the doings of Miss Etherington as the rest of us are.

"Last week I done a day in the mess room with my brother," he says. "It were bedlam. Like you've never seen. All them dinner baskets full of pies and stuff that wanted heating up. I put labels on them and laid them under a sheet on that big counter by the cooking range."

"How did you get on with the pole, Skinny? Fishing for tea, eh?" says Billy.

"It were padded so it fitted snug enough on my shoulder and I was quite happy. The cans from the boiler shop filled the whole pole so I had to unload 'em all before I went off again to the fitting shop, then the machine shop. Another load. Then the carriage shop, the wagon shop and the paint shop."

"Were that it, then?" says Billy.

"Nah," he says. "I was put to cleaning the brass 'til half past eleven, then put the pies in the oven and the cans on the stove. At twenty past twelve all hell broke loose. Cans and pies had to be put out in their correct places by half past and the men came in talking so loud they were like a load of turkeys in a tin shed. They ate the lot, then they were gone and it went dead quiet. I washed the tables down with hot soda water and the mess attendant thought up another list of things for me to do, to keep me out of mischief he said, 'til half past five. Then I went home."

"Were it better or worse than school?" Billy is showing mild interest. Skinny has come nowhere near braving the dangers of the machine shed, suffering the choking fumes, risking crushed toes, amputated fingers and dreadful burns.

"I went up the Golden Stairs," Skinny boasts, "and I shook Mr Eden's hand."

Well, you can't get grander than that. Billy blinks and whistles. The Golden Stairs rise like Jacob's Ladder in the office building between the loco shed and the sidings. At the very top is Mr Massingham's office, where he can see everything from his window. If the men are late for work they are sent up there and Mr Massingham tells them that if it happens again they'll never get another day's work. They have to thank him and come down the stairs which don't now seem quite so golden. Up there too is the engineers' office, where they draw tracks, sheds and engines for apprentices to trace.

When Dudley starts as a clerk he'll have to mix ink for them, collect newspapers from the station and run messages, which I would do better as I am a faster runner. If Dudley proves himself, he could then become a draughtsman. He'll trace designs for small jobs until he has *true knowledge*. He'll have to take evening classes in mathematics and mechanics and study the stations and levels of track, and he'll be expected to buy all his own instruments and technical books.

None of them asks what I want to be because I'm just the baker's boy. One good thing is they don't look down on me when Easter comes. I remember this as I grind expensive almonds, measure the sugar and drain the yolks off the eggs to make the Easter marzipan. I know the recipe by heart.

> MARZIPAN
>
> *1 loaf of sugar*
>
> *12 oz ground almonds*
>
> *3 oz sifted icing sugar*
>
> *Two whites of eggs*
>
> *One and a half gills of water*

At the back of the book are Father's personal notes and little ditties. This is one of his favourites.

> *He who spoils or adulterates the material*
>
> *He is a bungler*
>
> *He who just works the material*
>
> *Is a mere workman*
>
> *He who really improves the material – whatever it may be*
>
> *He alone is the master*

In woodwork today I almost finished my railway signal. I made the lever that will move the flag up and down. I bent the wire, looped it round a pin at the base and curved it into a lever. It worked, and I am mightily pleased. Next, I'll paint it black and grey and maybe put a red stripe across the flag.

"Once a railwayman, always a railwayman," says Billy gruffly.

Man cannot live by bread alone is what I think.

❦

"The Duchess is in Margate again! Come in, come in! I am ready!"

Edward seems to be alone in the house today and he is more than usually full of smiles and games.

"We must get on! Quickly, quickly!"

He whisks me past the stag's head in the hallway, through the willow-papered dining room, past Mrs Stafford Clark's desk, and out of the back door to the shed. In a trice we are in darkness. Curtains shut out the light and the rest of the world ceases to exist.

"What fun! So much better than having to draw to order. Politicians, the Queen, the Prince, the postman. The list from *Burlesque* is endless. My days are circumscribed by it. My professional reputation depends on it. But... today, my dear, we will forget work and think about art. That will please you, won't it?"

"Oh yes."

"Good, good."

His hands fly dementedly about like white gulls. They direct me to the back of the room, which is dressed for a scene I cannot work out. The stage is very bare.

"*Pygmalion and the Image – The Heart Desires*, from that great work by Sir Edward Burne-Jones. Nothing wrong with a composition which has been used before. They all do it. *We all do it*. And why not?"

He is more excited than I have ever seen him.

"Do you know the work? Perhaps not? Then let me drape you with sheets. Let us wrap your shoulders, so. And gather the folds about you... so. Then stand you in profile." His voice becomes gentle as he touches me.

"Just here. Chin up a little. There!"

I am swaddled. As he places a light cloth about my shoulders I feel his breath on my face. I have a rope twisted about my waist, and his hands caress me as he ties it. Another rope falls around my feet. He urges me to turn to the side and put my hands against my cheek. I'm thrilled by his attentions. I feel suddenly *elevated*. He darts back to the tripod and ducks his head under the cloth.

"Behind you The Three Graces are dancing but we can sketch them in later." He gasps. "Marvellous. Marvellous."

We flip between the ordinariness of the shed and sheets and the dreams in Edward's head. We are in a magic twilight, miles from the stench and clatter on the streets. He has a vision and I am part of it. The atmosphere changes, as it did the first time I was here. The air is thick with his concentration. I am aware of his eye, the camera's eye, the light and dark, the infinite possibilities of make-believe.

"Now turn your head a little, push your hair behind. My God! That's it!"

I listen to him breathing heavily as he works and little shivers run down my spine like fingers on a piano.

"They're getting very grand, these artists, don't you know? I love them, I love their wives, I love their houses. Oh yes, their artistic houses. I love everything about them, *but* they are getting a bit too grand," he says. "Burne-Jones was given a knighthood, no less. Leighton was given a baronetcy! Ha! One day before he died, poor chap. They're all turning into lords. That's what you get for being the acceptable face of the Royal Academy."

He sounds a little sad. Maybe even a little bitter. But the misery is gone in a moment.

"Do they not approve of your photographs, then?" I ask tentatively.

"Oh, no! Not of my photographs, no." He clears his throat and stands up straight. It always surprises me that he is taller than I think. "Nor of my work, my dear. You see I am only black-and-white!"

I turn my head to ask what he means.

"I work in black-and-white. No colour in my weekly masterpieces in *Burlesque*. I don't do oils." He separates these last five words and mimics a pompous voice.

I'm beginning to learn that the world of art has almost as many layers in it as society itself. But the actual rules are hidden.

"I am thus banned from ever being elected to the Royal Academy," he says. "But I did exhibit a painting there once, in a Summer Exhibition. Oils, my dear, are considered to have much greater value than black-and-white. A single oil could make you more than my entire annual wage as a cartoonist! Now you have ceased concentrating. Back to work! Take up your position! And... yes!"

I have strayed towards him as he talks. I say *talks*, but it is more like a confession. The darkness enfolds us and he is sharing something he has never shared before.

"Let's try another one," he says, stroking his beard, eyes suddenly bright with the next picture in his head.

"Let us do Antony and Cleopatra according to Sir Lawrence Alma-Tadema! Ha! Another titled artist. A dear man, of course."

Before I know what is happening, he has placed cushions on the floor and rearranged the sheets around me. Then he takes a dark cloth, which he says we must pretend is a leopard skin, and clasps it around my neck. He tells me to lie on the cushions and gaze with passion towards the back of the cave. Another cloth is hung from a hook in front of me to represent a column of sumptuous silk through which Antony, were he here, would be peering. Garlands of rosebuds to frame the picture are also missing. I am willing to do whatever he desires of me. I'm utterly and completely happy and want to treasure every second of this special day.

"What magnificent feet! What dear hands! What is this if not going to nature itself for inspiration?" His voice drips honey.

Somehow a whole afternoon passes. We have come to the end of it and must now set about putting everything away. The cloths which he turned into silk must be re-hung as curtains in Mrs Stafford Clark's Morning Room. I have to climb up on a chair to fasten them back into place among the imitation Van Dycks and

Kate Greenaway paintings. Nearby is that little table I noticed before, inlaid with many colours, smelling of frankincense and myrrh. He sees me looking at it.

"It is Moroccan. A little favourite of mine, too. Exquisite. The kind of thing they all have in their houses at Bedford Park. Liberty's oriental department, my dear. It keeps us all happy with treasures from the east."

When the curtains are safely hung, he asks me to follow him upstairs so he can show me where he works. His feet are already on the stairs when I stretch out a hand to adjust one of the Van Dycks and am astonished to find there is no willow-pattern behind the pictures. He has saved on wallpaper by cutting out squares behind the paintings. The room is not what it seems.

Ahead of me up the stairs he puffs out his chest, straining the buttons of his hound's tooth waistcoat. He is bursting to show me the Drawing Room, which covers the whole of the first floor of the house and is overfilled with a grand collection of chairs, tables and cabinets scattered with dozens of statues and lamps. Prints and pictures jostle for space on walls lined with embossed leather. It is all for show.

At the far end, beyond a piano adorned with statues, is a stained-glass window depicting a rampant lion on a scarlet shield bearing three red stars and plumes of golden feathers.

"Is that a coat of arms?"

"Hmm? What? Oh yes, in a way. I designed it myself," he says.

Van Dyck copies? Wallpaper cut-outs? A make-believe coat of arms? Is everything pastiche?

"Well, why not? Why not? We are all gentlemen these days. The world is changing so fast. All kinds of men are making money, lending money, mixing with titles, getting titles, making beautiful houses, shopping at Liberty's, throwing dinner parties, attending the theatre, marrying their models. Society is opening its doors!"

Then he draws back a curtain and shows me his inner sanctum. His high chair, his drawing board, his ink stands. This is where he spends his evenings after the Wednesday dinners at *Burlesque*. This is where he works throughout Thursdays and Fridays on his cartoons. He's proud of the engraver's globe he uses to see better. The sloped drawing board, not unlike an artist's easel, has jottings on it which must be work in progress. I can't stop myself from reading them.

Artist: Hello. Will you be my Muse?

Muse: I must first scatter the cinders, dust the furniture, prepare my lady's room, and lay the fires. But I may fit you in after six o'clock and before seven o'clock each day!

And then:

Artist: Hello Muse. Am I to be the wicked seducer who will ruin you or are you a naughty temptress who will bring me down? Which is it to be? Truly?

I quickly turn away.

"How does it all work?" I ask him in a whisper.

"I make the photographic prints and I place the tracing paper... so. Then I make the tracing and square it up."

Discarded tracings lie on the floor. The work looks long and slow. Tracing, squaring, piecing in, is very like sewing. I take it all in and realise how much of an illusionist he is.

"Once I have an outline I have scaffolding for shadows and lines, and I can use other photographs for reference and inspiration."

He tweaks his moustache. I spot a photograph of him wearing a sheet wrapped around his waist like a skirt, his bare feet just peeping out. He has removed his waistcoat and jacket, rolled up his sleeves and has a jaunty spotted neckerchief around his throat. His right hand waves a fan, while his left has gathered the skirt in preparation for a curtsey. He looks mightily amused.

"Ah. We have fun between the deadlines. The interminable deadlines! I have not your gift of speed you see, my dear. It takes me as long as it takes me. And that, indeed, may be rather a long time."

༄

Jack Stamp has brought me an orange. To smell its skin is to taste it. He says it was one of many thousands picked up off the shore after a ship was stranded in a storm. They have a basketful at home and this one was spare.

"Riches, Jack, what riches you have!" I am blinded by the brightness of it.

"Do I, Miss Etherington? I don't think so."

I take a minute to look at him. Jack, my little companion at the library, is not like other boys. Most days he has the look of a startled fawn. There is a yearning in him, for what I do not know.

"Now what is worrying you? Are riches a bad thing?" I ask. His knees are out of proportion, like saucers attached to his thin little legs.

"*Again, I tell you, it is easier for a camel to pass through the eye of a needle than for a rich man to enter the kingdom of heaven.*" He speaks solemnly. "What do you think about that, Miss? I never can understand it myself."

"I don't know, Jack. Nothing is certain. But I think it may be that being poor helps you understand other people. That's what the Bible means about rich people not being able to enter heaven. Because they haven't understood the people around them. But I am not the one to ask, Jack."

"I have no-one else to ask, Miss." He doesn't seem to think of his own father, who is a man of the chapel.

Every day his father takes out his cart filled with bread and stops for whoever comes to buy, almost as if he were spreading kindnesses. Women hurry from their houses, pulling their shawls about them, nod their heads and smile at him as if he is a priest. Sometimes he sends Jack in his place. The boy can scarcely manage but he does it as if his life depends upon it, which is how he does most things. His mother is somewhat strange, as she is so extremely small and keeps her eyes trained to the ground. I've watched her, wrapped in woollens, making her way to market each Thursday with a basket of eggs. I've seen her, too, with the moon still hanging in the sky, carrying bags of flour into the bakery. A single sack is almost as big as she is and maybe twice as heavy, so she doubles over and carries it on her back while the village sleeps. Her husband expects it of her and gives her no thanks. Then she goes back to fetch another. It is no wonder her little body is folding in on itself.

I have never longed for marriage as other women do. I've never yearned for children because I don't know what makes a family. I should always be afraid to lose a child, as my parents were lost to me. Whether I remain alone and earn my keep with my needle again, or whether I marry, as may become a possibility, it seems either way is hard labour. I cannot love as I have loved already. Perhaps we love truly only once, and for me it was the first time. The rest of life is making the best of things.

The orange turned into a strange dream that night. Suddenly I was enveloped in a luxurious cloak. Not a soft thing made of rabbit fur but one made of orange skins which had been cut into quarters and turned inside out so that they formed a mass of pustules shimmering with juice. Edward was there and he began to lift the bottom of my orange cloak and suck it clean. Dribbles ran down his chin. His eyes were greedy for the next skin. What a night I had with that dream.

*

March 2 1901
(In 1791 John Wesley, founder of Methodism, died)

Seeing in the dark
The narrow slit which you see in a cat's eye in bright daylight is never to be found there in the dim light of the evening. As night comes on, the narrow opening grows wider and

wider, allowing more and more of the waning light to enter. A cat cannot, of course, see anything at all in complete darkness, but in a light which would seem very dim indeed to ourselves it could readily detect a small object. That is one of the ways in which Nature equips the cat as a night hunter.

My knees brush the damp mulberry leaves and stroke my warts, which are getting bigger every week. I've slipped away after chapel into the back gardens of Colville Road, past the doctor's house and into the garden of Mr Massingham. The house is quiet, the sky is darkening and the only sound is my own breathing. Then there is movement in the upper window. Miss Etherington has lit a lamp and I can see her outline clearly. She comes to the window, looks into the garden and up at the moon. She stands there for a while. A cat slips across the grass. She takes off her shawl and drapes it on a chair. She undoes her bodice, takes off her skirt and stands in her shift. I begin to pant like Gyp and my feet grow into the earth. She lifts a jug of water and pours it into a bowl, lets her hair tumble around her shoulders like a shower of coins. She lifts her shift up over her head and stands before the bowl looking out. She could be gazing at the night or she could be looking at her reflection in the glass. She looks so sad. The cat miaows. She lowers herself over the ewer, her bare white breasts falling forward. It is as exciting as lying on the tracks beneath the train but is a great deal more pleasurable. I see the dark pink tips of her nipples dipping up and down before another cat arrives and jumps off the fence to snarl at its rival. I hold my breath. She lifts a cloth quickly to her chest and draws the curtains. She vanishes.

 I take a roundabout route on my way home. Going up past The Works, I pass Tom Stokes weighing cotton waste into bundles, large ones for the cleaners, small ones for the drivers. I catch sight of Mr Massingham in his dark grey suit and his bowler hat. The hooter is about to go, so Tom will soon be finished. In the machine shop, men carry on working. As I turn towards Sebastopol Road, the engine cleaners are arriving to start oiling, waxing and polishing. They even polish the connecting rods and dab them with petroleum jelly to protect against the weather, and they scour the brass with soot from the smokebox to make it shine.

❧

Rosie drew the curtains, turned to her bed and pulled out two envelopes from under the mattress. She kissed them and held them against her cheek. She already knew them by heart but she unfolded them tenderly as if they were new. As she read, the sound of Edward's voice came back to her and made her smile. Then she searched for the things he might have written but hadn't, and that made her eyes fill with tears.

Rosie,

My little one – what terrible thing has happened – where have you taken yourself off to – what did you see to scare you away so violently? Splashes of blood hung like rose petals among my precious plates – smashed to glass daggers they were. So many of my beautiful young girls in pieces. Are you all right my little one – that is all that matters? Are your pretty fingers healing? If I could only kiss those hands to make them better. I would forgo lunch at The Garrick to find them. All I ask is – do not judge me. You, above all people, above all the artist-turned-knights, must not judge me. That would be too much.

It was fun, though – little one – wasn't it? We had fun. How I should hate to hurt you.

Rosie pressed the scars on her fingers. They had healed well but she'd had to get used to a feeling of numbness in two of them. With her forefinger she traced the giraffe on the back of the envelope. Then she turned to the second letter. Its arrival had surprised her much more than the first. He might have sent one and then forgotten her. But he had written another, and what did that mean? No. She must resist his old charm. His appetite, for food and for other things, was monstrous.

Rosie,

Little one – life is dreary without you – when will you return? My Great Work is nearly finished and – yes – so much of it is yours. All our friends at the zoo are there - the old rhinoceros, the ostrich, the monkeys, the snake – in fact most of the animal kingdom – our kingdom which had you as its Queen and myself as King. They now have recognisable faces of the well-known and the admired members of the establishment, seated around a long oval table, set with best silver, about to dive into a stupendous dinner. Oh, how I do like to pull their whiskers and prick their pomposity! We opened our doors to show it off and thirty-five people came to see it. "The finest work".... "your best yet".... "you should work in COLOUR". They loved it – I wish you were here to tell. Thirty-five is a good number but not nearly so many as the seven hundred which Mrs Luke Fildes told The Duchess she had at the last Picture Sunday.

The Duchess is in bed again. She is suffering from neuralgia, sore throat, backache, headache, rashes, exhaustion, biliousness. She makes sure she is fair to all of them, giving them each a turn, so that sometimes I forget whose turn it is and then she is displeased. They are her seven (very ugly) dwarfs and she is their (slightly better looking) Snow White who sleeps in the forest for days on end while the world goes by. I don't let it stop me. I am busy about town with all of life to dip my beak into.

I take Polly for a canter across the Park each morning, show my face at the office of Burlesque, take lunch – Rules on Monday produced the best steak and kidney pudding. Then I had thirty to dinner last night for a gentlemen's evening. We had a good meal – caviar, clear soup, cold salmon, chaud-froid pigeons, roast lamb, haricots verts, roast chicken, Russian salad, jelly, anchovy savoury, ices, fifteen bottles of Champagne. I planned it myself. And tonight I shall amuse myself with a trip to the theatre to see Lady Windermere's Fan. It is a good life but it no longer has Rosie-time in it – ah, then I felt truly alive, truly arrived, truly that I had found my twin.

CHAPTER ELEVEN:

THE DRESS

I dream I am about to marry Edward. If I can find a dress to wear, then at last, we can be together. Should it be a demure high-neck in ivory silk or white organza? I flit round the haberdashers, finger rolls of fabric, toy with different styles of neck and sleeve. I need the gown that will make him love me, make him fall upon me as lustfully as a soldier returned from war. What would he love? Which part of me does he love best? The neck, the hips, the waist? I try the drop waist, the high waist, narrow sleeves, puff sleeves. I become a princess, an insect with muslin wings, ribbons and trails, a piece of stuff that floats in the breeze, a purse of desire covered in silk and sea pearls. If only I can find the dress, I will be there for him.

Then someone speaks, someone without a face.

"I think you might have to wait a long time for him at the station."

And I answer. "Yes. I know that. I have always had to wait."

Then the fantasy shatters into a thousand fragments.

"I know your meaning. Yes. I might find myself waiting for an age." I don't know who I'm speaking to.

The disembodied voice tells me he may not come at all. He may not know he is marrying me. He may have decided not to. He may not have asked me. In fact, he did not ask me, did he? He cannot marry me. He can never marry me *because he has a wife*. I have been a vain fool. I am like the blue butterfly he kept in his rosewood box, alive for one short spring, then pinned into place, skewered by ideas above my station. Vanity has been my greatest failing. For how long, I wonder, does a specimen last in its case?

One hundred years? Imagine the dust!

I wake feeling drained. I know I am no more than a specimen in his collection. Though my heart is heavy, my ears ring with joyous sounds coming from the garden as spring takes hold. I have survived a whole winter. The birds play their flutes and piccolos, making sounds much louder than their tiny bodies seem capable of. Melodies tumble around me, washing away the dream. I listen more deeply, try to unpick elements of the chorus much as I would unpick stitches from a dress. I hear tongue-curling, lip-rolling, throat-gurgling. They twirl and loop and tie knots in the air, they rattle, whistle and squeak like mice skittering through the trees. The old wood pigeon on the edge of the roof keeps up his steady cooing. Tulip, tulip, tulip. Twee, twee, twee. Reddit, reddit, reddit. *Trollop, trollop, trollop.*

⁂

"A dress that Tissot would have painted! The Duchess would love it. She would look so stylish. It would set so many tongues wagging. She could parade from one At Home to another, showing off her witty dress. Oh, such a witty dress! Now, which one?"

Edward reaches down an exhibition catalogue from his shelves and makes a *tum-te-tum* as he turns the pages. He has already been out for two hours this morning, first riding his new bicycle, wobbling, shouting at friends and falling off. Then riding his horse across the park. He loves to boast about how he keeps up with current thinking on the importance of outdoor activities.

He stops at a page displaying a painting of a ship hung with flags and a gathering of prosperous women on the scrubbed deck. They are all dressed in black and white. The title of the picture is *The Ball on Shipboard*.

"James Tissot. Cowes week. Women of fashion showing off their finery. Perhaps black and white was a thing that year. Do you like it?" he says.

"I do. It's not an everyday scene but I think it captures a moment."

"Ah, yes. They all say that. Ruskin criticised Tissot for producing *painted photographs of vulgar society*. Well, if that's what this is, then I think it is rather expert. My friend Mr Alma-Tadema lives in Tissot's old house in St John's Wood which is the same house, my dear, where Tissot kept his mistress. These days The Duchess goes there on Mondays to visit his wife. That is, when The Duchess is well enough to leave her sofa. When her nerves are good enough. So what do you think?"

"I think a black and white dress would be most unusual."

He often talks to me about artists and writers and their lovers who live nearby. Some have children out of wedlock. William Powell Frith is one such. He has twelve children by his wife Isabelle and seven with his mistress Mary, who lives a mile down the road. Wilkie Collins is another. He has a sort of second wife called Caroline who lives round the corner with a second family. George Cruikshank also keeps two households in Mornington Crescent and has ten children with his second love. There are so many of them that I think London streets must be thronging with men dashing from one family to another. I'm daydreaming now but Edward brings me back to the present.

"Smile away, smile away. I'm glad you like it. A dress in the style of Tissot would be just the thing! I need something to cheer up The Duchess and lift us up out of the fearful black fogs that sit over London on dark winter days, and indeed to get The Duchess out of bed in the mornings. The doctor has now ordered her to start the day by swallowing two pints of wine."

He tidies his moustache with his forefinger, then looks at me thoughtfully and points to a dress in the foreground of the picture.

I study it and we are quiet together. I can't see the gown in detail as the wearer is seated sideways with her body turned towards the painter. I'm impressed by its black and white simplicity, the black bodice, white frill at the neck, piping around the base of the skirt, the balloon sleeves with stripes which change direction where the wearer bends her elbow. It is a high society pelt which I think Augustus P. Reynolds would appreciate. It is complicated but I am fairly sure I can turn it into dazzling *haute couture*.

༺♉༻

The afternoon is taken at a gallop. It is all scuttling and shushing. Arnold and Freda are helping us arrange things in the shed. The Duchess is upstairs in bed, so Freda vanishes every now and then to attend to her. She returns out of breath, bringing the props that Edward has asked for.

"How is she, Freda?" Edward says, patting his stomach.

"She's complaining about your photography again, sir. Oh Freda! She says to me. Those endless photographs, Freda."

Dressed as suffragettes, Freda and I have been fighting all morning for women's votes. Big hats, heavy coats and, for some reason I fail to understand, heavy boots.

"I need the detail. The detail for my cartoon," says Edward.

He bobs up and down behind the camera, the single eye shining in its wooden box.

Back in the Morning Room, which is really The Duchess's parlour, I re-hang the curtains and step down from the chair. My eye is drawn to the desk, a fine walnut (or at least it appears to be a fine walnut, but one can't be quite sure in this house), on which a marbled notebook lies open. Each page contains a date, addresses of friends she has visited and menus for meals they've had. My heart lurches. I can't stop myself reading more.

The date is Tuesday of this week.

Bedford Park. Very nice house. Dinner of eighteen. Very nicely served. Silver service. Six serving maids. Caviar, artichoke soup, cold trout, quails well done, goose pieces in tomato sauce and garlic and parsley, Russian salad, beans with bacon, apple jelly, almond tart, anchovies, parmesan cheese. A delightful evening. The talk is of Gertrude Jekyll and her new way with gardens. I hope that the house and everything in it is enough for Edward. I could not contemplate his attack on a garden as well. Besides – no-one sees a garden.

"Come along, come along Freda, take the hats! Fetch the boots! Cook is wanting you for supper. The Duchess will be down soon."

His voice comes from the hallway, muffled by the stag's head and stuffed birds.

And I cannot resist putting the tips of my fingers to the page and silently turning it back. I itch for another tiny scrap of information about their lives. I long to read more of the neat looped handwriting of a woman I have not yet met but whose house I am in. I turn to a date from last week.

Maida Vale. No expense spared. Potted cheese, soles au gratin, ducklings, potatoes boulangere, sweetbreads in brandy sauce, watercress salad, cinnamon pastries, syllabub. There is discussion of bicycles and Elgar's Enigma Variations which Edward says is a musical cartoon! House very aesthetic. Many bottles of wine. Edward queasy after and I have my headache.

I am even fascinated by her shopping lists.

Deep blue velvet dress, six pairs of stockings from Barkers, leather gloves from Marshall and Snelgrove, cup of chocolate at Charbonnel's, took tea dress back to Madame Bonne as very ill-fitting.

Oh lordy. This is as good as a photograph. Here is her life on a page. I have no need to meet her, for I know her now.

Even so it's decided that I am, at last, to meet The Duchess. Plans for the Tissot dress are well in hand. She is to visit Madame Juliette's. The day arrives and the footman in his white gloves waits beside the glass windows and the embroidered handkerchief, the sample of all samples. At the appointed hour a carriage draws up. The Duchess alights and is ushered into the *premier magazine*. Madame Juliette welcomes her with a smattering of French words. She pulls up a gilded chair for The Duchess and they begin to talk about the dress. As arranged, The Duchess mentions my name and Madame Juliette calls.

"*Jeune fille!*" I run into the *salon* full of mahogany and mirrors, carrying my sketches from Tissot's *The Ball On Shipboard*. Trembling, I lay them on the gilded counter and The Duchess picks them up. Are her gloves the same ones mentioned in her diary, from Marshall and Snelgrove? She examines the drawings and looks up, searching for the hand that drew them, eyes sharp and curious.

"Edward is so clever to think of this! These are quite charming, my dear. Quite... no *very*... exciting!"

My eyes scamper over her face and body before I drag them back and manage a curtsey. In those few seconds I see an unusual face with eyes set wide like a deer, a deep forehead and foreshortened chin and mouth. The overall effect is not displeasing. The broad shape is that of a heart narrowing to the tiny tilting chin.

She will look very fine in the dress.

We discuss fabrics and colours. I say 'we', but I mean that she and Madame Juliette consult each other, lift down bolts of ivory and black silk taffetas and roll them out on the counter while I remain silent in my black glacé dress. But this is all pretence because it has been settled in advance. I will have to create the stripes with bands of black and white fabric, just as Tissot probably painted stripe by stripe. Madame Juliette leads the Duchess to the correct choices and explains what I will do.

"*C'est exquisite!* No-one else in London will have such a dress. Now my *jeune fille* will measure you."

I am so close to The Duchess now, close as a mother or a lover. I have her arm-lengths, the size of her bust and shoulders, the drop from her waist to the floor. And for a moment I have my fingers on her neck, for it is essential that the white ruff fits perfectly. The bodice, too, must fit like a second skin. The measurements reveal unusually long limbs, like those of a tall boy, as well as a very compact waist. It never entered my head before, but now it does, that she has never had children. Of course. It has always been clear to see, in their house and their domestic arrangements. I chastise myself for not having understood fully before.

"I should so like it in time for Picture Sunday," she says, her wide eyes turning on Madame Juliette. Her skin is not so much pale as bedroom grey, unused to sunlight.

"Ah. Picture Sunday, *bien sur*. Like many other great artists, your husband will be opening his house to show his works. That is no problem, plenty of time. Not until May, I think? The work is intricate but the *jeune fille* is good."

As she glides across the carpet, I see her multiplied by the looking glasses into a hundred Duchesses. The footman lets them out of the door to climb into the waiting carriage.

༺

March 29 1901

(In 1813 Dr Livingstone was born. He mounted three expeditions into the African interior to find the source of the River Nile. On his travels he endured great hardship, spread

Christianity and began what has become known as The Scramble For Africa)

How we began to classify the animal kingdom

The Greek philosopher Aristotle first thought of sorting living things into classes and divided them into Plants and Animals. It was not a very good system because he placed all flying things in one group and all aquatic things in another so there was no place for the penguin or the frog. In the 1700s a Swedish biologist, Carolus Linnaeus, refined it and introduced five levels of classification: class, order, genus, species and variety. Body parts, ways of getting food, size and shape helped to place them in their categories. This was called the binomial system. The first part of the name identifies the genus, the second part the species. So humans belong to the genus Homo and the species Sapiens.

We have decided to organise the animal kingdom, judge it by the way it looks and arrange it in levels of importance, a bit like humans do with each other. Here in Swanton Stoke I am of the big group called *railway people*, but I am also of the very small sub-group *baker's son*. The trains do the same by having First, Second and Third-Class carriages. Armies organise themselves like this too, so that some give orders and some obey. Just like at The Works. We are all sorted. But what happens if you want to jump from one to another? I think the wrath of God is likely to come down because he made man and woman in order, so order is important to Him. *And God blessed them, and said unto them, Be fruitful, and multiply and replenish the earth and subdue it.* We are all in our slots, like the books in the Reading Room.

I've started to run messages for her. For Miss Etherington. I've always thought I was born a good runner for a reason, and now the reason has shown itself. I stretch out my legs and take the road up past The Works, past the Hartley Arms where I first saw her in the blue dress in the twilight, and head out of the village towards Lord Hartley's hall. I fork right down the stony track to the Belle Vue tower, to find Young Joseph. I'm out of breath but can take the stairs two at a time, circling up to the top. He is seated at the window, looking down towards the sea and marsh with one foot across his knee like he owns the place, which he does. Or he will do one day.

"Take this," she said, then her tiny hands, smooth as the custard in Father's tarts, placed the message in my hands.

There were bright spots of pink on her cheeks, and her mouth hung open a tiny bit. A lock of shining hair fell down one side of her face.

Young Joseph looks at me as if I am quite the wrong person in the wrong place. He takes the message

"Did you see her write it?" he asks.

I look at my feet.

"How did she seem?"

She seemed to be suffering from the heat, her cheeks were coloured, her neck was taut as one of Lord Hartley's racehorses on a June morning, but her face was quite set.

What I tell him is that she sat writing and then she looked up and stared through the window into the distance as if she wished she was somewhere else.

He waves me away.

I clatter down the stairs. But on the way back I do the run faster. I am Cupid on winged feet. I keep steady down the track, then lengthen my strides as I turn away from the big house back towards the village. No-one will know I have gone and come back. Except Miss Etherington, that is.

I feel nature stirring all around, new smells coming off the hedges, out of the earth. I see nettles and grasses waving, all bright green and vigorous. The evening air is cold but pockets of heat rise off the track, promising an end to cold mornings, sore throats and painful chests. Until September comes again. In the half-light, the path glows white and a deer suddenly appears from nowhere in front of me. He stops and turns his head and his eyes meet mine. But in another second he is gone, leaping into the field, vanishing into the gloom.

All along I'm wondering if the messages from Young Joseph come and go only when she and I are at the library, or if they fly around at other times as well. And is Young Joseph usually quite alone in the Belle Vue as the sun sets, or does she sometimes meet him there? Does Miss Etherington, who is given to wandering, slip up the road in the balmy dusk to climb those stone steps and find him waiting for her? Or am I going mad with my secrets, my knowings and thinkings? It all began with my first sin, which was stealing the jemmy.

CHAPTER TWELVE:

THE LOBSTER

Mrs Massingham and I have had our lives turned upside down. The King, no less, has been to Swanton Stoke and the men have been working extra hard to prepare for him. They grumbled amongst themselves and complained about having to sweep the tracks. Never has there been such polishing or painting, or checking of points and signals. There's no Royal Train in these parts, so Lord Hartley had to order carriages with fine saloons to be brought in from another part of the country. This allowed him to greet the King on his own private railway platform before inviting him to enjoy the comforts of his house and grounds, table and cellar.

The great day has come and gone, but not before the tension reached breaking point. Mrs Massingham found it difficult to please Mr Massingham in any way at all. Her starched skirts, loops of grey hair, smiling face, her very self, fell short of his exacting standards.

"It isn't a matter of whether people are too grand for the likes of us. It is a matter of service. We are here to serve. No-one is interested in whether your suet is too soft or too dry, or whether your skirt is starched. The only thing that matters is that we make a good impression." So said Mr Massingham.

Now the big day is over, his back has slumped and his bowler hat has been laid aside. Supper is prepared and he has agreed that I should join them tonight. A large steak and kidney pudding takes up the centre of the table, sides straining under the pressure of meat and sauce.

"Mr Eden accompanied them in their saloon," he says.

He thinks Mr Eden has been touched by greatness because he has breathed the same air as the King, though in truth he is still Prince of Wales and she still Princess until the coronation, which is not for a while yet. I can't help but remember the girls at Madame Juliette's chattering about how the Prince's waist bulged to forty-eight inches because of his love of pies and puddings. But I don't pass this on to Mr Massingham as it might not be helpful.

"What did the Princess wear?" I ask.

Mr Massingham looks exasperated. His mind is on higher things. He is also not at all sure he can remember what she wore, and thinks it a ridiculous question.

"Hmm? Oh, she looked very fine indeed. Very fine. Queenly. Possibly dark blue. A tiara on her head. Yes. That was it."

"And the Prince?"

"Ah. The King looked like a King, one related to almost every royal family you care to mention. I would have considered it an honour to black his boots."

We eat in silence. Mrs Massingham is busy with vegetables but the goodness she dispenses does not seem to be received.

"Sent Piggott home for being five minutes late," says Mr Massingham, his mouth narrowing to a slit. "Said I never wanted to see him again."

"But Mr Eden was full of airs and graces and bestowed his own different kind of justice. He told me it is always easy to sack a man for being late or for drinking, but it is far better to make him see the error of his ways and mend them."

Mr Eden is a much kinder man than Mr Massingham. That hardly needs to be said.

"If he had to deal with them as I do, he wouldn't think like that. He's too busy keeping his eye on his place in heaven, that man, instead of making this world work on time."

And what isn't said is that the true reason for Mr Massingham's grumpiness is that he wasn't invited into the saloon with their Royal Highnesses.

"Only the chosen few," he says bitterly. He pushes his plate away the moment he has finished, and puts his hat back on. "Only the chosen few."

I lie in bed that night with tears coursing down my face. They pour like they have never done before. I feel I am a small child again, being looked after by strangers in a storm. I've run away from London and Edward Stafford Clark as I had to. But his words have stayed in my head and he has stayed in my heart. His house bewitched me. I see the Moroccan table in my dreams. And now I can't rework my life as if it were a gown in need of repair because the things that happen to us change the way we are. We can move on, cancel meetings and friendships, but we can't stop feelings and ideas. Oh dear. I am overwhelmed by it all. I sense that my life is already over. And if this is so, then nothing from now on matters very much. Especially if there is no God. I've been turning over what Augustus P. Reynolds told me at the zoo, and I've decided that the soul cannot exist without God because only faith allows us an afterlife. Nothing else does. Perhaps the soul is more like a ghost of someone who has gone before, and perhaps after I am gone, my spirit will continue to linger in this village.

Though Mr Massingham's hand lies heavy on the shoulders of the workers, everyone here lives with certainty. They know their place. It couldn't be less like the house of Edward Stafford Clark, where every rule was made to be broken. In truth I no longer belong any more to one place rather than another. Who are the Massinghams to invite me to their table when they wish, then make me feel I don't quite belong? I toss and turn. The problem is a matter of urgency. The little money I had is used up. If I am to continue to stay alive, I must do whatever is necessary to look after my earthly needs. Because no-one can break my heart again. No-one can prise it open, then walk away leaving it gaping. No-one can play tricks on me again. From now on I will be in control of the decisions I make.

"You don't have long, dear girl," Mrs Massingham said to me this morning. She spoke tenderly, as one who has suffered herself and is keen to protect another. "A woman has few choices and only a small window of time in which to make them. After that she must make the best of her lot. As a child, my dear, I think you lacked the advice of a wise old woman like me. You didn't have your parents or your village keeping watch over you. Perhaps that makes it difficult for you to know what to do. To tell right from wrong. Harder than it is for most girls."

༄

April 9 1901

(In 1882 Dante Gabriel Rossetti died. He helped to found the Pre-Raphaelite Brotherhood of painters who promoted a love of nature and craftsmanship, the expression of true emotions in art and a renewed appreciation of old English myths and legends)

Market day is a thousand times better than Chapel. Listen to the noise! See all the people who have come to visit! A herd of bullocks off the marsh is fenced into a corner, the whites of their eyes bulging in panic. Sheep churn in their pens as sheepdogs worry them this way and that. Carts line up outside the pubs. Gigs pull in beside the haberdashers and fine foods store. Stalls and canopies have appeared from nowhere overnight. Strangers, farmers and housewives mingle. Smells fight with each other. Cheeses, fish, apples, horse dung, old meat and fresh flowers, all make one great stink.

And suddenly there is a hare! Big as a dog with a fine bony face and legs like pistons, dashing from one end of the street to the other as if it was on its way somewhere but took a wrong turn. Some stand and stare. Others see nothing at all, as they are too busy choosing chickens or sorting piles of cabbages. This is how things can happen in this world. Sometimes nobody sees.

Then there's a commotion in the yard of The Bull. Mother and I step across to see what's happening. And there is Old Balaclava, one eye black like a lump of coal, his body rigid as a broom, dressed in white shirt and smart tie as if he were on his way to Buckingham Palace. His war medals are pinned to his jacket for all to see. He's been throwing weights in the yard to prove his strength, drunk too many beers, and is now fighting with Rough Jimmy.

He takes a swing with his good arm at Rough Jimmy, but misses him and falls over.

Rough Jimmy appears to relish the moment.

"The honour of White Blaze is at stake," says Old Balaclava, finally getting his words sorted out. His bowler hat has flown off and his white moustache twitches.

White Blaze is one of Lord Hartley's horses which Old Balaclava helps to train for the races. We all know that Old Balaclava loves horses more than he loves humans. Perhaps this is no surprise as he was one of the soldiers in the Charge of the Light Brigade, one of the few who survived to tell the tale. In case we forget, he is forever refreshing our memories. He took a lance wound to his ribs and neck, and a ball from the Russian infantry went clean through his right eye. He was nursed by Florence Nightingale herself, or so he says. And when he came home, he did one better and met the Queen, who gave him a pair of woollen stockings, a scarf and some mittens. Though I don't think she knitted them herself.

Mother pulls me away, so I never see if Rough Jimmy beats the hero of the Light Brigade, but I think he does. Rough Jimmy believes that when armies tire of making war on each other they make war on ordinary people, and the wars on ordinary people can be more terrible. They can be bloody as the Old Testament, which has more killing in it than any other story I can think of.

After the excitement at the market I want more tingles up my spine, so after we get home I creep along the secret path to Mr Massingham's back garden, hoping to catch sight of Miss Etherington in her window. I might even get to see her apple dumplings again and feel the frog jump in my trousers.

But once I'm bedded in the mulberry peering between the branches, I find she is not upstairs but downstairs in the back parlour, and she isn't alone but is with the mill owner Mr George Childs. I chew my lip and think he is unlikely to be a friend of Mr Massingham's and even less likely to have dropped by as he was passing.

He talks urgently, as if he is telling her of a great sadness or a deep feeling.

She stands in front of him, holding her neck very stiffly. She backs towards the window. I touch my five warts, which are growing like pig's nipples, as I puzzle over the scene unfolding in front of me. I feel a little like David in the Old Testament who saw Bathsheba bathing and took her for himself, even though she was a married woman. David made it worse by telling lies and making sure her husband Uriah died in battle. I've not lied like David did, but I have seen like David, and I have hidden, and now my store of secrets is growing. I think, yes, I am convinced, that Mr Childs from the mill wants to kiss her. I cover my eyes with my hands but still manage to peep between my fingers. She moves behind the chair and keeps it between her and Mr Childs. And suddenly Mr Childs turns on his heel and departs. One minute he is there and the next he is not. As he didn't leave time for a goodbye, she must have made him angry in some way.

I'm better at running and delivering loaves than I am at understanding the way a beautiful woman deals with the people around her. I bet that even Dante Gabriel Rossetti couldn't paint her true loveliness. I'm proud that I know about him because she is the one who showed me his pictures of damsels with flowing hair and curly lips. She told me, too, about his sister Christina, who wrote sad poems and wanted to matter in the world.

&

"Degas! Poof! Oh very *je ne sais quoi*, my dear. All tutu and powder-puff, all spied from behind or from the side or up the skirt. Oh, dear me. *Yes.* Lovely calves. Firm limbs, young flesh trained to a purpose, feet at ten to two, shoulders with such elegance, layers of skirt like swans' feathers, slices of *mille feuille*, a thousand leaves, halos on the posteriors. Oh yes. Not to put too fine a point on it. Am I getting carried away? Then again, my dear, he did some fine things with…"

"… With how we look?"

"Well, yes, how we look at things. No more need for the classic arrangement of figures. His subjects are glanced from a doorway, caught in a mirror, *en passant*, so to speak."

"So, it isn't so very different from photography. You snatch things as you see them."

"I do. *I do.* Though I don't cut people's legs off as he does, or their arms. Or even their upper bodies."

He chortles, strokes his beard. His eyes are soft brown and, I'll own up, he is by no means handsome.

"Ha! Here is my work of art – a pair of feet! A big toe! That is what Degas has to say to us. Oh yes! I like it very much. *Très amusant*, my dear. Owner of the most beautiful hands and feet that you are."

I am never more alive than when I am here.

We are alone today. The house is ours. It is full of pools of flickering light. Amber, woodland green and cornflower blue shine through the stained glass. Every chair, fabric, object and picture has been chosen and placed by him. The house is where his art and his life meet. He calls it his *house beautiful*. It is where he announces to the world who he is. It is where he plays. It is where we meet.

"The Duchess is in Margate. Freda and Arnold have the day off. The Duchess is very happy down there. In the house of her parents, with a turret and pretty bargeboards and the sea close by. In August she takes a whole month there. Sometimes she stays until the end of November. It leaves me alone to devote myself utterly to my outdoor activities and the rigours of *Burlesque*."

He smiles as if we are sharing a secret.

He asks how the Tissot dress is coming on. It is a joy, I tell him, and yes it will be ready for Picture Sunday. This is the day before the sending-in date for the Royal Academy's annual exhibition, when artists open their studios to show their work. Luke Fildes, Lawrence Alma-Tadema, William Powell Frith, John William Waterhouse, invite members of society to view their works at home. It doesn't seem to be a show so much as a competition.

"And you will open this house?" I ask.

He turns away, sucks in his breath and blows it out again like one of the animals at the zoo.

"All in all there is so much less for people to enjoy this year, so why not? The season is curtailed by the war in Africa. The Queen's dancing days are long over. So we all need a little uplift."

Because he doesn't bring it forth, I feel I can't ask to see the grand invitation we have been working on all this time. I no longer know what my place is. He shows me some of his works for *Burlesque* and it reminds me that I am lucky to be here at all, so close to a man who has such a reputation, who works for such a famous journal and is admired by so many people.

He pulls out a sketch of a lady in a flowing dress, her knees outlined beneath the folds. The face is undoubtedly Freda's. It is a cartoon about the new Anti-Tight-Lacing-Society, which is becoming popular with women with an artistic temperament. Another sketch is of a skin of an African woman, hanging like a limp dress over the back of a chair. *Peau de femme*, says the caption beside it. Another is of a slave in chains, sitting inside a zoo cage. The caption says: "Am I not man also? Am I not the white man's brother?"

He brings out another curiosity to show me. It is a cartoon of three soldiers at Ladysmith, one in a kilt drinking hot chocolate, one opening a tin of chocolate, another dipping a finger in. "The Queen. God Bless Her," says the caption.

"I got the idea from this, he says and hands me a copy of a letter.

Dear Lord Lansdowne, - The Queen commands me to inform you of her anxiety to make some little personal present as soon as possible to each of her soldiers serving in South Africa. Her Majesty has decided upon sending chocolate, which she is given to understand will be appropriate and acceptable. It will be packed for each man in a tin that has been specially designed for the occasion...

"A cup of chocolate wouldn't go far," I say. "A luxury like that is an odd present in the middle of a war." We exchange smiles.

"Stupid drawings of mine. Stupid. Stupid."

⁂

Another week, another day, I am at his house again. He takes me into his studio and wraps me in a white sheet. I smell the starch Freda has rinsed through it, and know the work that went into ironing it, though Edward has now tugged it into hills and valleys so that it looks like an unmade bed. I've let the slate-coloured wrap around me drop behind my back. I am lying down, facing away from Edward towards the back of the shed. My flesh is cold and probably mottled. He is breathing heavily.

"Beautiful. Beautiful. Gently does it. Let it down. Just so. The ice-maiden melts. Velazquez, would that you were with me now!"

I scarcely breathe. My body is, it seems, willing to do anything and I am not at all sure whether it is for the sake of the art, for the sake of the man or for the sake of the moment.

We were caught in the rain at the zoo. Edward rushed me back to his house in a Hansom cab and offered me the warmth of the Morning Room to dry my clothes and drink a large glass of brandy. Gold swirling in a glass balloon, it lit a fire in my throat and made me fuddled. He gave me a wrap but then he said he had a better idea.

"*The Toilet of Venus*, the only female nude by Diego Velazquez. Painted two-and-a-half centuries ago, my dear, but powerful as yourself. She was the goddess of love, you see, the most beautiful of the goddesses. Her son Cupid sits and holds up a mirror to her."

But I have said no to a mirror. Because I am not stupid. I can see that, while Velazquez shows the reflection of her face, a mirror in the exact same position would show all sorts of other parts and not the face at all.

"Ah, my dear. This is heaven," he says.

My elbow is propped up on a pile of pillows, and my hair is rolled in a knot.

"Turn your head a quarter round to the left. Lower knee forward, upper leg outstretched. That's it."

I am under his spell. My stomach tickles, my flesh glows. We are cut off from the outside world. His voice comes out of the darkness as he fidgets with his black cloth behind the camera. Together we are making something daring, something lasting, something I have never had before. I hear his every movement. There is a *tum-te-tum* while he busies with his glass plates. Then he holds his breath and takes a picture. Then he starts again. And I am held, ecstatic, in the moment. I feel his gaze running over my body like the bow across a cello. I am no longer an invisible woman in a looking glass or the unknown maker of an exquisite gown. I am at the centre of the picture. I no longer hold the pencil making the drawing. I am being treated like a goddess. We are, together, in a land which is not real, but it is not all fiction either. We are somewhere between the two.

"It is an ancient tradition. Ancient as art itself," he whispers through his whiskers.

I often look back on this day, re-live each moment. I believed it was art and forgot one very important thing, which was that he wasn't creating anything but only *taking photographs*. There was not a paintbrush or a pencil in sight.

⁂

Lordy me! How did it happen? The last knockings of summer when The Duchess was in Margate, the sun was glaring, the parties were over, the streets were empty and all of London was dozing in the heat. We had the house once again to ourselves.

"I love it! Love it! The whole city is ours for the day. We can do as we please!" says Edward.

We are alone, and we are doing our favourite thing. I am dressing and undressing and Edward is busy with his camera, puffing and gasping and straining his waistcoat. But this time we are in the Morning Room where The Duchess's diary lies on the table. It is a magnet which I must not be drawn to. The Kate Greenaway paintings are to the left and the Van Dycks which are not real Van Dycks to the right.

One of them is the famous *Cupid and Psyche*, which was painted for King Charles I. It is really about Psyche's sister, though she isn't in the picture at all. She was so jealous of Psyche's beauty that she forced her do difficult things like sorting chickpeas from lentils and finding golden wool. She also made Psyche visit hell to steal an elixir for beauty from Proserpina, Queen of Hades, and take it home in a sealed casket. But on the way back Psyche couldn't resist opening the lid, and a cloud of darkness rose out of it and enveloped her in a deep sleep. Cupid flew in on winged feet, found her almost naked and desired her so fiercely that he stroked her back to life. Edward told me the story.

We have had the most wonderful day. We walked in the park and he put his arm through mine. We visited a department store where we were astonished by carpets from India, carved elephants from Africa and new designs from Wedgwood. Afterwards we returned to the house and watered the ferns in the glass case. Then we dined on obscenely pink lobsters, which Edward had specially delivered because I told him I had never tasted one. As he laid it before me, I thought this might be the best day of my life.

"Pluck it from its shell, just so!" he says. It tastes of sea breezes. With the heat outside and the creature on my plate, I must be dreaming and yet I'm not.

We sit at the dining-room table, the very table where he has held his dinners with renowned guests and too much rich food, as I've read in The Duchess's diary. And here am I! Sipping the wine Edward has poured for me, winking in its pretty glass. It is my first wine. Around us hang his photographs of woodland scenes, peopled with nymphs and satyrs, that captured me on my first day here. I am giddy and no longer feel the slightest bit faint when I'm with him. On the contrary, my heart clops along like the horses' hooves on Rotten Row. I never know what he will have us playing at next.

I never stop to think.

I forget how many glasses of wine we've drunk but everything has become very blurred.

In the heat and quiet we throw all manners away.

"This day is a very special one," he says, as he brings in sheets and a large pot. "It is our day, my dear. I want the texture of flesh. The flesh itself is so important, you see. It is, after all, the very thing of which we are made."

I am his paintbrushes and his oils. And dare I say it? I am his muse. I will do anything he wants of me.

And here I am, bare as the day I was born, one elbow over my head and the other raised towards it, a white sheet falling around me, one foot slightly raised. The house closes in and holds us tight. My nipples tingle as his head vanishes behind the camera.

"Frederic Leighton. *The Bath of Psyche*. Done ten years ago. Delightful, my dear. The body here and now. The very skin itself in its purest form. As it is. As you are now. *Delightful.*"

It's that Psyche again. She is too beautiful for men to approach, so her parents make a plan to sacrifice her. But, instead, she is taken to Cupid's palace to live quite happily until her sisters are overcome with jealousy. She has one failing, which is that she is given to gazing at her reflection in the water, indicating vanity.

We do a lucky dip of scenes all afternoon. Clothes on. Clothes off. Clothes half on. He is singing for joy and I am in a kind of trance.

"Artists have been aided by each other's compositions since time began. I am pleased to say that I now have an aid and an adjunct. You and my camera."

And all at once I am sitting, my gown half open, not a stitch beneath it, upon that Moroccan table with the filigree of inlaid woodwork beneath my thighs. Here I am, opening my legs to him, the table gleaming beneath, flashing its patchwork of woods. The scents of sandalwood and rosewood rise up, the gown rustles around my calves, the pink lobster floats in my mind. I am his.

"Oh my dear... my dear... what secrets you reveal to me."

And we are held by the spell of the table, never touching but just looking.

Edward took many photographs that afternoon.

CHAPTER THIRTEEN:

THE PIER

June 2 1901

Sea Breezes

The sea-breeze is caused because the sun heats the land more quickly than it does the water. The air over the land then rises, as heated air always does, and other air from over the cool ocean flows in to take its place. But water, though it gets hot more slowly, keeps the heat which it absorbs for a longer time than the land, and hence it often happens after sunset that the air over the sea is warmer than that over the earth. When this happens a land breeze arises, and blows briskly out to sea.

The shingle at Highcliff is crowded like a railway platform. The new pier is almost finished and is fine as anything in London. I am sure of this, though in truth I am only guessing. The "crabs have walked". They bring in the money and the town is merry. I'm excited about seeing my cousins again. We've been to the boatbuilders and watched cousin Tom helping to make the best boat ever for Flinty Daredevil. It has a fat belly of new wood, a mast thirty feet high and beds for sleeping on. Tom says Flinty comes every day to check everything is to his liking. Filch, Reg, Ron, Skinny and I run through the town, dodging down the lokes, through the yards, round the sheds. The cottages have their windows flung open and signs out saying CRABS FOR SALE. The kitchens are full of chatter, interrupted by crunch and pick as the crabs have their legs broken and their insides rearranged.

"One minute to do a crab, that's my best," says Aunt Mary, hollow eyes lighting up with pride. These women are famous all over the world for their nimble fingers.

"Is the pier nearly finished?" I shout as I chase after Skinny.

It lies below us, stretching far out into the waves wrapped in railings, painted white like the icing on Mother's wedding cakes, with domes and lamp-posts instead of candles. It is a miracle that will allow us to walk out on the sea! We'll be like Jesus on the Sea of Galilee, except that this is the North Sea and engineers have had a hand in it, not the Holy Spirit. On the tip is a pavilion with a roof like a helmet. Dancers and singers will come to put on shows in there and Father says they will lay temptation before the weaker men and women among us.

The crab boats are pulled high up on the beach, where fishermen sit with their lines and crab pots. Some mend nets, while others stretch their legs out and enjoy the sun on their old walnut faces, talking of this and that. Uncle Henry's eyebrows shoot up and down as he works on a pot, lacing nets into hooped frames, not unlike Aunt Mary when she knits his stockings, except his fingernails are black. Over by the gangway, steam is pouring off the coppers where the whelks are being boiled alive. Piglet Long has kept some back and pulls them out of their shells to make bait.

"Before I married the girl of my dreams," he says, "my father told me this. Never buy her a drink, never make her a cup of tea, and yer marriage will last." Their laughter rumbles up from deep inside their chests.

A dark smudge out to sea moves closer and reveals itself to be a vessel. Flinty Daredevil rows it hard like he is showing off. He steps into the shallows and draws the boat up the shingle single-handed. He tips his lobsters onto the stones, black and glistening, claws waving, and his girl's mouth twists into a smile. He chats with the men as if he is one of them, but his smooth skin reminds us that he knows Latin and is not really one of us at all. He flings himself down onto the pebbles to cut the muscles in the lobster claws, then heads off up the gangway, long legs flashing, to put them on the London train. They'll travel further than I have ever done, all the way to Liverpool Street station.

Filch is perched on the backside of a horse beyond the groyne, pulling a bathing machine into the waves. He is barefoot and the horse moves slow as an elephant, trailing the white carriage at a stately pace. I think it is early in the year for the bathing machines, but some ladies are already taking the air and want to sink themselves in salt water to loosen their joints. One appears, right now, climbing down the ladder into the sea, clothed from chin to calf in a blue bathing gown edged with scarlet. Other machines are already lined up, waiting for women to throw some of their clothes off and show their white meat like picked crabs.

"Ah, he is a good lad," says Piglet Long, watching Filch sitting patiently in the shallows on the huge piebald.

Everyone chuckles at Piglet because he not only keeps visitors in his house all summer to milk their money, but is on the beach whenever the weather is hot enough, offering to carry ladies onto the pleasure-boats so they can keep their feet dry.

☙

The house is dark when we come home to Sebastopol Road. Father sits alone in the gloom, eyes down. Mother and I have enjoyed our day at Highcliff, but as soon as we see him our good spirits are spit in the wind. Gyp has his little nose between his paws, eyes darting back and forth, whimpering as if Father has been angry with him.

But Father's voice is calm as he recites Psalm 41.

Blessed is he that considereth the poor: the Lord will deliver him in time of trouble.

The Lord will preserve him, and keep him alive; and he shall be blessed upon the earth: and thou wilt not deliver him unto the will of his enemies.

The Lord will strengthen him upon the bed of languishing: thou wilt make all his bed in his sickness.

I said, Lord, be merciful unto me: heal my soul; for I have sinned against thee.

Mother takes his hand and leads him to the stairs.

"Oh, come now. It will work through, sure as jam comes to the boil. We're all poor. Them as well as us," she says. I watch her go up the stairs behind him, prodding his back with her fingers. He is stiff and upright as ever, always a strong white leek among the wilted ones, while she looks small and, though I shouldn't think it, a bit wormy.

"Early start, same as always," says Mother. "The oven must be lit. There are loaves to be made. The village will expect their daily bread and you will give it to them, payment or no payment. What would they do without you?" Then she mumbles. "What *we* will do is another matter."

Now this sets me thinking about whether Father has somehow sinned, or has found out that someone close to him has sinned. My head crawls with worries about the awful thing upsetting him, and whether it has anything to do with my own secrets and wrongdoings.

Nobby Stokes comes clattering into my bedroom, all hot breath, boots, sweat and dirt. He throws himself down and I'm relieved to see him. I pull my blanket up and roll over to make myself think about other things.

"Nobby?"

"Hmmm."

"Nobby?"

"Yes."

"Do you think Miss Etherington is special?"

"I think she's trouble."

"In trouble?"

"She carries trouble. She will cause trouble."

"Not pretty, then?" I say.

"Not enough meat on her for me. I like more to grab hold of. I've no time for all her fancy drawings and that. I want one who can make a good bacon and leek pudding and darn my socks."

As I see it, rich people have servants. Poor people have wives. Rich people have time. Poor people don't.

"You know what Rough Jimmy says? He says that one day women will be better than men. One day they'll decide things for us and make everything kinder. He says they are the clever sex."

Nobby snorts. "She's a ripe fruit that needs picking soon, or she'll go over. That's my last word on it," he says.

Then he tells me the story of Mrs Nettle at Old Barton, the gatekeeper on the railway who is forever holding up the trains while she is cooking.

"This time it was her dumplings," he says. "'Ya mucky varmin',' she says, 'I'll not have my dumplings spoilt. The train can wait!'"

I can't hold back a laugh. It is a tinny sound in this house where the air is heavy as a pile of hymn books.

And then he tells me the one about the old archangel Mr Eden. He is returning from a night out in his evening dress and his pumps, smart as you can get, when the train breaks down. The wagons pile into each other, fires break out among the broken sleepers and what does Mr Eden do? He takes himself to the middle of the accident and settles down in his black tail coat and his white gaiters, his white silk scarf curled around his neck. He whips out his sketchbook and starts to draw.

We think this so funny that we can't stop grunting and giggling until Nobby chokes up and the fleas jump.

"What's all this reading yer doing now? Those books by your bed. If it's not one, it's another," he says.

I've finished *Treasure Island* and *Little Lord Fauntleroy* and *Children Of The New Forest*. Now I am reading *Tales From Shakespeare* and have got stuck on a story about a black man who kills his wife because someone got hold of her handkerchief.

"It's good, Nobby. It takes me out of here."

He grunts. "I've no time for it myself. Books ain't real, so what's the point?"

"I don't think I know exactly. Except we are all about stories, telling them and believing them." I don't add my belief that the Bible is all stories too.

Nobby's bed erupts as he blows off again.

"Don't forget, lad. The most important thing in life is work. Paying the rent, paying the bills, keeping our heads above water. Books is for people who don't need to work. In my book you get on or you get wrong."

∾

Mrs Eden is sitting for me. I'm drawing the rough shape of her face and wondering what to do with her tipped-up nose.

"You are so lucky," she says. "To have a talent."

I say nothing, for I find it is the best way. She likes to talk and she likes me to listen. We find things to do together, to fill her time. Though her delicate frame contains a strong spirit, I notice she is getting thinner all the time. Her wrists are so tiny the bones stand out. She yearns for London.

"Of course, the upper classes," she stops mid-sentence as she is not quite sure whether she is one of them. She usually thinks of herself as higher than everyone but occasionally admits that there are people above her. Lord Hartley is one of those. She continues after a short pause.

"The upper classes feared that the railways would encourage an already disturbing tendency towards equality. They tried to prevent it happening."

"Really?" I've decided that the tipped-up nose can be done with charm. Then I need to capture those cheeks like wishbones. I would like to work on her pale grey eyes but am using only pencil and paper so colour means nothing.

"They thought it would be frightful to have the lower orders wandering aimlessly around the country, mixing with all and sundry."

Her voice is as precise as a darning needle.

"They made travellers book their passage at least one whole day in advance, giving their name, address, date of birth, age, occupation and reason for the journey, to make sure that they weren't travelling for the wrong reasons."

"What sort of reasons are those?" I ask.

A tidy frown appears on the palest of foreheads.

"Well, I can't say I know exactly," she says. "But Mr Eden assures me the rich travel to spend money, which is good for the nation's prosperity, while the poor travel for... well, I don't really know what. Jonathan is of the belief that idleness can damage national prosperity. If a poor man is hungry, then he will work. But if he has too much to eat then I fear, I do fear it... he goes to the public house."

"Oh. I see. Is it the same reason why people have to pay to get on to the new pier?"

She sucks in a breath.

"I believe it is. They want the right kind of people, not those who bring their own food and want merely to admire the views. They want *select* people with deep pockets. That is what railways are good at, don't you agree?"

She adjusts her pose and extends her long neck. She is close enough for me to touch her dress. In the hours I have sat with her I've learned much. I know she suffers from biliousness after buttery sauces, that she has long wakeful periods at night when she doesn't like to disturb her husband, that she sometimes sleeps in the next room, that she gets rashes on her hands when she eats chocolate. Yet she still knows almost nothing of me.

She has gathered that I'm able to enter a room full of railway men and have them drawing their hearts out by the end of an evening. And that I can have the roughest of them settling down happily to draw a bowl of roses working only with the colour pink. She may not know I've brought Rough Jimmy into the Institute as a model for them to draw. They compare his face to a railway map, his nose to the black funnel of an engine. He is grateful for a few hours in the warm with a hot drink.

I can tell Mrs Eden admires my skill because her grey eyes flicker with admiration. She and her husband promote the men's art classes because they want them to be raised up out of their narrow lives, led away from drunkenness. And I must own up that I'm thirsty for admiration, not only from the Edens but from the men. I see the way they look at me and it reminds me of the way I was looked at before, in such a different place, by a man with a camera and a love of art. I wish for it again and take what scraps of appreciation I can.

"Jonathan is keen also that every man should receive an education," she says. "That every lad he takes on must pass an exam in reading, writing, arithmetic and dictation. And in company time, *company* time my dear, they will soon spend an afternoon a week learning essential skills."

And what, I ponder, will happen to little Jack Stamp once all his friends have joined the railway and are enjoying these extra lessons? Will he be sweating in the bakery for the rest of his life?

"I am thinking." She waits to make sure she has my full attention. "I might start a tapestry. A day-to-day picture of my moods. I will use beautiful colours, of course. But mostly I will keep a record of my sadness. It will allow me to see how my feelings change from one month to the next."

It is a statement but I hear a need for reassurance too.

"Yes. Yes," I say. "Which colours would you choose?"

"What's most important is the colour I use for unhappiness. Because I want it, oh, to look glorious. I don't want clouds of black or grey. I think perhaps blue might be best, for it is pretty and is a favourite of mine."

A bleak smile. Then she changes the subject to plan one of what she calls her "little suppers".

I can't count how many times the Edens have sat me down with George Childs. I am like an adopted daughter whom they wish to see respectably married. But I've done nothing to encourage this. They invite him in order to discuss their plans for the new railway. Land is being purchased in advance and, between the fish pie and the raspberry tart, they are astonished to discover that land in Staithe is owned by women because the fishermen are so prone to drowning that their wives have taken on the houses.

Mrs Eden and I usually listen attentively while Mr Eden and Mr Childs work out the details of their ambition to build a huge embankment to control the flow of water on and off of the marsh. They want to dredge and deepen the channel, change the scour of the tide. She and I exchange glances because she is as disbelieving as I am that they can impose their will on the sea. They conjure wharves, warehouses, cranes and lifts out on the edge where the herons now stalk. They speak of attracting investment, creating a new company, organising directors' visits. The blue-eyed Mr Childs is putting in all his savings and hoping for bounty. Mr Eden is convinced the plan will lift the fortunes of Staithe, and Mr Childs feels he has the blessing of the Almighty.

"Know this, my man. That the humble path may also be a heroic one. The battle of our lives can be fought along backwaters and marshes, railway platforms and ticket offices, just as well as on the heights of Balaclava or the fields of Waterloo," says Mr Eden.

God and money work well together and somewhere along the way I have been thrown into this endless talk like a dowry, and it is understood that I'll become the property of George Childs and live with him in his windmill. The word marriage wasn't mentioned until the other day when he appeared unexpectedly at the Massinghams' house and made his proposal. I was taken aback. He came so close to me that that I slipped behind a chair for protection. I said I couldn't give him an answer of any kind as I needed time to think.

I have too much hidden within me to show him an honest face, too much still to mourn before I can understand the value of what he is offering. But deep down I am sure I have no appetite for it.

CHAPTER FOURTEEN:

THE THIRD EYE

June 18 1901

(In 1815 the British, led by the Duke of Wellington, won a decisive victory over the French, led by Napoleon Bonaparte who had declared himself Emperor of most of Europe)

The colour in a rose

The secret of its colour is one of the greatest mysteries of the rose. The flower has no colour, really, in itself. The red which we see at this moment was in the sun ten minutes ago, ninety million miles away. What the rose-petal does is to split up the sun's beams of light into their component parts. If it is a red rose, it keeps for itself the greens and the blues of the prismatic colours, and reflects the reds to us, but exactly how it performs this peculiar feat is still a mystery.

The diary is my teacher. It puts ideas in my head like Miss Etherington does. She does it in person, while my diary is invisible to everyone except me. She makes my heart beat and my diary makes my brain work. If what it tells me about the colour red is true, and we only see it because the rose has hoarded all the others, then maybe people are the same. Father and Mother have been there since my world began, but they have a life in their bedroom which is hidden. Even more is concealed in all they do *not* say. They talk to each other about jobs to be done, people to be helped, eggs to be taken to market, prayers to be said, but not what they feel.

Miss Etherington is different. She gives me books, ideas, stories about art, glimpses of her bare bubbies, which I must keep forever locked inside me. So I have a hidden world too. Perhaps concealing things is part of being a grown-up and I am half way to becoming one of them. Yet I'm not sure that Billy has secrets in the same way. Then another thought plummets into my brain, bigger than a goose's egg, which is that we only see the parts of a person we choose to see. Like the rose, we absorb the greens and blues and allow ourselves to see only the scarlet and pink.

Mother spends all afternoon making crow pie. This is not good. The crows live in the spinney cawing their heads off, especially when they gather in the mornings and evenings. One evening they are there, the next morning they are on our kitchen table and Mother is not plucking but skinning them and the black feathers are sticking to her fingers.

"I'll soon have you stewed under a crust," she tells them.

Then we have the punishment of eating them.

"Only the breast and legs, for the back is bitter. A dozen should do," she says.

I say every bit of them is bitter, and there are about a dozen too many. They'll sit on my plate tonight, all bones and foul dark paste in a pastry wrap, squatting in their own jelly. It is no wonder people tell each other to go eat crow. Even Gyp doesn't care for it.

"It's cheap and it's food." Mother sucks her gums and will have no whimpering, which means that every bone will have to be picked clean before I see an end to it.

※

The hot days of summer have arrived. Rosie walks to the marsh with Jack Stamp. It is evening, and the spectacle of ants taking flight stops them in their tracks. Suddenly the air is filled with tiny wings which get snagged in their eyelashes and hair, fly down Rosie's neck and up Jack's shorts. The sun lights up the insects creating the illusion of summer rain. Rosie and Jack swat and wave them away as they cross the crusted mud tracks down to the edge of the sea.

"History, Jack," says Rosie, "is a debt which the living pay to the dead."

Jack thinks it is more to do with knowing your kings and queens and telling stories to make people feel good about being British.

"It is also made up of many truths. Not one viewpoint, but many," she says. "It is about how you see things."

He wonders if that includes the things you aren't meant to see. Or all the little things, like flying ants, which people forget to look at.

They pick their way through mauve sea lavender, their faces drying and lips tightening in the hot wind.

Rosie gives Jack a small box and says it is for him to keep. Inside he finds a piece of amber, no bigger than a thumbnail, a droplet of resin so old he can never know its age. He holds it up to the sinking sun and sees a fly trapped inside, legs dangling, wings extended, antennae pointing upwards.

"It's for you, Jack," she says. "A little piece of history. Not the history of men, or battles, or money-making. Just a fly caught in a moment, like a photograph catches people."

"Thank you, Miss."

Jack can't find words good enough to say how grateful he is. He places it tenderly in his pocket and thinks it is another secret to keep from Mother and Father.

"You know, Jack," she says. "Women are good keepers of history, maybe better than men. Sometimes for no better reason than that they live longer. They keep boxes of letters and photographs, and like to tell stories about the past."

As her own mother disappeared from her life when she was young, she has become increasingly aware of what she missed.

Jack nods. He is sure now that something from her past life is troubling her.

The sky alters. A few minutes ago it was like a Chinese lantern, scissored silver tissue backlit by the orange of the late afternoon sun. Now it is a mass of clouds in layers coloured from grey to indigo, arching over them like an angel's wing. Behind them the barley fields shimmer dark gold, millions of tawny stems drooping their whiskered heads, plump with grain. A wind blows dust over the wheat fields, which seem already to smell of bread.

❦

The day I discovered Edward Stafford Clark's other life was the day my dreams were shattered. It will always be the most significant day of my life, whether I marry Mr Childs or whether I don't. It was an un-wedding day. It remains lodged within me.

My memories stalk the present, then slink away again knowing they're not wanted.

I've begun to think this summer is ours. Today he is interested in the actual process of disrobing. The way women unwrap themselves like presents. He is interested, too, in the curious undergarments we wear beneath our gowns. He and I are full of purpose. We are working hard. Time passes quickly. Freda and Alfred have taken the opportunity, while The Duchess is away, to visit their families in Dorset and Kent. But then there is an unexpected knock at the door and a messenger from *Burlesque* asks Edward to go to the office immediately. The editor is not happy with his work. Edward's face turns to ash and he is utterly cast down.

"I must go. The grindstone awaits. The accounting, the defending, the re-working." He looks round at the scenes we have created.

"I must leave. Make yourself ready in your own time, and go when you have composed yourself, my dear. Do not fret over restoring everything to its place. I will do that on my return. Forgive me, special one. Pray excuse me," he says. Then, with a gallant bow like the hero leaving the stage, he is gone from the room. I hear some to-ing and fro-ing in the hallway, circles of panic as he finds his coat and hat before the door closes behind him. The house creaks. Then it settles and seems to watch me. It's the first time I've had the freedom of the place with no-one else here. The doors are open, the rooms beckon, and his voice isn't in my ear telling me how to look at things.

I can't resist. I go up on tiptoe, float through, leaving no trace of my presence. The house feels different. When Edward is here, he makes it sing, summoning light and colour. Now it is empty it is filled with shadows and whispers. It breathes out what has been and breathes in what might have been. I think all houses hold on to the dreams of their owners. This house knows there is an interloper moving through its dim interiors. Every part of it reflects an aspect of himself. I run the tip of my finger around the golden urns and green leaves that he has painted on the doors. I scan the paintings and the willow wallpaper. A ray of sun strikes the stained-glass panel, scattering yellow and blue ribbons of light. I am in awe of the sheer number of objects – furniture, vases, clocks, ornaments, little things he has picked up and wanted to possess.... It is quite fantastical.

I hear the whispers. They say *continue*. I glide across the decorative tiles in the hallway, past the antlers and up the stairs. A glass box on the landing contains a collection of seashells with a label which tells me they come from Highcliff in Norfolk. Above is more stained glass etched with an E for Edward and an M for Marguerite, the initials of himself and The Duchess, snaking round each other in scarlet and gold. I swallow hard.

I slip up to the first floor and hold my breath on the landing. I don't know it yet but this is the last moment of that part of my life. Often have I questioned myself. Was I blinded by my own vanity? Did I deceive myself? The make-believe is about to be ripped away. Think of it as you will. The end is coming. I creep forward. I am nothing really, and have always been nothing. I am no more than a worn sheet being sewn sides to the middle.

In his inner sanctum I tenderly sort through his drawings. Sheets of paper they may be. But they have the power to make me laugh or cry. I know his work well enough, but these are different. These drawings have not been done to order or to deadline. They aren't the result of an evening of drinking with friends from *Burlesque*. They are on scraps of napkins and old theatre programmes. Here, there, everywhere, he is trying to draw freely without his 'invaluable adjunct'. Faces, hands and feet, people plump as chickens, tottering on stick legs, women with huge hair. I come across a sheaf tied with ribbon. With trembling fingers I untie it. There are drawings of me, done with a simplicity of line, a minimum of fuss. But this is not what strikes me first. What hits me, like a punch in the stomach, is that these are my most private parts, places that no man has seen apart from him, exposed and examined. There is passion in them. He invites the viewer in as the honeysuckle beckons the bee.

   I'm shaking so much that I must lay them down, switch my attention to the other drawings. In this blinding moment my mind is sharp as a diamond-cutter. It forces me to admit what I have long known but have not allowed myself to think. I am sure as a dog is of its master that the drawings before me are ordinary. Now that he is not here to dazzle me with his charm, I can see that his work is stiff and workmanlike. They are professional but nothing more than that. Am I right? Is my judgment skewed by the anger growing within me? Am I being unkind? I am full of doubts about my new power to think and see. Who am I to say? For I know nothing more than what he has taught me. I track back through events, his methods, the use of the camera, his frustration at drawing to the clock, his jealousy of his artistic friends, his rudeness about the Royal Academy. I question the joy he has taken in our little expeditions and our dressing up days, and the private world we made together.

   Once more I turn to the drawings released from their ribbon. I unfold a napkin and see myself. Hips, breasts, mouths are jumbled and rearranged like a puzzle. There is a kind of freedom here, something I haven't found in any of his other work. Is this, then, the true artist at work? Has he used me for the sake of art after all?

   Used. Used. Used. The word jabs its finger into me.

   Something draws me up another staircase to the top of the house. I open a door on the landing and find a marble bath, veined like cheese, with a wood trim, where he develops his photographs. Hanging above it is the clothes-line on which he dries his prints. This must be the room he calls his laboratory. A wasp drones against the window pane, banging its striped torso against the glass, a crazy random thing with no sting left.

   Upward I go, one final staircase to attics where the air becomes stuffy. Ahead is Freda's room with a truckle bed and corner fireplace, tiny as an eggcup, where she must warm her hands in winter. I push open a half-closed door to the left and find an easel standing in front of shelves full of cameras, magazines and old glass plates. Very gently I lift a camera down, turn it towards the window and peep through the lens. I expect to see the rooftops on the other side of the street but instead I see only the shelves. I turn the camera this way and that, and find it contains a dog-leg with a cleverly placed mirror designed for deception. The holder can seem to be photographing one thing while he is in fact photographing something quite else. It is a 'secret camera'. My mind is racing now.

   Old editions of *Burlesque* are stacked on the lower shelves alongside copies of

The Camera Club Journal. I feel like a burglar now, moving things around, flipping through the stuff of someone else's life. On the highest shelf, densely packed, are his glass plate negatives. Heavens! There must be thousands of them. Moving quickly now, I climb on to a chair and reach up. They're awkward to pull out, but once I've loosened the first few, the others come easily. They are heavy so I lower them carefully before taking take them to the window and lifting them to the light.

It is a while before I breathe again.

I see naked women. Then more naked women. All of them are naked. Some are in groups or in pairs, others rolling on the floor. They hold each other. They kiss. One woman lies on a bed, another is wrapped in sheets. One wears a mask and only a mask, another wears her stockings and only her stockings. The nudity goes on and on. I scramble up and down, levering more plates out, holding them up, seeking the next shock. One woman rides a bicycle, another sits with her legs akimbo on a chair. And there is a photograph of Freda under the blankets in her bedroom, sleeping unawares but photographed all the same with her mouth open. I didn't know he was interested in Freda too.

Many are young girls. With his Third Eye he has caught them coming out of school, skirts flying revealingly in the wind, hair slipping out beneath their hats, mouths sweet with innocence. So young.

There is no-one to hear my cry as the plates fall to the floor. One schoolgirl after another goes down. I cut my hands on the shards of glass as I don't fully understand what I'm doing. I see glass on the floor but it is far away from me. Everything is in chaos. My heart thumps and my face is wet. So many of them. There are so very many of them. And I am just one more. Abruptly I stop still. In that frozen moment I remember another time when things came apart and I was alone in the world, when the oars dipped in and out of the water and pulled me away from my parents.

I search inside myself, try to find solid ground as a girl might reach for a steadying arm when she has fallen. But there is nothing there, only emptiness. I have been stupid. I've taken a generous hand that has been extended to me and have ignored the conditions that came with it.

My tongue is dry as a lump of wood, my knees shake, my heart bangs. I am aware of the usual clop of horses in the road outside, but the sound is different. I understand that I've been part of a game. I must have known but I trusted him. We had, I thought, something that many people never have. We had our own world where all things were possible. We played as I have seen children play, in the way Elsie and Nelly described in our attic room at night when our fingers ached and our necks felt full of needles. The truth is that this summer has been the first time I have played in my life. He and I stepped in and out of paintings He didn't even need to tell me what to do. He loved my drawings, my face, my body. We seemed to be the greatest of friends. Was he promising more when he talked to me about artists setting up house with their mistresses? Did he drop ideas in my head about a possible future for us? I try to remember but I can't recall that he said anything that definitely planted hope. There was no moment of physical intimacy but we had every other kind of intimacy. I sift through hundreds of moments but I find nothing. He has left no fingerprints.

Somehow I get back to my rented room, scarcely knowing if I am crossing this thoroughfare or that. My landlady Mrs Thomson keeps a clean house in Kentish Town. It doesn't run with rats like some of the places in Islington or the East End. It isn't that I ever thought I could be anything to him. No, I'm not being truthful with myself. For if that were the case, then why would the city, the houses, all the people, be drained of colour, nothing but monochrome now? Life falls away like a vast landslip ahead of me. I pass the night at Mrs Thomson's which lasts for an eternity. I don't expect to sleep but lie under the sheet, listening to the city. I think of all the thousands of human hearts spending time with each other, loving. For what is more important than to touch another's heart? What is more important than love? No matter how I try to divert my mind with colours and shapes, or with great paintings and their composition, the horror of the glass plates come before me. My bedroom window is ajar and by dawn I can hear the trams and the bells of London tolling. They tell me to leave.

And this is a strange thing. As I lie there waiting for the light, my joints ache. My knees, hips, elbows, wrists and neck are pierced by knitting needles of pain. First my calf muscles cramp, then the arches of my feet tighten hard enough to break the bones. The first trains on the nearby track pulse in time with my anguish.

By the first birdsong I have decided what I will do. I rise and see the pale face of a stranger in the mirror. I pack my bag, stowing away my sewing things, my sketchbook, my pencils from L. Cornelissen & Son, my brown serge dress for autumn, woollen grey dress for winter, summer and winter shawls, my second pair of boots. I put on my pale blue summer dress. No frayed cuffs or worn hems, for I have kept myself neat. I glance at the sketches I made at the zoo, drawings I chose not give him, the early attempts at the tiger's face, the ostrich, the flamingos. It seems long ago now. I pay Mrs Thomson. She frowns, then swiftly cleans and bandages my cut hand.

"But where will you go? What will you do?" She despairs.

I promise to send her word of where I am.

But first I must take my black glacé silk dress so I roll it in layers of tissue and brown paper and make my way to Madame Juliette's. She receives me in the mirrored room, dark with the chandelier unlit, ghosts lingering in the looking glasses. She sees the bandage on my hand and thinks the worst.

I hand her my parcel and beg her leave.

"You are too good to lose, *ma cherie*. I know a woman who can help you."

Her nose twitches at the scent of bad news, her eyes gleaming at the possibilities of what my hasty departure could mean. But I give away nothing other than the appearance of a rabbit about to be skinned alive. The descant of pain in my joints has ceased but my head is now circled with iron nails. She hasn't spoken for a moment or two and I sway in the gloom.

"A glass of water, *ma cherie*."

The doorman's shoes squeak on the polished floor as he hurries to fetch a glass. The water is the first thing to pass my lips since I was with Edward the day before. It tastes different, oily and heavy, as everything now seems new and different and distant.

I make my escape, return to Mrs Thomson to collect my bag, and walk swiftly, astonished to find that my body still functions, to Liverpool Street Station. I buy a ticket to a part of the country which Edward called Poppyland, which he visited with titled and talented friends, close to Highcliff where he found his collection of shells. I ask for the last stop on the line.

CHAPTER FIFTEEN:

THE BAG OF EELS

August 6 1901

(In 1809 Alfred Lord Tennyson, the poet, was born. His best known works are The Lady of Shalott and The Charge Of The Light Brigade)

The week when everyone goes home. Railway workers aren't born railway workers. They start somewhere else, out beyond Sebastopol Road in the land of wheat and cows, not among the slap-slap of the drive belts, the hooters and the washing dusted with soot. So when the summer heat brings almost everything to a standstill they go back to the place they still call home.

Billy has put himself in the way of Mr Massingham, cutting his hedge, weeding his path, calling him "sir".

"It's the tradition. It's the way in," he says. Pleased with himself, he is. Especially because he's now discovering the special things that only railway people know.

"I tell you something useful. If you blow down the gas pipe in the Railway Institute, the lights go out all over the village."

He wipes his nose and rolls on his heels as if he is a station master already.

"It's a hard life," he says. So is being a baker, but working alone with white floury hands is not as adventurous as working with a gang of men with blackened hands.

"Six days a week, hot metal, choking fumes, amputated fingers, ten hours a day," he says. These days his voice squeaks like a violin, then suddenly growls like a cello. While mine is the same as it always has been.

"You stink," I say. "Like you've come out of a barrel of herrings."

He sniffs his sleeve.

"So I do. That's what you get for a good night's work. Out with my brother labelling the carriages last night. Working the fish trains. It was so dark I couldn't see what was what. And fish juice doesn't stay put. It likes to spread itself around." He raises his eyebrows importantly.

High summer is also the time for fish. First the 'specials' run from west to east, bringing girls all the way from Scotland to work on Wellmouth quay, smoking, salting and selling fish. They're well kippered themselves by the time they go home. Then trains loaded with fish travel east to west and, more often than not, stop over here to wait in the sidings and spread their pong. It makes a change from the soot, bones, hay, potatoes and manure. Then come the holidaymakers with their trunks, bicycles, hats, babies, nurses, nannies, medicine chests, caged birds and cricket bats. Is there anything they don't leave behind?

⁂

As the temperature rises in Swanton Stoke, Rosie realises she has been here almost a year. It was autumn when she stepped off the train. The letters from Edward Stafford Clark keep coming. Every two weeks an envelope arrives with a funny drawing on the back of it. A man in a top hat chasing an elephant. A monkey snatching a woman's handkerchief. She doesn't reply because she has too much to say and nothing to say. But the letters keep thoughts of him alive and she often sits on her bed in the evenings, reading them again and again. Though she searches, she can find no sign that he feels he has done anything wrong.

Rosie,

The saddest thing. Polly was jostled and injured in Kensington High Street. It has been a catastrophe waiting to happen for the roads these days are pure Bedlam. A plethora of horses and carts jostling for space. She was too far gone to be rescued so I took her to our friend Augustus P. Reynolds to be slaughtered for feed. I put her with all the other horses left by the hansom cab owners, but A.P.R. removed her and promised she would be humanely killed before being fed to the lions. I trust him absolutely. I am so drear without you. But I am desolate without Polly too.

I stayed on after the zoo closed and I almost thought I could see you there floating through the dusk. But no. Small compensation was a grandstand view of reptiles being fed – I tell you because it reminds me of you and me. There were two boa constrictors, each one ten or eleven feet long, trying to swallow the same stodgy pigeon. The smaller one swallowed the pigeon with some determination. Then the larger snake hinged its mouth open, pinned the small one and slowly but surely eased it in. After that it could no longer curl itself up but lay there, three times as fat, skin stretched so hard that the scales separated and it was almost painful to see.

If we were they, which of us would be the larger and which the smaller? Who has swallowed whose heart for slow digestion over an unknown period of time? Which of us was the biter and which the bit?

I am cheering myself up by organising new country tweeds and riding dress. And I fancy a cycling suit might be in order. Though my girth is not what it was. Sweet youth is what I miss. Sweet innocence. The girls I might have known but never can now. With you it was different. We shared a pair of eyes, we shared dreams. Didn't we? I believe that a love without shared dreams is a compromise. You accepted all my facets with delicacy. Like a butterfly, you flitted into my house, through my pictures, across my lens, you stepped from my real space into my imagined space. You saw my desire to be a great artist – as great as any of them! And you knew what it meant to draw to order. You straddled the licit world of art and the illicit world of my photography. Who else could have done that? Who else will ever do so again?

Rosie,

Let me tell you what would have happened if I had not become an artist. I would have been an engineer. Yes. Perhaps on the railways. Maybe that is what I should have done. I could have used my Third Eye, the Invaluable Adjunct, in another way. I might have dreamed of rivers to span and land to flatten, instead of youth and beauty.

It is a constant wonder to me that The Duchess took me as her husband because she had money while I had none. She likes to mingle with the rich and famous, and my work gives her an entree, though it does not give her quite the social standing she would really like. We have her banking friends to dinner and they love my stories and I love their money. Ha! Men of industry and commerce are the wealth-creators now, not the old aristocracy. They are building the new country houses and filling them with art. A force for good, I am sure! Millais had money pouring in from them before he died. He was making thirty to forty thousand pounds a year from his paintings of women in mob caps. They say patronage is no longer in the gift of the church but now lies in the hands of the middle classes, and that art has been captured by commercial advertising. You have only to look at Millais' soap bubbles. I do not believe, though you well might, that art is a noble mission, only that it is a mission. Reproduction is the key and there is nothing wrong with that.

I have had the drawing room entirely redecorated. The floor is now parquet, there is a new sofa, yellow shades, extravagant curtains. A.P.R. has sent me Polly's hoof as a memento and I have had it mounted on brass and placed in a very important position. With it came news that might interest you. The dark-coloured horse with the stripes on its front and back legs, the one with two toes like an antelope's, is not a zebra at all but is actually related to the giraffe. There has been a row about it of course – a professor denounced it as a fraud but the man who found it produced the skin and skull to prove him wrong. There was a Scientific Meeting of the Society and the explorer won them over, so the animal has duly been anointed a member of the giraffe family and named "okapi". Ha! I have had fun with that one in the pages of Burlesque.

As to Polly's hoof, I am not sure whether The Duchess is more despairing of me for being too sentimental about it, or more angry with cook for drinking away the beer. By the gallon. So I think she is for the chop!

Rosie,

I have been reflecting. Perhaps there is a touch of fiction in all our lives? A cartoon must have elements in it which are real but then it needs a dash of fiction to make it fly. That is what I have been taught ever since I became a junior at Burlesque when I was sixteen years old. A likeness is made first of something ordinary like the label on a good claret or a stuffed bird on a wall, then an element of lunacy is added to make it absurd. That is my trade. They say it makes me an astute commentator. But you have always understood this, as naturally as you know how to blink and breathe. The truth is, my little one, that you have it – the talent, the eye and the hand, the feeling – whereas I must work into the night and use my tools slowly like (a rather fat) tortoise to earn my living, in black and white. I need a deadline. I cannot work without it. It takes a deadline even to drag stillborn kittens out of me.

I must tell you. I went to see the one-act play Madam Butterfly by David Belasco last night. It was about a tea-house girl in Japan who is taken by an American in a sham marriage. She falls in love with him but he leaves and she waits for a long time for him to return and to send a signal when his ship comes into harbour. He comes but he does not send the signal, and he brings an American wife with him. I was quite cut up by it, and very pleased that The Duchess was not with me as she would have disapproved. As it is, we have to shun any of our friends who consort with ladies of ill repute, or actresses or dancers. The thing is this. It is not entirely clear whether the Japanese tea-house girl made a commercial transaction with the American, or if she really gave him her heart. What would you say to that? I wonder. I spied the great Verdi in the stalls. Perhaps he was looking for an idea for his next opera.

Rosie,

The worst has happened. They have made me chief cartoonist at Burlesque. The Duchess is overjoyed. The door is slamming shut, Rosie, and I shall be left with nothing but lunch and supper to look forward to. The work has lost its joy for me since you went away. I am forever to wear a deadline around my neck. I am forever the court jester, never the artist. You showed me the colour of coral, the colour of dawn, the promise of youth. You showed me all you had.

※

August 10th 1901

(In 1675 the Greenwich Observatory was established to further the exploration of navigation techniques and astronomy. The site it occupies is significant because the Prime Meridian runs through it)

I push the handcart up the street towards the station and see clouds of white smoke rise up from the station into a forget-me-not-blue sky. The milk trains have long gone to Finsbury Park. Sunlight filters through the smoke, touching the leaves on the trees. It is the kind of day when the world bursts with possibilities. Today I could become an explorer, or a writer. Or a new idea has come to me. Maybe I could be a teacher? This day (I feel it in my warts) could be a wonderful day.

At the station I see Young Stokes, two years older than me, carrying his postbag. He walks along the platform past the Third-Class Waiting Room, The Ladies Waiting Room and the First-Class Waiting Room. A few moments later I spot him again, delivering a shovel and a coal-pick to the Peterborough train. I peer into the machine shop, where steam is as all-powerful as God, right here, right now, on this grand day at the beginning of the new century.

Then Young Stokes walks towards me carrying an oblong basket across his chest.

"One for Miss Etherington. Take it on your cart, would yer?"

It is made of wicker, like the ones at Lord Hartley's. His are packed with pies and pickles and brought out at shooting parties. This one weighs almost nothing. I sweep a path of white flour off the floor of the cart and set it down gently. I am not a frequent visitor to the front door of the Massinghams. I'm more familiar with the back door, the cat's eye view from the mulberry bush. The back window is my magic lantern where I watch Miss Etherington's performance with her jug and ewer. I can't stop myself coming back for more.

I hear bees busy in the hives nearby as I step towards the door. A cat is curled on the step, warming its tabby coat in the sun. It opens its green eyes as I knock, then scats around the corner. As it happens Mrs Massingham is out, so Miss Etherington answers the door herself and looks surprised to see me. But then she spies the basket and looks as if she has suffered a sudden stab of pain. I hold out my offering proudly.

"An important delivery, Miss."

"Thank you, Jack. Yes. Important. It may be." Her voice is shaky. The pale blue sky does that thing where it appears to lift away into outer space.

She puts the basket on the floor, with me standing right there, handling it as if it were filled with danger. My eyes pop and I won't budge now even if she asks me to. Her slender fingers undo the leather straps, and inside I see a pile of black and silver coils, like a bag of eels in the sunlight.

"Oh, no!" she cries. Her hand flies to her mouth, her forehead creases up and her eyes brim with tears. Thank goodness the tears don't drop because if they did, where would I put myself?

She lifts the eels and they turn themselves into a gown of black and white silk taffeta. She plucks at a sleeve which is shaped like our fire bellows at home. This is curious but it must be some smart fashion thing. It smells of lavender and wine and cigars. The tiny pearl buttons down the back must have been sewn on by a mouse.

Miss Etherington is like a deer caught in the moonlight. She appears to have forgotten I am there at all.

There is a card with few words written upon it but it is torn down the middle. Two jagged edges. The writing slopes, loops and spits with anger. She lets it fall so I pick up the pieces and put them together before handing them back.

How dared you to presume to dress me even as you attempted to rob me of all that I hold dear. May God be your judge. You are beneath contempt and beyond redemption.

"No, no, no, no." Miss Etherington's voice shrinks to a whisper.

She sinks to her knees and leans her head against my apron, which is covered in flour though she does not notice.

"Oh Jack. Am I a bad woman? Am I a woman who wants to cause harm to the people? That is what she thinks of me."

"I don't think so, Miss. I think you are… er… lovely, Miss." My face is hot as hell and, while I might have secretly dreamed of being this friendly with her, I haven't an idea in my head what to do now. I touch her hair with a dirty finger.

"How did The Duchess find out where I was? From him? From his letters? Oh God. She wore this, loved it and paraded in it. And then she discovered." Her voice is almost a whine.

"It must be a terrible thing." She says this almost to herself as she picks herself up.

"This is a gift made of thorns," she says. "She is casting me into the darkness but she doesn't know I am there already. Apart from you, Jack, too young to know, and Rough Jimmy, too poor to help, I don't think I have made many friends in this world....." Her lips wobble and my groin fires up.

She is all warm and trembling. A marrow is sprouting in my trousers. I am an allotment on legs. There is nothing for it but to step away from her soft hair and shuddering shoulders. She is an insect caught in a net without hope of escape. She tidies her hair and skirt, as if this will restore order. She steadies herself. I breathe so hard I think they must hear it on the quarter-past-nine to Liverpool Street.

Which Duchess did she mean? Not Lady Hartley, surely. Lady Hartley would certainly not be pleased if she knew that messages were being exchanged between her son and Miss Etherington. But Lady Hartley wouldn't bother herself with parcelling up a dangerous dress and sending a nasty card. A lady who can't cut the top off her own boiled egg or lay out her own gowns for dinner, would not wave a glove in the direction of Miss Etherington. No, this is a Duchess from London who Miss Etherington once made a dress for – the like of which has never been seen in Swanton Stoke. I am not sure it is what people here would call beautiful, as it has no colour and no ribbons. I'm shaking hard now, like her, but must hurry back to the cart and the bakery. Father is stretched on account of a wedding in the village. I've been delivering loaves while he finishes making bridal slices and Genoese cake for the celebration on the bowling green.

"Will you take the basket upstairs, Jack?"

The wicker creaks and my boots clump on the stairs. I don't need to ask where her bedroom is and I step into it before I remember to make a show of asking the way. Anyway, she is too fretful to notice I am there already. My eyes drink it all in, the cover on her bed, the jug and ewer by the window, the stoppered bottles on her chest of drawers, the view of the garden. Can she see my hiding place behind the mulberry bushes? It feels a bit like being in a holy place. She motions under the bed and I shove the basket in there. Then I am off out, quick as Gyp after a rat.

The final Saturday hooter goes. It must be one o'clock. The fish and shellfish hawkers from the coast have arrived and are standing on the station platform ready to go house to house with their baskets.

Father and I have delivered trays of bridal slices filled with jewelled fruits and light perfumed Genoese cake to the wedding party, as well as to the driver of the bridal train, Bob Porter, who sends up a shower of cinders to celebrate.

"Hurray!" Everyone shouts, excited by the power of the train, the toot of the whistle and the sense of being connected to the whole outside world.

The wedding couple step on board the eight-minutes-past-four. The guard has kept the carriage locked to keep others from going in, so the couple are sure to be alone in there. Fog horns are blown many times over, according to a code not found in the Rule Book. They trigger a line of explosions along the line as signalmen telegraph news of the wedding before the honeymoon train builds up its steam and heads westwards.

The rest of us are left to carry on as normal. The pattern of the trains is the pattern of our lives, the line is our track from birth to death.

CHAPTER SIXTEEN:

THE POPPIES

August 13 1901
Grouse shooting begins

(In 1704 the Battle of Blenheim was fought in Germany. Thanks to the combined forces of the Duke of Marlborough and Prince Eugene of Savoy, the French and Bavarians were soundly defeated)

The small blue butterfly
The Cupido Minimus is so tiny that its entire wingspan is no more than one inch wide. It needs sheltered, sunny habitats and depends upon the kidney vetch from which it takes nectar and in which it lays tiny bun-shaped eggs. It has a life cycle which lasts about one year, from the point when the female lays her eggs to the point when the caterpillar pupates and metamorphoses into a butterfly. It favours grassland habitats on chalk, limestone, coastal areas such as dune systems, and man-made environments such as disused railway lines. It is easy to overlook and dusky in colour.

The entire road is being whitewashed. Bedrooms and living rooms are being chalked, and windows left open to dry in the sun and wind. Men play cricket during meal breaks. It feels as if it will never rain again.

We boys take to the fields during the harvest. Men move slowly through the fields, backs bent over their scythes, advancing in a steady line, sharpeners hanging from their hips in leather pouches. Behind them come the women tidying the mess into sheaves, heads bound in white sails of stiff cotton to keep the sun from burning their faces. We are called upon to do our bit too. We wait and watch. When the men have cut round the field margin and pressed towards the middle they leave a small square of wheat standing where all the rabbits hide. We are prepared. We raise sticks and chair-legs, ready to shack them as they try to escape and dash for safety. We are pumped up like the soldiers must have been at the Battle of Blenheim. I land a blow and my first rabbit falls. *I am a man. I am a man.* I watch the poor creature tense and its legs quiver. I sling it carelessly to one side as other boys do with theirs, and think that I shan't take it home to Mother but will give it instead to Rough Jimmy.

"Now, that'll do nicely," he says, his black and white beard bristling like a pile of hedgehogs. Beneath his curly leather hat, his face is so brown that his eyes shine white like cuckoo spit.

I've found him down by The Tin House at Bell's Loke, where Mrs Maynard lets him sleep in her shed and sometimes gives him hot porridge in the morning, even though she has seven children to feed first. He's happy to eat the leftovers with a dab of honey from Mrs Maynard's bees. The Tin House is made of corrugated iron like The Tin Church. Rough Jimmy says they send buildings like this to India for British people to put together to make them feel more at home.

In return for my dead gift he plays a tune on his forehead with his knuckles. He treats his head like a drum and get notes out of it.

"How's yer career plans, lad?" he says.

I tell him about Billy getting close enough to Mr Massingham to polish his bowler hat, and say I am considering becoming a teacher.

"I tell yer, tiddler, you'll be baking bread long after this lot have stopped living by railway-time. The world has forgot about nature, summer and winter and the great miracle of the world around us. They only think of herding people into factories and making money. But bread," and his white eyeballs turn skywards, "that's another thing. It takes wheat from the fields, moisture from rain and energy from the sun, and makes these things into food for us. And you, creator of dough, you bring it to our table. Bread is sent from heaven. It is a gift from God."

Father read from John's Gospel last night while Mother and I sat with him in the darkness, for he only lights one lamp in the evening now to save money.

For the bread of God is he which cometh down from heaven, and giveth life unto the world.

Then said they unto him, Lord, evermore give us bread.

And Jesus said unto them, I am the bread of life: he that cometh to me shall never hunger; and he that believeth in me shall never thirst.

"Your father is a good man, boy."

Rough Jimmy rubs his nose, which is a worry because he has so many black veins wriggling there that I'm afraid one might burst. I tell him I have recently decided that goodness comes in a variety of ways and some of them are dark and sad. Good is smiling to all the neighbours but not smiling at home. Good is not having any money and eating rook pie. Good sometimes means keeping secrets to keep other people safe. This is what I tell him.

⁂

Another letter from Edward has arrived hard on the heels of the basket containing the black-and-white dress. I search it for the things he does not say.

Rosie,

Apologies, apologies, apologies – there was nothing I could do. The good Duchess found discarded paragraphs I had written to you and the odd picture here and there – I do not hide these things. She took violently against the Tissot masterpiece you made for her and considered it Out Of Order. She does not understand how generous it was of you to make it for her, or how patient you were with me and my photography. The endless photography! This is what she cries at me and has done for many years. She locked herself in her room for two days. Then she came out and followed the tracks you left behind, my dear, just as I did. She went back to Madame Juliette, from there to Mrs Thomson in Camden, where she obtained your forwarding address.

Then the dress turned into a weapon and she sent it back to you. Take care of it.

Rosie,

I do not want to be seen as a villain. Do not take me for a bad man.

I have put distance between myself and him. Half a day's train journey, to be precise. Real distance isn't so different from distance in a drawing. A table looks smaller when you are far away from it. Therefore he should look smaller to me as I am far from him. I have given myself time and the distance to separate truth from fiction, or fantasy from love. So powerful are these things that they can melt my mind. And now Edward is not staying put where he should be but is travelling towards me.

Rosie,

I am here - at last – and am come to pay homage to my Galatea. I am come to

Highcliff in the land of poppies. It is as I remember it, though new buildings spring like mushrooms overnight and it will soon be changed for ever. Mabel Lucie Atwell is here and everyone is turning their children into her pictures and vice versa. Edwin Lutyens is here too and I have had several encounters with him already. He is busy designing a large house for one of the new millionaires on the crumbling clifftops, and is taking the air at the same time. The crabs from these waters are the sweetest I've tasted anywhere. And the lobster unsurpassed!

I am staying in lodgings which are comfortable enough, run by Mrs Birdwood. I see her as a hamster – you could draw her and have her exactly. Well-meaning. With teeth.

The mistakes I've made gather round me for a vigil, unforgiving and prayerless as I try to sleep. The night is somehow insubstantial and translucent, a death mask of the day. The summer light is never-ending, never closes its eye, never says it's time to rest. It spills across the ceiling and throws a silver cloak over the trees. It watches the inside of my brain. The endless glow prevents the essential sleep. Nature is at its most restless. Almost mad. Fields and gardens are full of rustlings, twitterings and moonshine killings. My nerve-ends are raw. This room, though spacious, feels lead-lined.

If what Mr Darwin says is true and there is no God, then I'm not sure what will happen to my soul. I am still not sure the soul can exist without religion. Without it, where do we go after death? Who shall I haunt when I am gone?

What was it that Edward said about the soul? No, it wasn't the soul, it was *The Souls*. A group of country house people who decided to live inside their heads and leave all practical things for their servants to do while *they* concerned themselves with ideas, mathematics and art. I am both things. I am a kind of servant but I also *like to think*, though it doesn't do me any good.

I can no longer slip through London streets invisibly, known only by my stitches. Now I live among people who know me by name. I have learned, too slowly perhaps, that it wasn't just Edward who looked at me differently but other men do too. Yet I'm not like most of the other people here, born to a specific place and job. I don't have a front parlour of my own. They believe I've stepped from the train like a free spirit and that not all free spirits are good. Some have offered friendship and I've resolved that I must try to make a home here. And just as I do so these letters start arriving. I'm afraid my past will catch up with me and I will never be able to hold up my head at all.

The fact that I wake suggests I must have slept, and yet I feel I haven't slept at all. I gaze dumbly at the furniture, hear sounds of men and shunting trains. As I do, I realise that a painting works on the viewer in the same way that a loved one works on the lover. If the meaning of a painting is partly hidden, we are repeatedly drawn back to it to work out what it is saying. In the same way lovers are drawn back to each other if questions between them lie unanswered or too many things remain unsaid. A painting which keeps us guessing is a painting with great power. I hurt inside. Oh Lord, I hurt. But I comfort myself with the thought that hurt carries love on its back. Those who haven't touched us can't hurt us. Only those we care about can do that.

☙

George Childs has brought me to Highcliff for the opening of the pier. His hand is on my arm and he is riding a wave of happiness.

"Sir Arthur Conan Doyle is here," he says. "Returned from South Africa with enteric fever, so he has come to let some good sea air into his lungs. They say he is in a house by the bowling green, writing a new story."

Everyone has dressed up for the great occasion and the whole town is buzzing. I'm wearing a dress which is the colour of pink roses, made from a bolt of thick cotton Mrs Eden had put away for a rainy day. I've attached gathered muslin to the waist and embroidered tiny roses into the bodice. Mrs Eden insisted we sewed together – she continued with the increasingly colourful embroidery of her sadness, and I stitched my new frock.

"What a capital day this is. But you are pale. Are you sure you are quite well?" says George.

I reassure him that I am well but rather tired.

In truth I am tense as a new bride, sad as an old widow and anxious as a new mother, all at once. Of all the people in Highcliff he might have chosen to stay with, Edward is lodging with Mrs Birdwood, who may be a bit like a hamster but she is also George Childs' sister.

I'm sure Edward won't pass up the opportunity to poke fun at a seaside town trying to make something of itself with a new pier. My head swivels, my eyes rake the crowd, expecting to see him suddenly prancing like a dancer, fizzing with energy, making people laugh.

"It is the rule to walk on the sands in the morning, venture along one cliff for a mile in the afternoon, and then another mile in the opposite direction at sunset," says George. "With the new pier people will be able to stroll along it at night."

Visitors throng the promenade around the entrance to the pier. Men in straw boaters, children in sailor suits, women in their best lace and white hats. Mr Eden lifts his hat grandly above the crowd while Mrs Eden feels the strain of being close to so many people whose names she doesn't know, who she's never seen before and has no intention of seeing again. She has a handkerchief to her nose.

"It is a somewhat *villainous* structure. From here the bandstand looks small enough for performing fleas," says Mr Eden.

"To be able to land visitors and goods at all states of the tide, be it high or low water, must be a good thing," says George. "Think of the commercial advantage. The Highcliff Esplanade Company has extended the foreshore into the sea by a thousand feet. That could quadruple the number of visitors."

Below us on the beach we watch holiday makers being pulled along in goat carts and children building sandcastles. Big white tents have sprung up along the base of the cliff to house coconut shies and aunt sallies. I scan them all in search of a portly gentleman making merry. Might he be wearing a white straw hat today? I search and find nothing. Then suddenly I realise everyone in my small group is looking at me, questioningly, as if to ask whether they are missing something too.

"Is a bandstand the same as a pavilion?" I say, a bit foolishly.

Mr Eden stiffens.

"A pavilion would be a *catastrophe* for Highcliff. It could no longer belong in the same social *echelon* as Bournemouth if it didn't have a bandstand."

"Oh, but wouldn't visitors find it a little dull if they came all this way and there wasn't enough entertainment?" I can't stop now.

"If Highcliff is to remain above vulgarity, then it must avoid not only the horrors of too much entertainment but also the pitfalls of advertising, the sale of goods and the proximity to anything that might be deemed a whelk stall."

Mr Eden looks very disappointed in me.

George squeezes my arm and coughs. He is irritated but I don't care. Even when he is annoyed his cheeks colour and lips swell every time he looks at me. I wonder if I can marry him after all. He's pleasant enough but I feel nothing for him.

On the stroke of one o'clock the magnificent ironwork gates to the pier are unlocked with a golden key. We move inside for luncheon, which has been laid out in the Hotel d'Homard. The railway company has invited a party of pressmen and photographers to admire the pier, the promenade, the cliffs, the fields of poppies, the new hotels and tell the rest of the country about it all.

The Massinghams are here too, eager to admire the new wonder and to mingle with dignitaries. They come over to speak to me, which is an act of kindness since we see each other every day anyway. Mr Massingham is wearing the shirt I took off the washing line only this morning.

"What is your opinion of the new structure?" he says, sounding rather formal.

"I think it is a thing of fantasy, a figment of the imagination made real, a work of art in wood and iron."

He looks bewildered at my flowery words and remains determined to retain his gloomy demeanour.

"It is important to keep the memory of what has gone before, even on such a day of celebration," he says. "The truth is that this town has been shaped by endurance and hard work. It was not made for pleasure. You don't remember, like I do, the number of times the old jetty was ravaged by the sea and wind, or how many vessels have been broken against it. Nor do you remember the money lost on those jetties. Each one was constructed in hope. Each one was broken and auctioned off in pieces."

"Sanitary conveniences for women were considered an unnecessary addition back then," Mrs Massingham whispers in my ear, smelling of crab.

She smiles knowingly.

Mr Massingham is aware that his wife has said some silly thing which he can't hear, so he valiantly carries on with the conversation.

"The chairman of the commissioners also *happens* to be the owner of the Hotel d'Homard, which *happens* to be in prime position just opposite the pier. That is how things work around here." He goes on to describe how the commissioners incorporated all the finest attributes of the other piers into their design but carefully excluded anything that would lower the tone.

Lord Hartley stands on a podium and proposes a toast.

"Success to the pier, prosperity to Highcliff and prosperity to the railways! A fishing village which was all but inaccessible to the country, home to no more than a handful of families and a few donkeys and goats, can now be enjoyed by all."

Mr Eden murmurs with pleasure and looks for a moment as if he might have swallowed a demon drink or two.

I slip away out of the Hotel d'Homard and walk along the front where a band is playing. I think I might have caught sight of him through the window of the hotel, so I bunch my skirts to quicken my steps. But then the figure turns round and it is not him at all, only a man like any other with a small beard on a sunny day. The band plays on.

"You are a strange creature today. A cat on hot bricks. Are you feverish?" says George, who has followed and swiftly caught up with me.

I feel flustered and strained from hiding so much from him, as well as from all the others around me. I've no choice but must simply take whatever path opens in front of me. The fact is that this is actually all I have ever done but I have still landed myself in trouble. My cheek twitches.

George and I stroll along the clifftop with many others, a fair number of them twirling parasols. He enjoys a sense that he's rubbing shoulders with important people, even *artistic* people. One of them is definitely artistic because he wears white silk robes and a turban round his head.

"Even Prince Edward has been known to come here when he is bored. They say he eats the local gentry out of house and home."

He's trying his best to make me laugh but little does he know how familiar I am with the girth of Prince Edward's waist.

"Speculation. Speculation. Speculation. The town is full of it. Not on the scale of London but very similar. Everyone is here to show their money or to make it," he says.

Not everyone. My cheek twitches again. My past and my future are in danger of colliding today and my emotions are being wrung through Mrs Massingham's mangle.

We reach the highest point of the cliff, where a family has laid out a picnic with a silver teapot, cups and saucers. An assortment of sons and daughters wearing straw hats eat slabs of fruit cake off delicate china plates. Beyond them the field is ablaze with poppies, their blooms flashing like a million red handkerchiefs. Claude Monet would have loved it. The poppies are only here for a short time so everyone wants to seize the moment, the sunlight, the colour.

Way below, close to the line of the surf, boatmen set up wooden platforms for ladies to climb up and onto their boats. The men have swapped crab pots for crinolines.

August 16th 1901

(In 1819 The Peterloo Massacre took place in Manchester. The King's Hussars charged thousands of demonstrators demanding the right to vote. Eleven were killed and six hundred injured)

We cousins are out on the marsh, trusted with the sheep that belong to Uncle Henry Squinty Clink's brother Tom, who is busy with boatbuilding, and they also belong to Filch, who is taken up with bathing machines. Reg, Ron, Skinny and me are on The All-Night shepherd's watch that we do once every summer. They bring a horse and Reg trots down the dirt tracks ahead of us, across the banks and wooden bridges over this half-sea-half-land on the edge of everything. He needs no reins but guides the horse by talking.

Long after we would normally be asleep, the sun still crouches low in the sky. Its rays weave silk webs over the marsh and we whoop and jeer in the strange light. We are treeless out here, not a trunk or a branch or a leaf is anywhere to be seen. Instead there are fresh water drains running towards the sea, swallowing the colour of the sky, doubling it like liquid arithmetic. We have blue above, blue below and blue to either side of us. Coiling and squirming beneath the surface of the water are eels we want to catch for eating or selling.

"We could be babbing, if only we had worms and wool," says Skinny. "If we gave them to mad Margie Pringle, she could sell 'em for us."

Babs are sticks with hooks. Aunt Mary puts worms on them, then old wool to snag the eels' teeth when they bite. We all let out a cry when we spot one jumping out of the water, a muscle in flight, and Skinny looks pleased as a man on his wedding night. The swans are silent, bright white on the dark of the marsh. Every now and then one of them turns a watchful black eye twisting a long neck made of angel scraps. We fall silent all of a sudden. Listening.

The sheep make silly noises, scattering droppings in grassy hollows. We move them on to drink at another freshwater drain, then on again to a patch of salty grass. I'm not sure who leads who, them or us. There's one sheep track down to the sea which they say is the smugglers' path. Old Uncle Henry's brother used to help the smugglers by driving his flock over their tracks before the law turned up. No-one says anything about it. We're all tongue-tied. These days when a tin of tea or roll of silk turns up in the cottages, it is still accepted without a word.

Suddenly Reg has all his clothes off and is riding naked like an ancient god. We all leave off our clothes and run with bare bottoms, knobs dangling in the marsh air, whooping and jumping. The sheep run with us, bleating like dafties, bells tinkling hour beyond hour as if summer has no end.

Sometimes we drift close to the cottages where ducks fuss on the pond like old ladies arguing over whose chicks are whose. Birds skim low as my shoulder across the green while night stands at the open door of tomorrow. The moon and the sun, pinned overhead, are so like each other that I can't tell one from the other.

Down at the edge of the sea is the huge shingle bank, a buttress against the sea rolling and murmuring beyond. Three years ago it burst and the ocean moved in. "The water's over!" everyone shouted. Soon autumn will come and the village will be watching the bank for signs of danger again. Last time it came they called it "the rage". Dogs swam in through bedroom windows while furniture swam out. Drinking water was spoiled in the wells and the village went without food and clothes until their homes dried out. That was when the sea turned the windmill into an island.

The heat finally broke, the rain poured non-stop for two or three days and the parched fields swallowed it gratefully. This was unfortunately the moment that the directors of the new Railway Company chose to come from London to inspect the route for the new line to Staithe.

"It was most badly-timed," said Mrs Eden, spreading her embroidery and smoothing out the bumps.

"Was it?" said Rosie, scarcely summoning an interest.

"The ground was sodden, the directors were not dressed for the weather and their shoes sank deep into the mud. The windmill was shrouded in rain, the lanes ran with water, the whole proposition looked most unpromising. Indeed, they were worried about flooding from the river as well as from the sea. The marsh was, well, *marshy*."

Rosie agreed it was a shame they chose that weekend when there had been such good weather only a week before.

"Mr Eden is concerned they have taken away the wrong impression. The concern, you must understand, is not just for himself. It is for the people of Staithe and for Mr Childs, who has committed so much energy and money to the project."

Rosie put her hand to her mouth in shock. She wished him no ill.

They sat, both of them, still as stoats listening for a fox, letting the situation sink in.

"Oh, Good Lord," she said.

It seemed that a cruel trap had been laid for George Childs. He had been a willing foot soldier to Mr Eden, buying land for the new railway. Privately she had always thought this little line would have to be extremely robust if it was to cross the marsh and brave the sea. Both she and Mrs Eden thought so. Yet as women they hadn't been listened to. They sat by while the men re-arranged the map as they pleased, ignoring small practicalities like soggy ground. Enterprise and engineering was all.

"How do you think Mr Childs will take the bad news, if it comes?" said Mrs Eden.

"I think he will take it very badly," Rosie said quietly. She thought George had little experience of disappointment and disadvantage. She suspected he wouldn't react at all well if he saw his dream of a good life sink in the mud. The decision to marry him had been settled as easily as buying a piece of meat at the butcher's. It was the only way forward if she was to avoid going back to sewing night and day. Mrs Massingham's advice was that a woman in this day and age must have a husband. But Rosie also felt oddly drawn to his windmill and the whispering reedbeds which surrounded it. She felt they would keep her safe. If the sea broke its banks, then she would climb up the tower and stay dry. She would have no need to step into a boat, watch oars dipping in and out and be rowed away from all she knew.

"The directors fear the operation may be fraught with setbacks," said Mrs Eden, choosing her words carefully. "It is a little bit like making mayonnaise."

"If you don't stay with it, if you don't beat the mixture, it doesn't take," said Rosie.

She was surprised that Mrs Eden had ever made mayonnaise. Then again, it required a level of patience and skill that the lady of the house might believe was hers alone.

How much impact could one summer drenching have on the grand new railway?

"Mr Eden is very worried. The pursuit of knowledge is close to his heart, as you know. His very desire is to assuage the misery of his fellow creatures," said Mrs Eden. She added that knowledge was the kneeler on which we bent before God.

"But what if knowledge *replaces* God? De-thrones him, tells us the world was made by nature itself and that the Bible is just a wonderful story handed down through the generations?"

Oh, let it all come out, Rosie thought. Why not?

"Darwin's theory," Mrs Eden replied, unruffled, holding her needle up to the light. "Darwin is not a good name to mention in this household. 'That horrible Darwinian theory' is what Jonathan calls it. Death, he says, without the rituals of Christianity, prayers, hymns, readings and tributes, is made mean if we take too much notice of Darwin. If you follow his arguments, the death of a human is nothing more than the death of an animal."

A shiver went down Rosie's spine.

"Because of the Queen, we have lived in an age of mourning," she said. "Forgive me. You are not shocked by this conversation?"

"Not at all. Your questioning mind gives me pleasure, my dear. It is a breath of fresh air," said Mrs Eden.

Rosie then suggested that if her employer followed the path backwards through the centuries from Darwin, she might conclude that religion had flourished only because there was no science to explain the world to us.

"In the absence of explanations, we made it up," she said. "Religion and imagination occupy the same space in our heads. Don't they?"

Imagination, she thought ruefully, was one of the many attributes that George Childs did not possess. It was the certainty of his outlook that made her fear he would handle disappointment badly.

Mrs Eden stitched away silently at the tapestry of her moods, which now looked rather wild and colourful.

"This is food for thought," she said. "No wonder Jonathan says that unbelief is spreading like typhus through the suburbs of the great metropolis. Are you not muddling our desire for story-telling with our need for answers?"

Rosie took a different view again. "Stories are another thing for which we have to thank the railways, for they love to travel by train. Mr Dickens's instalments went all over the place by steam. They turned us all to reading. And the advertisements on station platforms brought art to people who had never seen it before."

Mrs Eden sighed. "The world is being rearranged, it is true, but we must maintain belief. We must believe, most of all, in the people closest to us, otherwise we are all lost."

She smiled sadly at Rosie, who saw that Mrs Eden as they were talking had sewn a quantity of sapphire into her composition.

❦

August 24 1901
(On Saint Bartholomew's Day in 1572 the French Huguenots who were Protestants rose up against the Catholics in the French War of Religion in which millions of people died)

Fairy Rings
The deep green circles, called fairy-rings, which you so often see in the pastures and on the downs, have nothing whatever to do with elves or fairies, or with anything that is half so romantic. They are generally caused by the circular growth of a small toadstool called Marasimius Oreades. It grows to a height of about two inches and is of a pale brownish colour and pleasant odour. When young it is as good to eat as proper mushrooms.

I cannot concentrate on pressing my wild flower specimens because I keep remembering Miss Etherington in her pink summer dress at the opening of Highcliff Pier. It isn't that the dress was so beautiful I wanted to crush it to my face, or that she was so pale I thought she might be ill, or that she looked helpless as a kitten. It was that I caught sight of her sitting on a bench with Flinty Daredevil. We cousins stay away from him because of his baby face and his crazy streak. But that day he wasn't a mad fisherman with a polished chin and a girl's mouth. Oh no. He wore a blazer and white trousers and might just have stepped off the London train. There he was, cool as you like, posh as they come, making sweeping gestures as if he was describing the building of his boat. It was only a short moment but it was long enough to see she was very taken with him. And as for him? He was another one under her spell.

❦

At last, I sleep. But then Edward walks into my dream. Or to be more precise, he rolls into it. We lie on our bellies at the top of broken white cliffs with the sea far away beneath us. We elbow to the edge of the precipice and look down at rocks which are sharp like broken teeth. We gaze at the sea and sand and the little people living down below. He turns to me. I want to ask him if he loves me. He looks at me, into me, deep inside me, and moves his head towards mine. I don't need to ask him. He kisses me and I shape myself to him. He pulls back and comes again. We roll over and over, right along the edge. I don't need to ask him. I never did and I never will. He doesn't need to ask me. The unanswered questions can be satisfied with pure logic.

I am an oddity, unable to fit in with the norms of society. Why is it that when I throw caution to the wind and break the rules, I find certainty? It is all wrong that it should be this way. It should be that if I follow the conventions, I find solid ground. That is where certainty should be, yet it is not. Instead, I find correctness inside the forbidden, happiness outside the allowable. My head hurts with thinking. Perhaps it is simply the case that there is nothing more powerful than an emotional truth felt by two people, and the fact is that the circumstances of my life will not allow it.

CHAPTER SEVENTEEN:

THE LEATHER FOLDER

George Childs is extremely agitated. His eyes, normally kind, have the look of a lizard about them. As I show him into the front parlour, his shoes click on the floor and he says not one word. I imagine this might be what he's like when he does business. As we pass Mrs Massingham's oval mirror in the hallway, I am so put off by the anger in his eyes that I can't imagine ever being joined to him. He seems a little mad and I'm not sure why. Things are settled. The first banns have been read, the future is set and I know my duty now is to find good things in my new circumstances. His spirits have lifted and his good financial prospects have made him pleasant enough to be with. But at this moment, standing before me, he is filled with menace. I may be wrong but his rage is so great that I feel he could even become violent. I can hear Mrs Massingham in the kitchen, where she's been topping and tailing crab apples, tossing them in a pail on the hob to make jelly.

I smell the sugar melting and know she has brought it to a rolling boil. I hear her skimming foam off the top and tapping it on to a plate. George Childs is oblivious.

He stands by the long table in the parlour where a vase of late roses hang their heads, autumn dew still upon them.

"I'm so sorry if you have received bad news," I venture, words dropping down an empty well. "Mrs Eden warned me that the railway company might withdraw from your plan, put off by bad weather. I have been worried for you."

I think I hear him counting under his breath.

"Woman! Do not concern yourself with matters beyond your competence."

His blond eyelashes blink rapidly and beads of sweat appear on his upper lip. He holds up a leather folder, worn around the edges.

"I do not need to explain to you what I have here because this appears to be an area of life in which you *do* have expertise, in which you are apparently extremely competent. I don't know what," he pauses, "what they are. I am almost speechless. But not quite."

Flecks of saliva fly from his mouth.

"My sister, at whose boarding house the eminent cartoonist Edward Stafford Clark is staying, made a check of his room when he was out taking the air this morning. And she found these. These, how can I put it, *unspeakable images*. She might have been distressed to find such a thing under her roof at all. But when she recognised the face in the photographs, she could feel only horror. *Horror!* The prospect was awful to her. That a member of her own family, her own brother, was about to marry a woman of ill repute! She was disgusted. I don't need to say that she came to me in great distress and great haste, and I have come directly here."

I've been waiting a whole year for this moment. Now it has come, I am almost relieved. I am hauled out of the shadows. No more hiding. I'm flushed but mute. What is there to say?

He raises his voice and lowers his face close to mine. Too close. He speaks slowly.

"There is a law against this. Men are sent to gaol for peddling pictures like these. Sent down! Sent down for years of hard labour."

I'm startled by these new facts. A tingle runs from the base of my neck down my arms. The room rocks a little so I put my hand on the wall to steady myself. Mrs Massingham's spoon hits the side of the pan as she stirs the apples.

He jerks his head away.

"I am puzzled, truly perplexed. Wrapping yourself in sheets? Holding a broom upside down? Putting a saucepan on your head and smiling like an inmate of Bedlam? Was this some sort of jape?"

He is panting now but pauses to gather himself.

"Don't tell me. I would rather not know."

Abruptly he slams the folder down on the table and throws his hands in the air.

"Had you wanted to come and spend your life with a man who is financially ruined, and yes you are right in thinking that I am ruined, then I would have been happy. Oh, much more than happy, to take you. But this...this...is something I cannot accept. I am undone, utterly undone. I have built *all* my dreams on marshy ground."

He puts his face in his hands. Then quickly he looks up, wipes his mouth and glances out of the window before turning and looking me slowly up and down as if to say that this will be the last time he will ever see me. Then he walks out of the room, out of the house, away down the road.

I feel the rowing boat nudge through in the floodwaters, as if I am that girl again in one of her many guises. I am the shopkeeper's daughter, I am the seamstress working into the night, I am the woman who dreams she can become an artist, I am the fool who trespasses into another woman's life. There are only two truths I can be sure of. One is that I loved Edward. The second is that I am only truly myself when I put pencil to paper. I hear the oars in their rowlocks but it is Mrs Massingham with her spoon.

*

Darkness falls, and the world of the human gives way to the world of the animal. People sit by their firesides, curl up in their shelters, light their lamps to ward off what they cannot see. Autumn is descending on Swanton Stoke. Trees are already losing their leaves, extending their gaunt branches skywards. Some have retained their summer foliage and cast grotesque black shapes across the streets. Jack thinks the moon looks like a half-used nutmeg tonight. Black clouds slide like shrouds across it. From far off in the distance he can hear a train coming, working its pistons, set on its course, making a beeline for Swanton Stoke. But it is not yet anywhere near.

He runs with long strides, then stops and tucks himself into the bushes to wait and listen, then runs on again. She is a small figure in the flicker of light and shadow, her skirt swinging, head held up, hair tied at the back, heading towards the Belle Vue. A barn owl floats up, a huge flake of white ash, keeping pace with him for a few seconds. He smells crushed apples, mint, and dusty old nettles. The birdsong is sad as a requiem. The summer is over. He waits for the charcoal sky to turn to ink.

Without warning, a pony and trap comes clipping towards him from behind and he sees the silhouette of a man whipping the pony in the direction of the oncoming train. The shoulders of the driver are set square. Something in the use of the whip, and the speed at which he goes, indicates to Jack that he is in a fury. He brings the trap to an abrupt halt, throws down the whip and strides towards Miss Etherington. She does not remark at his being here at this strange hour. Jack thinks the figure is Mr Childs but he can't be sure. He thinks he hears a voice which sounds dark, clogged.

"If you can't be mine...." The leaves swish in the wind and Jack strains to catch what is said next. He thinks the voice says she should belong to no-one.

The train comes into view, unstoppable, smoke rolling out in a long pale tongue across the fields. It huffs and screeches. The engine blocks out the last rays of light in the sky, and the two figures became hard to see against the moving carriages. *Clickety clack. Clickety clack.* Do the two figures come together? Do they pull apart? Do they stay upright or fall to the ground? Jack waits inside his cloak of leaves while the train passes, truck after truck, hauling itself towards a well-earned night of rest. *Clickety clack. Clickety clack.* Finally it has gone, and so has the pony and trap. The trap has gone the way it came, hooves tapping away into the distance. All is silent, no-one to be seen. No-one at all. Did she climb into the trap with him? Did he take her away? Jack breathes easily again. A hedgehog levers itself across the grass, a ball-shaped brush searching for supper. Jack slips through the shadows to where he last saw her.

He stops, listens, and hears a breath and a moan somewhere close to the ground. He runs towards it.

"Jack. Is it you?"

"Yes, Miss."

"Will you do something for me? One last thing?"

"Yes, Miss."

He did not ask why she was lying on the ground.

"Will you go back to the Massinghams' house? Mrs Massingham will be out now, so no-one will be there. The door is not locked. Go inside and up to my room."

It sounds as if it is difficult for her to speak, and the ground does not seem the best place for her to be at this time of night.

"Fetch the wicker basket from under the bed and a leather folder which lies between the mattress and the bed frame. Take both to Rough Jimmy. Tell him they are for safe-keeping and tell him where I am and that I need help. Then go home."

"Yes, Miss."

He feels like Cupid bending over Psyche in that picture she has shown him. He wants to stroke her.

"Will you do exactly as I say?"

"Yes."

Her hand takes his and squeezes. It is very cold.

"Be brave, Jack. You're a good runner. See how quickly you can do it, yes?"

And he is off, carrying his heart like an egg yolk in the palm of his hand. Bushes, stones, lamp posts, houses, trails of grey smoke, all blur together as he runs. There is no barn owl now.

His hands turn into jumping fish but he finds the door handle. He enters the cold house, scrambles up the stairs, finds the bedroom, retrieves the basket, presses his fingers under the mattress and pulls out the folder. Hands full, he heads back down to the hall. Glancing behind him through the kitchen door, he sees something that looks like a leg hanging from a hook over the kitchen table, dripping into a bowl. He gasps but then catches the sweet heavy smell and knows it is a muslin bag hung up to strain juice for crab apple jelly. He needs two hands to carry the basket and folder so he has to move slowly, ease out through the front door, step along Colville Road, down the main street towards Bell's Loke and find Rough Jimmy. What will he do if he's not there? A knife of anxiety stabs through the sweat of fear sliding down his back. He moves from lamp post to lamp post and arrives at The Tin House in the thick of the dark.

Rough Jimmy at first is not aware of his presence. Jack watches him for a moment. The old man has made a tripod of sticks and lit a small fire in the middle. A black pot hangs from the sticks with the promise of supper. The boy thinks the man's face, lit by the glow, looks as cosy as if he were at home in a normal parlour.

He remembers what has to be said. Then he spouts his words

Rough Jimmy takes the basket and folder straight into the hut and comes out again. He douses the fire, then grips Jack's arm.

"No. Tiddler-that-once-was. I'll take yer home first. Come with me."

Jack starts to shake, and by the time they reach Sebastopol Road he is no longer steady on his feet. His mother takes him in. She is curt with Rough Jimmy and all but slams the door in his face. Then she wraps a blanket around her son and puts him by the fire which, by some miracle in these hard times, has been lit.

September 24 1901

(In 1493 Christopher Columbus embarked on his second voyage to the Americas taking seventeen ships and one thousand two hundred men. His aim was to create permanent British colonies in the New World and look for precious metals)

This is a night the village will not forget. This is the night Rough Jimmy carries Miss Etherington back. He walks under the streetlamps holding her in his arms, her skirts dangling, her head on his chest. Everyone knows she is dead as no-one could bury a nose so deep into Rough Jimmy's clothes like that. No-one alive could bear such a stink of woodsmoke, animal guts and old sweat. As they said later, telling the story again and again, men going to work on the nightshift stopped in the street at the sight before them. Rough Jimmy, hideous as a monster from the forest, beard hanging over her pale oval face, breath foul as a septic nostril, hands rough as cobbles, walked slowly on, carrying the body of the spirit who came from nowhere. He walked carefully past the Astley Arms, up Colville Road and into the front room of the Massinghams' house, where he laid her on the table in the parlour. They say her face was smashed, a cheek gone, an ear gone, hair matted with blood, neck darkened with bruises.

I don't see it myself as I am squatting in front of the fire in my father's house. I cannot speak. It is no matter what people ask me. I cannot speak. Billy comes to the door and tells Mother that Miss Etherington's body has been found and brought home. Mother doesn't let him in but I can hear what he says at the door, taking fast gulps as he does when he is very excited.

"She were like a rabbit hit by a stick after the harvest," he says. "Blood and guts everywhere."

Father lines himself up in front of the fire, pushes his jaw forward, looks into me, then puts his hands behind his back and addresses me as if I am a meeting.

"Now what? What, Jack boy, has been going on?"

He is impatient, angry, shocked, all at the same time.

My jaw trembles and I cannot think of the right answer.

"What, and I repeat myself Jack. What have you seen? Of more importance, perhaps, *where* have you been?"

This is worse than anything that has ever happened.

I cannot tell him about my secret passageway into people's back gardens. I cannot tell him about watching Miss Etherington undress in the window. I cannot tell him about what I saw between the leathers when I stopped by the last lamp before Bell's Loke and peeped inside. I cannot tell him that I saw pictures of her with her legs wide open and her breasts right out and her hair down around her shoulders and her lips apart. I cannot tell Father these things.

I have sinned in thought, word and deed.

Some words tumble out but they come with long gaps like a row of pictures. I tell him about running messages between Miss Etherington and Master Joseph from the big house, and about Joseph waiting for her at the Belle Vue. I tell him about following her up the road to the Belle Vue and about the pony and trap, about the train coming and the trap racing away. But I do not tell him about the wicker basket or the black and white dress because I don't think he would be very interested in those.

September 25 1901

(In 1066 the English fought off the Norwegian army at the Battle of Stamford Bridge. Greatly weakened, the English army fought against the Normans at the Battle of Hastings and lost)

At first the village thinks Rough Jimmy killed Miss Etherington. No-one is sure whether the death took place on railway property or not because her body was found beside the railway line but not right upon it. The special railway policeman is here all the same because it is Friday, which is pay day. As usual, the bank sets up a table in the front room of the house on the main street. A brown blind is drawn across half the window bearing the letters BB. The clerk from the goods office walks down the hill with the railway policeman and a sack barrow with a Gladstone bag padlocked to it. They collect the money, then walk back up the street to The Works, where it is divided into brown paper packets for the men. There is a sound of thunder made by the men's boots as they advance on the Time Office to queue in the right order to collect their money. Each one is called by number. If a man is unfortunate enough to miss his turn, then he is made to wait until the end.

Everyone says it is lucky that the special railway policeman is on his weekly visit. He takes a room at the Hartley Arms and the first thing he does is ask for Rough Jimmy to be brought in.

"Fetch the vagrant," he barks.

Rough Jimmy is inside the room for two whole hours. Afterwards he shuffles back down the road, hiding his face. The railway constable opens the windows, pulls in deep breaths of fresh air and seems to be in a very a bad temper.

"What is the workhouse for but taking people like that off the streets?" he shouts.

Later in the day he pays a visit to Mr and Mrs Massingham, where Mr Massingham accuses Mrs Massingham of bringing shame upon his house by showing kindness to stray women.

"She was orphaned. She was a fast learner and had a good heart," says Mrs Massingham. "She was a lost soul."

Then he goes to Mr and Mrs Eden's house, where Mrs Eden more than once calls for the smelling salts. Then he returns to the Hartley Arms, where he has a bottle of whisky and a tumbler by his bed, and is not seen again that day. While he is busying himself in this way I sit with Father, listening to his prayers and Bible readings and repeating after him when he asks me to. Mother makes shortbreads, which she arranges in crossed pairs to look like a castle, then drenches them with sugar before setting them in front of me. After I have gone to bed Mother and

Father murmur in their bedroom deep into the night.

No-one asks why she was out at night walking on the lane towards the Belle Vue. I remember she said that it isn't who says what that matters. It is who sees what and how they see it.

On the second day the special policeman takes off in a carriage to Staithe to speak to George Childs because he has learned of his engagement to Miss Etherington. But when he arrives he finds that no amount of knocking will bring Mr Childs to the door. The policeman finds a back door ajar and lets himself in. He enters the mill room and finds Mr Childs hanging from an iron rafter, a rope around his neck, his legs slack in the air, his tongue turned black. The special policeman informs the next of kin, Mr Childs's sister Mrs Birdwood of Highcliff, who tells him a thing or two about Miss Etherington which makes his eyes pop out. By nightfall the story that Miss Etherington is a prostitute, a gold digger and dishonest to the core has spread through the village and Father has doubled the hours of prayer and Bible readings so that I am sitting into the night with him until I am too tired to move my lips. The policeman is satisfied his job is done.

On the third day I creep away to find Rough Jimmy down by Bell's Loke. He is sitting by the shed watching the birds peck at windfall apples and breathing in the sweet rotting smell. At first I think he has rubbed earth over one eye, but then I see that he is one big bruise.

He looks up as if he has been expecting me.

"Right on time, lad," he says.

I look at him, full of questions.

"I buried her quick. No-one was there. But we'll go now and give her a proper stone."

He takes me to the shed, where there is an oblong stone wrapped in old sacking. Jimmy puts it on a barrow and together we push it up the street to the churchyard. We don't care who sees us. We take it to a spot by the very edge of the churchyard which is almost in the next-door field, and there in front of me is an oblong of freshly mounded soil.

"Closest to consecrated ground we can get, eh? They don't want her in the churchyard but they won't be bothered to move her from here. Half-in, half-out. Best I could do."

One eye is so swollen he can barely see through it.

Jimmy has already dug a slit in the ground to set the stone in. The turned earth smells rich. The air has turned cold. Memories of her flip round in my head, thick and fast, and a lump rises in my throat. He presses the earth down with his big old boots.

"I'm no stone-cutter. But I've worked on it. What d'ye think?"

There is a name and a date, that's all. For a few minutes I am struggling too much with seeing her go.

"It's a bit rough. It's good, though," I say.

I don't want to hurt his feelings and I know that each letter has been done with more care than anyone else could ever have given it. My head aches with holding back my tears.

CHAPTER EIGHTEEN:

THE WICKER BASKET

September 30 1901

I meet Billy down on the allotment where women aren't allowed. They never have been. Vegetables is man's work. He waits under the old apple tree.

His chest seems broader than before and he is altogether bigger than me now. He doesn't look happy.

"What you up to?" I ask.

"Nuthin'," he says.

I think he will be bursting with things to ask me, but he isn't. What's more he isn't even *pretending* not to be interested.

We sit with our backs against the tree trunk where there is a big hole in the bark with mushrooms growing out of it. Best not to look at him.

"How's it going?" I ask.

Billy has just started as an apprentice at The Works. But he isn't boasting about it.

"What have you been doing?"

"Chipping boilers. It makes you deaf, like so deaf you hear ringing in your ears all night. When you use a chipping hammer you might as well stick your head into hell, it makes so much noise."

"Still, you got your hearing back now," I say. Then I ask about the others.

"Skinny is on riveting. He makes a coke fire and gets the rivets white hot without burning 'em. The danger is that if he loses one, the fire turns to a mess of white sparks and the riveters fill the air with swear words and Skinny loses his courage and can't do it again for a day or two. Then he has to start all over again."

Billy rubs his eyes and shoves his chin in his hands.

"You tired out?"

"It's the smoke and the stink, all day every day."

"It'll get better maybe," I say.

He starts to undo his trouser buttons and I think he's going to have a piss but has forgotten to stand up first. I look away but he doesn't piss, he just sits there. So I turn back and there he is with his John Thomas out and looking every inch like a red caterpillar. Yes, a *red* one. I take a second look and whistle.

"What's that for?" I ask.

"It's their *initials semi*," he says.

I think for a while, then say: "You mean initiation ceremony?"

"Yes. That's the one. They wait until you're alone. Then they hold you down and pull down your trousers. And you don't know what's going to happen next. Then one of them dips a brush into a pot of red paint and dabs it all over your knob."

More thinking is required.

"It shows you're tough. It shows you're one of them," he says gruffly.

"Well, you are now then, aren't you? Have you tried washing it off?"

"It's stubborn."

He is beginning to look a bit more cheerful. He can see I'm moved by this unexpected event. It has overtaken the importance of the Miss Etherington tragedy in his mind, and he thinks it has in mine. But of course it hasn't.

※

Everything has been decided. It is over. I am never to return to school, to the room with the long wooden desks and windows too high to see anything on the outside. I will not now study trigonometry, or learn my table of solubilities, or the chemical names of common substances. My diary has them all, laid out alongside the results of the county cricket championships and posh school records for running the mile, long jump, high jump, hurdles and throwing the cricket ball. I will never have a chance to spend Wednesday afternoons in the Railway Institute where Mr Eden encourages his youngest workers to raise themselves up through knowledge.

Father believes I've slipped off the straight and narrow, what with roaming wild on the marsh for The All-Night and knowing too much about Miss Etherington. He thinks my mind has been addled by the new pier and borrowing books from the library. Thanks to Miss Etherington I have read *Robinson Crusoe* and *Great Expec-*

tations and have sucked the marrow from every word. She warned me that English literature was a luxury which was not permitted in schools so you had to find it for yourself. In Father's view I've been led astray and need to be reminded of who I am. I must be removed from harm's way. I will be restored to Grace through hard work, for which I will, in later years, be grateful. I must rise at four each morning, open the bakery, light the ovens, prepare the dough and help Father. He is too tired to carry on for ever, and Mother is getting too worn out to be much use.

My warts have gone.

I am to give up my shorts and start wearing long trousers.

෴

I no longer keep a diary but have an exercise book where I store my thoughts and memories. As she said, a painting which leaves you guessing brings you back to it again and again. The memory of her calls to me. The missing pieces of her entice me back.

It wasn't for long that I looked at the photographs inside the leather folder that night, but the moment will stay with me for ever. She was all flesh, sitting on a small table with a top made of coloured woods, like a jigsaw puzzle. Foreign-looking. It must have been the devil to make, all those little pieces twisting and turning like a shoal of fish. Yet I didn't linger over it, for it was *how* she was placed that grabbed me. Between her legs was something like a sea creature emerging from a shell. I was filled with wonder. It was like seeing a rainbow for the first time. No. It was more than that. It was like stealing raspberries, or eating my first crab or peering into the future. I held her in my trembling fingers.

And I want to cry when I think there was a time when I would have talked to Billy about it. And we would have laughed and straightaway set up a big stone to throw smaller stones at. I might have said the thing I saw was like a snapdragon. And he might have come back saying it was more like his Grandad's knobbly ear. And I might have said, no, it was like a pudding spilling honey. And he might have got the last word by saying it was like an old ham sandwich. We would have split our sides.

But not now because we are all grown.

Lord Hartley died in January. Young Joseph took on Swan Hall and it seemed like the very next day he put an old railway carriage into the garden at The Tin House. He said Rough Jimmy could live there as long as he liked, and promised him a shilling a week for the rest of his life. Jimmy also makes a bit of extra money these days catching adders. He brews up clarified snake fat for rich men and women in London to rub on to their sprained ankles and aching backs. He also sends baskets of live adders to London Zoo, where he seems to have a connection with a person of some influence that I wasn't aware of before. I sometimes see his former sparring partner, Old Balaclava, with his one eye. He is now a beggar and sits outside The Bull with a placard around his neck.

Once village tongues had stopped gossiping and judging Miss Etherington, Jimmy brought me the wicker basket for safekeeping.

He said that Flinty Daredevil had finished his boat with the thirty-foot mast, the fish hole and the beds to sleep in, and he had called it the RE and painted the letters onto the hull himself. Rough Jimmy asked me if I thought it wasn't a coincidence that those were the initials of Miss Etherington, and he wondered aloud about whether Flinty had been another admirer.

"I saw her with him the day the pier was opened. He looked like he was lost to her," I say.

Rough Jimmy leaned his arm against the door frame as if he was settling in for a long discussion.

"So she had a third admirer, did she?" he said.

"She was sad. That is what I remember," I said.

"She were born at the wrong time, I tell you that," Jimmy said. His eyes were rimmed with white scum.

I keep the model I made of the railway signal on the shelf above my bed and I keep the wicker basket underneath the bed. I no longer share my room with Nobby, so all of the space is mine. The basket reminds me of the owl pellet which Billy and I found all that time ago. It is a leaving.

Mother leaves rag rugs, Father leaves his book of recipes, the men leave clean carriages and trains that run on time, Flinty Daredevil leaves his boat, I leave my diaries. We all make leavings for people to find one day in the future.

What is inside the basket? Sometimes I undo the straps and lift the lid. The inside is lined with oilskin to make it waterproof. A compliment slip from someone called Madame Juliette of Marylebone High Street is tucked down the side. Almost of its own accord, the dress flops out like the body of a deflated zebra, then crackles and expands, fairly doubling in size. I lay it out gingerly. The neck is trimmed with a small white ruff, bodice tight and pure black. The skirt is made of sweeping vertical black and white stripes, finished with a horizontal black band. It puffs out like a balloon. I touch the tiny hand-sewn seed-pearls on the back and appreciate the handiwork. It is magnificent.

Underneath is a pile of letters from the cartoonist at *Burlesque*. They make interesting reading and keep me puzzling for hours on end. He writes of drops of blood scattered like tears among his broken plates, and I remember the bandage on Miss

Etherington's hand when she arrived at the station in the half-light. I guess that she had found the photographic plates, then dropped them and cut her hands on the shattered glass.

I have her sketchbook too. The first half is filled with exotic creatures. Elephants and giraffes mingle with winged monsters and wraiths. The second half is a gallery of coiled creeks, wintry seas, fields and marshes. I recognize Staithe windmill, the Tin Church, Mrs Massingham's mangle, corners of the Works, distant figures, faces. Sometimes she uses a bold single line. Sometimes she makes mere suggestions of shapes. They are smudges in a way, but I know them as dunes or sheds or birds.

She drew everything she saw.

The bottom of the basket is where I keep the leather folder that still contains the photographs that were seared into my mind that night. Since then, my body has thickened, my brow has grown heavy and I am no longer the boy I once was. I am changed on the outside. But I am forever changed on the inside too.

As well as the photographs I saw in the lamplight, there are others, including a set of eight taken in sequence. Some nights I lay them out on my bed like a pack of cards, feeling a little guilty as they show Miss Etherington peeling off her layers. The pictures are beautifully staged. In the first she is wrapped in a dark cloak over a dark glossy skirt, the canyons of fabric caught in a swishing motion. In the second, the outer shell has been shed, revealing a frilled white shirt and ribboned white petticoats pinioned by a corset. Next, the corset is off, held at arm's length, dangling from her white hand like a spare set of ribs. Then the shirt is cast aside, then the petticoats, and there she is in a shift that overwhelms her body. In a few minutes she has made the journey from respectable Victorian lady to woman of any station in her underthings. All women look equal in their underwear. Then she sits with one lace-up boot removed, one black stocking half off, one leg hoisted over the other ready for unlacing. The boots are the worn workaday ones I knew so well. Only in one photograph does she look directly at the lens. It is a full gaze, sensuous and questioning. In the last, she has picked up a book, her head is bowed, strands of hair escaping on to her shoulders. She doesn't remove the shift. She has bare feet and her toenails are like perfect little seashells. The camera loves her.

⁓

News of Mr Childs spread quickly through the streets. His name appeared in the newspaper.

Sale particulars for Staithe Mill at the hour of six of the clock in the afternoon of the tenth of January nineteen hundred and two. To be sold by auction the estate of George Bartholomew Childs of Staithe in the said county, a bankrupt.

Mr Eden held his head high and told anyone who dared ask that the man had been prone to hot-headedness.

If we miss the news when it first appeared, we have no need to fret because it always comes round again. We catch up with it in our privy, where we sit in comfort leafing through the squares of newspaper nailed to the wall, before we wipe our arses with it. I must have spent hours learning about Captain Scott's expedition to the South Pole. Half-sentences were sometimes all I got, but I enjoyed thinking about what the missing words might have been. It was in this way that Edward Stafford Clark suddenly announced himself to me. I was reading the opinions of an art critic on the work of a certain cartoonist when it occurred to me that this man might be him, Miss Etherington's letter-writer. The paper said his greatest achievement was a work called *Invitation to Dine*, which had never been finished but was admired by guests who saw it hanging in the hallway of his house. The paper devoted half a page to it. I was cold in the privy but carried on sitting there and studied it. The cartoonist had turned an array of important people into wild beasts. A man with an extra-large head and protruding ears had become a monkey. An overfed, oily man with a sinewy neck looked like a boa constrictor. The grand person at the head of the table was a lion, slack-skinned, haughty and watchful. An enormous woman sat bolt upright, cocooned in the feathers of an ostrich. *This has a quality which I have not seen before or since, a sharp eye and imaginative wit combined with a gloriously supple hand*, said the newspaper. *The earlier work was done by a very good mechanic, the later work is dreary, and dare I say it, bad-tempered. But this is Stafford Clark at the peak of his powers.*

I know some of the creatures sitting around that table. I have seen them in Miss Etherington's sketchbook.

My father's book of recipes is now mine. The brown paper cover is torn and spattered with grease but the word *Recipes* is still easy to read. Inside, my father's hand has set everything down as meticulously as another man might write his diary. It begins with *Edna's Special*.

> EDNA'S SPECIAL
>
> 1lb of sugar
>
> 2oz of butter
>
> 4 table spoonfuls of syrup
>
> 2 tea spoonfuls of vinegar
>
> Melt the butter, add the sugar and syrup and dissolve over a low heat and boil well for approx 10 mins (test in water for setting).

The headings scrawled across the pages sum up his life's work, which now is mine too. Best-quality plain slab, prima donna, rock buns, cream buns, milk bread, yeasted scones, Swiss rolls, doughnuts, high-class Genoese, ginger biscuits, éclairs. The book is patched and glued. Flour falls from the creases when I open it.

༶

It is now three years since Miss Etherington stepped from the train in a cloud of smoke. I must not flinch from this as I write. In that year I said goodbye to the boy I was, and to the school I was at. I lost Father's good opinion, though I don't know that I ever had it. Now I have the weight of his work on my shoulders and it will only get heavier as time goes by. I had my first taste of a woman, though it was no more than second-hand. I saw her nakedness. I witnessed the strange code which adults live by, and learned that nothing is quite what it seems. I came to know there is an invisible world which is made of ideas and stories. I have accepted that I am a keeper of secrets, which may fester and trouble me for years to come. I have seen the closest thing to an angel, but she was unfortunately unable to deliver me from the bakery. Or perhaps I was her angel, the last person to see her alive, and I failed to save her. Nothing is ever like you think it is going to be. Father was right. Nobby was right. Rough Jimmy was right. Hard work is my friend now.

Every morning, in the wet or the frost or the fog, I pummel and stretch the dough with as much love as I can muster. I lay it in the wooden trough, leave it to rise, sweep the floor spotless, stoke the oven, shift the flour sacks, knock back the dough, lay out the loaf tins and feel the dawn lay its hand upon my shoulder. I wipe the flour from my eyes and hair. I am now the man people look and laugh at because his eyebrows are like snow. I am the one who sets off with the handcart in my apron to deliver to every street. I talk to every customer, give them a smile and know their names. I know who can and who cannot pay, how it affects the way we live and where Father gets his goodness from.

Give us this day our daily bread

The first year of the new century came like a strong wind, blowing through the railway lines and station platforms, sweeping us towards the future. I stood in its path and it tossed me about like one of thousands of autumn leaves, then dropped me back down and hurried onward. Somehow or other, I have stayed put.

Acknowledgements

I have always been fascinated by repositories of history, the stories we pass down, the objects we keep, the houses we live in and the landscape we inhabit. Even the lists, jottings and recipes we leave behind are fascinating.

I am indebted to the kindness and generosity of the late Phyllis Youngman and James Meek in the North Norfolk village of Melton Constable for sharing their extensive collection of memorabilia of the M&GN railway works before it was shut down as part of the 1959 Beeching cuts. I also want to thank residents of Melton Constable who spent an evening with me recounting their memories. Their experiences helped me create Swanton Stoke as the backdrop to this story, which is entirely imagined.

I am also very grateful to Marian Skipper for the many chats we had about her father Jack Gaskin, who grew up in the Melton Constable village bakery and later ran his own much-loved bakery in Hindringham.

When I visited the Sambourne House Museum at 18 Stafford Terrace, Kensington in London, I felt this was the kind of home that my character Edward Stafford Clark would have inhabited. Linley Sambourne was a legendary illustrator, cartoonist for *Punch*, photographer and great grandfather to Lord Snowdon who remained happily married to his wife Marion until his death in 1910. Edward Stafford Clark is quite different as he is a less accomplished, less successful, more insecure personality, and works for *Burlesque* magazine. Both were drawn to the use of female models and the camera.

Other authors have been interested in some of the same subjects and I have drawn on their greater expertise. I would like to acknowledge *The Ark in the Park* by Wilfred Blunt; *The Zoo*, the story of London Zoo by J. Barrington-Johnson; *Linley Sambourne House* by Daniel Robbins, Reena Suleman and Pamela Hunter; *Public Artist, Private Passions* Linley Sambourne exhibition catalogue; *Exposed, the Victorian Nude* Tate Britain exhibition catalogue; *Forty Years Of A Norfolk Railway*, the reminiscence of William Marriott, engineer and traffic manager of the M&GN joint railway 1883-1924; *Melton Constable, Briston and District (a portrait in old picture postcards)* by Rhoda Bunn; *Melton Constable, Briston and District (a further portrait in old picture postcards)* by Rhoda Bunn; *Claimed By The Sea* by Chris and Sarah Weston: *Time and Tide* by Alan Childs and Ashley Sampson; *Salthouse, the story of a Norfolk village* by Frank Noel Stagg and the people of the village; *The Story Of Cromer Pier* by Christopher Pipe; *Poppy Land in Pictures* by Elizabeth Jones; *Glaven Ports, maritime history of Blakeney, Cley and Wiveton in North Norfolk* by Jonathan Hooton; *A Country Camera 1844-1914* by Gordon Winter.

I am deeply indebted to my brave independent publishers Waterland Books; to writer-editor-photographer Cameron Self for committing to *The Sitter* and for his steadying hand; to the former chair of the Suffolk Book League Jacqueline Knott for being its first reader and urging us forward; to Nick Stone, designer and polymath, for making it such an exciting creative process and to the Reverend Alison Miller for proofreading.

Most of all I want to thank my husband Richard Girling from the bottom of my heart for living with Rosie, Jack Stamp and Rough Jimmy and for gifts from his bottomless bag of spellings, commas and full stops.

Caroline McGhie, 2025

Biographical Note

Caroline McGhie is an award-winning journalist, known for reshaping the coverage of property and lifestyle during Britain's boom-and-bust cycles. She had a weekly column in The Sunday Times for seven years, contributed features to The Sunday Times Magazine, was part of the launch team of The Independent on Sunday Review, had a weekly column in The Sunday Telegraph and fronted The Sunday Telegraph Life section. She has also had regular columns in The Financial Times, The London Evening Standard and Country Living. She emphasised the importance of the home in present-day social history and as a repository of love and memory, as well as money. She was named Property Journalist of the Year seven times and also won Property Scoop of the Year, Environmental Property Writer of the Year, was nominated for a UK Press Award and awarded a Lifetime Achievement Award. She has lived in North Norfolk for over thirty years and is dedicated to working in fiction and memoir, and walking on the marshes. This is her first novel.